Forge And Furnace

A Novel

by

Florence Warden

Double9 BOOKS

Forge And Furnace
A Novel
by Florence Warden

ISBN: 978-93-73404-76-9

Published by

DOUBLE 9 BOOKS
2/13-B, Ansari Road
Daryaganj, New Delhi – 110002
info@double9books.com
www.double9books.com
Tel. 011-40042856

ABOUT THE AUTHOR

Florence Warden, born Florence Alice Price on May 16, 1857, in Hanworth, England, was an English actress and prolific writer. She began her career on the stage before transitioning into a successful literary path, writing under the name Florence Warden. Her novels often featured elements of mystery, romance, and social intrigue, reflecting the tastes and concerns of her era. Throughout her life, she published many works that gained her recognition and a loyal readership. After marrying, she was also known as Mrs. G. E. James, though she continued to use her pen name professionally. Warden's personal life was notable for her long-term partnership with fellow author Gertrude Warden, an unconventional relationship that defied the social norms of the time. She died in London on May 11, 1929, at the age of 71. Florence Warden is remembered as a versatile and determined woman who made her mark in both theatre and literature, contributing significantly to the cultural landscape of Victorian and Edwardian England.

CONTENTS

CHAPTER I
A PAIR OF BROWN EYES

Thud, thud. Amidst a shower of hot, yellow sparks the steam hammer came down on the glowing steel, shaking the ground under the feet of the master of the works and his son, who stood just outside the shed. In the full blaze of the August sunshine, which was, however, tempered by such clouds of murky smoke as only Sheffield can boast, old Mr. Cornthwaite, acclimatized for many a year to heat and to coal dust, stood quite unconcerned.

Tall, thin, without an ounce of superfluous flesh on his bones, with a fresh-colored face which seemed to look the younger and the handsomer for the silver whiteness of his hair and of his long, silky moustache, Josiah Cornthwaite's was a figure which would have arrested attention anywhere, but which was especially noticeable for the striking contrast he made to the rough-looking Yorkshiremen at work around him.

Like a swarm of demons on the shores of Styx, they moved about, haggard, gaunt, uncouth figures, silent amidst the roar of the furnaces and the whirr of the wheels, lifting the bars of red-hot steel with long iron rods as easily and unconcernedly as if they had been hot rolls baked in an infernal oven, heedless of the red-hot sparks which fell around them in showers as each blow of the steam hammer fell.

Mr. Cornthwaite, whose heart was in his furnaces, his huge revolving wheels, his rolling mills, and his gigantic presses, watched the work, familiar as it was to him, with fascinated eyes.

"What day was it last month that Biron turned up here?" he asked his son with a slight frown.

This frown often crossed old Mr. Cornthwaite's face when he and his son were at the works together, for Christian by no means shared his father's enthusiasm for the works, and was at small pains to hide the fact.

"Oh, I'm sure I don't remember. How should I remember?" said he carelessly, as he looked down at his hands, and wondered how much more black coal dust there would be on them by the time the guv'nor would choose to let him go.

A young workman, with a long, thin, pale, intelligent face, out of which two deep-set, shrewd, gray eyes looked steadily, glanced up quickly at Mr. Cornthwaite. He had been standing near enough to hear the remarks exchanged between father and son.

"Well, Elshaw, what is it?" said the elder Mr. Cornthwaite with an encouraging smile. "Any more discoveries to-day?"

A little color came into the young man's face.

"No, sir," said he shyly in a deep, pleasant voice, speaking with a broad Yorkshire accent which was not in his mouth unpleasant to the ear. "Ah heard what you asked Mr. Christian, sir, and remember it was on the third of the month Mr. Biron came."

"Thanks. Your memory is always to be trusted. I think you've got your head screwed on the right way, Elshaw."

"Ah'm sure, Ah hope so, sir," said the young fellow, smiling in return for his employer's smile, and touching his cap as he moved away.

"Smart lad that Elshaw," said Mr. Cornthwaite approvingly. "And steady. Never drinks, as so many of them do."

"Can you wonder at their drinking?" broke out Christian with energy, "when they have to spend their lives at this infernal work? It parches my throat only to watch them, and I'm sure if I had to pass as many hours as they do in this awful, grimy hole I should never be sober."

The elder Mr. Cornthwaite looked undecided whether to frown or to laugh at this tirade, which had at least the merit of being uttered in all sincerity by the very person who could least afford to utter it. He compromised by giving breath to a little sigh.

"It's very disheartening to me to hear you say so, Chris, when it has been the aim of my life to bring you up to carry on and build up the business I have given my life to," he said.

Christian Cornthwaite's face was not an expressive one. He was extraordinarily unlike his father in almost every way, having prominent blue eyes, instead of his father's piercing black ones, a fair complexion, while his father's was dark, a figure shorter, broader, and less upright, and an easy, happy-go-lucky walk and manner, as different as possible from the erect, military bearing of the head of the firm.

What little expression he could throw into his big blue eyes he threw into them now, as he pulled his long, ragged, tawny moustache and echoed his father's sigh.

"Well, isn't it disheartening for me too, sir," protested he good-humoredly, "to hear you constantly threatening to put me on bread and water for the rest of my life if I don't settle down in this beastly hole and try to love it?"

"It ought to be natural to you to love what has brought you up in every comfort, educated you like a prince, and made of you—"

Josiah Cornthwaite paused, and a twinkle came into his black eyes.

"Made of you," he went on thoughtfully, "a selfish, idle vagabond, with only wit enough to waste the money his father has made."

"Thank you, sir," said Chris, quite cheerfully. "If that's the best the works have done for me, why should I love them?"

At that moment young Elshaw passed before his eyes again, and recalled Christian's attention to a subject which would, he shrewdly thought, divert the current of his father's thoughts from his own deficiencies.

"I wonder, sir," he said, "that you don't put Bram Elshaw into the office. He's fit for something better than this sort of thing."

And he waved his hand in the direction of the group in the middle of which stood Elshaw, rod in hand, with his lean, earnest face intent on his work.

Josiah Cornthwaite's eyes rested on the young man. Bram was a little above the middle height, thin, sallow, with shoulders somewhat inclined to be narrow and sloping, but with a face which commanded attention. He had short, mouse-colored hair, high cheek bones, a short nose, a straight mouth, and a very long straight chin; altogether an assemblage of features which promised little in the way of attractiveness.

And yet attractive his face certainly was. Intelligence, strength of character, good humor, these were the qualities which even a casual observer could read in the countenance of Bram Elshaw.

But the lad had more in him than that. He had ambition, vague as yet, dogged tenacity of purpose, imagination, feeling, fire. There was the stuff; of a man of no common kind in the young workman.

Josiah Cornthwaite looked at him long and critically before answering his son's remark.

"Yes," said he at last slowly, "I daresay he's fit for something better—indeed, I'm sure of it. But it doesn't do to bring these young fellows on too fast. If he gets too much encouragement he will turn into an inventor (you know the sort of chap that's the common pest of a manufacturing town, always worrying about some precious 'invention' that turns out to have been invented long ago, or to be utterly worthless), and never do a stroke of honest work again."

"Now, I don't think Elshaw's that sort of chap," said Chris, who looked upon Bram as in some sort his protégé, whose merit would be reflected on himself. "Anyhow, I think it would be worth your while to give him a trial, sir."

"But he would never go back to this work afterwards if he proved a failure in the office."

"Not here, certainly."

"And we should lose a very good workman," persisted Mr. Cornthwaite, who had conservative notions upon the subject of promotion from the ranks.

"Well, I believe it would turn out all right," said Chris.

His father was about to reply when his attention was diverted by the sudden appearance, at the extreme end of the long avenue of sheds and workshops, of two persons who, to judge by the frown which instantly clouded his face, were very unwelcome.

"That old rascal again! That old rascal Theodore Biron! Come to borrow again, of course! But I won't see him. I won't—"

"But, Claire, don't be too hard on the old sinner, for the girl's sake, sir," said Chris hastily, cutting short his protests.

Mr. Cornthwaite turned sharply upon his son.

"Yes, the old fox is artful enough for that. He uses his daughter to get himself received where he himself wouldn't be tolerated for two minutes. And I've no doubt the little minx is up to every move on the board too."

"Oh, come, sir, you're too hard," protested Chris with real warmth, and with more earnestness than he had shown on the subject either of his own career or of Bram's. "I'd stake my head for what it's worth, and I suppose you'd say that isn't much, on the girl's being all right."

But this championship did not please his father at all. Josiah Cornthwaite's bushy white eyebrows met over his black eyes, and his handsome, ruddy-complexioned face lost its color. Chris was astonished, and regretted his own warmth, as his father answered in the tones he could remember dreading when he was a small boy—

"Whether she's all right or all wrong, I warn you not to trouble your head about her. You may rely upon my doing the best I can for her, on account of my relationship to her mother. But I would never countenance an alliance between the family of that old reprobate and mine."

But to this Chris responded with convincing alacrity—

"An alliance! Good heavens, no, sir! We suffer quite enough at the hands of the old nuisance already. And I have no idea, I assure you, of throwing myself away."

Josiah Cornthwaite still kept his shrewd black eyes fixed upon his son, and he seemed to be satisfied with what he read in the face of the latter, for he presently turned away with a nod of satisfaction as Theodore Biron and his daughter, who had perhaps been lingering a little until the great man's first annoyance at the sight of them had blown over, came near enough for a meeting.

"Ah, Mr. Cornthwaite, surely there's no sight in the world to beat this," began the dapper little man airily as he held out a small, slender, and remarkably well-shaped hand with a flourish, and kept his eyes all the time upon the men at work in the nearest shed as if the sight had too much fascination for him to be able readily to withdraw his eyes. "This," he went on, apparently not noticing that Mr. Cornthwaite's handshake was none of the warmest, "of a whole community immersed in the noblest of all occupations, the turning of the innocent, lifeless substances of the earth into tool and wheel, ship and carriage! I must say that this place has a charm for me which I have never found in the fairest spots of Switzerland; that after seeing whatever was to be seen in California, the States, the Himalayas, Russia, and the rest of it, I have always been ready to say, not exactly with the poet, but with a full heart, 'Give me Sheffield!' And to-day, when I came to have a look at the works," he wound up in a less lofty tone, "I thought I would bring my little Claire to have a peep too."

"Ah, Mr. Cornthwaite, surely there's no sight in the world to beat this."

In spite of the absurdity of his harangue, Theodore Biron knew how to throw into his voice and manner so much fervor. He spoke, he gesticulated with so much buoyancy and effect, that his hearers were amused and interested in spite of themselves, and were carried away, for the time at least, into believing, or half-believing, that he was in earnest.

Josiah Cornthwaite, always accessible to flattery on the matter of "the works," as the artful Theodore knew, suffered himself to smile a little as he turned to Claire.

"And so you have to be sacrificed, and must consent to be bored to please papa?"

"Oh, I shan't be bored. I shall like it," said Claire.

She spoke in a little thread of a musical, almost childish, voice, and very shyly. But as she did so, uttering only these simple words, a great change took place in her. Before she spoke no one would have said more of her than that she was a quiet, modest-looking, perhaps rather insignificant, little girl, and that her gray frock was neat and well-fitting.

But no sooner did she open her mouth to speak or to smile than the little olive-skinned face broke into all sorts of pretty dimples. The black eyes made up for what they lacked in size by their sparkle and brilliancy, and the two rows of little ivory teeth helped the dazzling effect.

Then Claire Biron was charming. Then even Josiah Cornthwaite forgot to ask himself whether she was not cunning. Then Chris stroked his mustache, and told himself with complacency that he had done a good deed in standing up for the poor, little thing.

But rough Bram Elshaw, whom Chris had beckoned to come forward, and who stood respectfully in the background, waiting to know for what he was wanted, felt as if he had received an electric shock.

Bram was held very unsusceptible to feminine influences. He was what the factory and shop lasses of the town called a hard nut to crack, a close-fisted customer, and other terms of a like opprobrious nature. Occupied with his books, those everlasting books, and with his vague dreams of something indefinite and as yet far out of his reach, he had, at this ripe age of twenty, looked down upon such members of the frivolous sex as came in his way, and dreamed of something fairer in the shape of womanhood, something to which a pretty young actress whom he had seen at one of the theatres in the part of "Lady Betty Noel," had given more definite form.

And now quite suddenly, in the broad light of an August morning, with nothing more romantic than the rolling mill for a background, there had broken in upon his startled imagination the creature the sight of whom he seemed to have been waiting for. As he stood there motionless, his eyes riveted, his ears tingling with the very sound of her voice, he felt that a revelation had been made to him.

As if revealed in one magnetic flash, he saw in a moment what it was that woman meant to man; saw the attraction that the rough lads of his acquaintance found in the slovenly, noisy girls of their own courts and alleys; stood transfixed, coarse-handed son of toil that he was, under the spell of love.

The voice of Chris Cornthwaite close to his ear startled him out of a stupor of intoxication.

"What's the matter with you, Bram? You look as if you'd been struck by lightning. You are to go round the works with Miss Biron and explain things, you know. And listen" (he might well have to recall Bram's wandering attention, for this command had thrown the lad into a sort of frenzy, on which he found it difficult enough to suppress all outward signs), "I have something much more important to tell you than that." But Bram's face was a blank. "You are to come up to the Park next Thursday evening, and I think you'll find my father has something to say to you that you'll be glad to hear. And mind this, Bram, it was I who put him up to it. It's me you've got to thank."

"Thank you, sir," said Bram, touching his cap respectfully, and trying to speak as if he felt grateful.

But he was not. He felt no emotion whatever. He was stupefied by the knowledge that he was to go round the works with Miss Biron.

CHAPTER II
CLAIRE

Bram wondered how Mr. Christian could give up the pleasure of showing Miss Biron round the works himself. Christian's partiality for feminine society was as great as his popularity with it, and as well known. The partiality, but not perhaps the popularity, was inherited from his father—at least, so folks said.

And Bram Elshaw, looking about for a reason for this extraordinary conduct on the part of the young master, and noting the wistfulness of that young man's glances and the displeasure on the face of the elder Mr. Cornthwaite, came very near to a correct diagnosis of the case.

Bram was always the person chosen to carry messages between the works and Holme Park, the private residence of the Cornthwaites, and the household talk had filtered through to him about Theodore Biron, the undesirable relation of French extraction, who had settled down too near, and whose visits had become too frequent for his rich kinsman's pleasure. And the theory of the servants was that these visits were always paid with the object of borrowing money.

Not that Theodore looked like an impecunious person. To Bram's inexperienced eyes Mr Biron and his daughter looked like people of boundless wealth and great distinction. Theodore, indeed, was if anything better dressed than either of the Cornthwaites. His black morning coat fitted him perfectly; his driving gloves were new; his hat sat jauntily on his head. From his tall white collar to his tight new boots he was the picture of a trim, youthful-looking country gentleman of the smart and rather amateurish type.

He had a thin, small-featured face, light hair, light eyebrows, and the smallest of light moustaches; pale, surprised eyes, and the slimmest pair of feminine white hands that ever man had. Of these he was proud; and so his gloves kept their new appearance for a long time, as he generally carried them in his hand.

As for Claire, she not only looked better dressed than either Mrs. or Miss Cornthwaite, but better dressed than any of the ladies of the neighborhood. And this was not Bram's fancy only; it was solid fact.

Claire Biron had never been in France, and her mother had been an Englishwoman of Yorkshire descent. But through her father she had inherited from her French ancestors just that touch of feminine genius which makes a woman neat without severity, and smart looking without extravagance.

In her plain gray frock and big yellow chip hat with the white gauze rosettes, the little slender, dark eyed girl looked as nice as no ordinary English girl would think of making herself except for some special occasion.

Bram had not the nicely critical faculty to enable him to discern things. All he knew, as he walked through the black dust with Miss Biron and pointed out to her the different processes which were going on, was that every glance she gave him in acknowledgment of the information he was obliged to bawl in her ear was intoxicating; that every insignificant comment she made rang in his very heart with a delicious thrill of pleasure he had never felt before.

And behind them followed the two older gentleman, Mr. Cornthwaite explaining, commenting, softening in spite of himself under the artful interest taken in every dryest detail by the airy Theodore, who trotted jauntily beside him; and grew enthusiastic over everything.

Before very long, however, Mr. Cornthwaite, who was getting excited against his will over that hobby of "the works" which Theodore managed so cleverly, drew his companion away to show him a new process which they were in course of testing; and for a moment Bram and Miss Claire were left alone together.

And then a strange thing, a thing which opened Bram's eyes, happened. From some corner, some nook, sprang Chris, and, hooking his arm with affectionate familiarity within that of Miss Biron, he said—

"All right, Elshaw; I'll show the rest. Come along, Claire."

And in an instant he had whirled away with the young lady, who began to laugh and to protest, round the nearest corner.

Bram was left standing stupidly, with a feeling rising in his heart which he could not understand. What was this that had happened? Nothing but the most natural thing in the world; and the impulse of sullen resentment which stirred within him was ridiculous. There was, there could be, no rivalry possible between Mr. Christian Cornthwaite, the son of the owner of the works, and Bram Elshaw, a workman in his father's employment. And Miss Biron was a lady as far above him (Bram) as the Queen was.

This was what Bram told himself as, with hard-set jaw and a lowering look of discontent on his face, he quietly went back to his work.

But the matter was not ended with him. As he went on mechanically with his task, as he bent over the great steel bar with his long rod, his thoughts were with the pair, the well-matched, handsome pair of lovers, as he supposed them to be, who had flitted off together as soon as papa's back was turned.

Now what did that mean?

If it had been any other young lady Bram would not have given the matter a second thought. Christian Cornthwaite's flirtations were as the sand of the sea for multitude, and he would bring half-a-dozen different girls in a week to "see over the works" when papa could be relied upon to be out of the way. Christian had the easy assurance, the engaging, irresponsible manners which always make their possessor a favorite with the unwise sex, and was reported to be able to win the favor of a prude in less time than it takes another man to gain the smiles of a coquette.

And so where was the wonder that this universal favorite should be a favorite with Miss Biron? Of course, there was nothing in the fact to be wondered at, but the infatuated Bram would have had this particular lady as different from other ladies in this respect as he held her superior in every other.

But then a fresh thought, which was like a dagger thrust on the one hand, yet which brought some bittersweet comfort for all that, came into his mind. Surely Miss Biron was not the sort of girl to allow such familiarity except from the man whom she had accepted for a husband. Surely, then, these two were engaged—without the consent, or even the knowledge, of Mr. Cornthwaite very likely, but promising themselves that they would get that consent some day.

And as he came to this decision Bram looked black.

And all the time that these fancies chased each other through his excited brain this lad of twenty retained a saner self which stood outside the other and smiled, and told him that he was an infatuated young fool, a moonstruck idiot, to tumble headlong into love with a girl of whom he knew nothing except that she was as far above him, and of all thought of him, as the stars are above the sea.

And he was right in thinking that there was not a man in all that crowd of his rough fellow-workmen who would not have jeered at him and looked down upon him as a hopeless ass if they had known what his thoughts and feelings were. But for all that there was the making in Bram Elshaw, with his dreams and his fancies, of a man who would rise to be master of them all.

Out of the heat of the furnace and the glowing iron Bram Elshaw presently passed into the heat of the sun, and stood for a moment, his long rod in his hand, and wiped the sweat from his face and neck. And before he could turn to go back again he heard a little sound behind him which was not a rustle, or a flutter, or anything he could describe, but which he knew to be the sound of a woman moving quickly in her skirts. And the next moment Miss Biron appeared a couple of feet away from him, smiling and growing a little pink as a young girl does when she feels herself slightly embarrassed by an unaccustomed situation.

Before she spoke Bram guessed by the position in which she held her little closed right hand that she was going to offer him money. And he drew himself up a little, and blushed a much deeper red than the girl—not with anger, for after all was it not just what he might have expected? But with a keener sense than ever of the difference between them.

Miss Biron had begun to speak, had got as far as "I wanted to thank you for explaining everything so nicely," when something in his look caused her to stop and hesitate and look down.

She was suddenly struck with the fact that this was no common workman, this pale, grimy young Yorkshireman with the strong jaw and the clear, steady eyes, although he was dressed in an old shirt blackened by coal dust, and trousers packed with pieces of sacking tied round with string.

"Ah'm reeght glad to ha' been of any service to yer, Miss," said Bram in a very gentle tone.

There was a moment's silence, during which Miss Biron finally made up her mind what to do. Looking up quickly, with the blush still in her face, she said, "Thank you very much. Good-morning," and, to Bram's great relief, turned away without offering him the money.

CHAPTER III
SOMETHING WRONG AT THE FARM

It is certain that Bram Elshaw was still thinking more of Miss Biron than of the communication which Mr. Cornthwaite was to make to him when he presented himself at the back door of his employer's residence on the following Thursday evening.

Holme Park was on the side of one of the hills which surround the city of Sheffield, and was a steep, charmingly-wooded piece of grass and from a small plateau in which the red brick house looked down at the rows of new red brick cottages, at the factory chimneys, and the smoke clouds of the hive below.

Bram had always taken his messages to the back door of the house, but he was shrewd enough to guess, from the altered manner of the servant who now let him in and conducted him at once to the library, that this was the last time he should have to enter by that way.

And he was right. Mr Cornthwaite was as precise in manner, as business-like as usual, but his tone was also a little different, as he told Bram that his obvious abilities were thrown away on his present occupation, and that he was willing to take him into his office, if he cared to come, without any premium.

Bram thanked him, and accepted the offer, but he showed no more than conventional gratitude. The shrewd young Yorkshireman was really more grateful than he seemed, but he saw that his employer was acting in his own interest rather than from benevolence, and, although he made no objections to the smallness of the salary he was to receive, he modestly but firmly refused to bind himself for any fixed period.

"Ah may be a failure, sir," he objected quietly, "and Ah should like to be free to goa back to ma auld work if Ah was."

So the bargain was struck on his own terms, and he retired respectfully just as a servant entered the library to announce that Miss Biron wished to see Mr. Cornthwaite. And at the same moment the young girl herself tripped into the room, with a worried and anxious look on her face.

Mr. Cornthwaite rose from his chair with a frown of annoyance.

"My dear Claire, your father really should not allow you to come this long way by yourself—at night, too. It is neither proper nor safe. By the time dinner is over it will be dark, and you have a long way to go."

"Oh, but I am going back at once, as soon as you have read this," said Claire, putting a little note fastened up into a cocked hat like a lady's, into his unwilling hand. "And perhaps Christian would see me as far as the town, if you think I ought not to go alone."

But this suggestion evidently met with no approval from Mr. Cornthwaite, who shook his head, signed to Bram to remain in the room and began to read the note, all at the same time.

"My dear," said he shortly, as he finished reading and crumpled it up, "Christian is engaged at present. But young Elshaw here will show you into your tram, won't you, Elshaw?"

"Certainly, sir." Bram, who had the handle of the door in his hand, saluted his employer, and retreated into the hall before Claire, who had not recognized him in his best clothes, had time to look at him again.

"A most respectable young fellow, my dear, though a little rough. One of my clerks," Bram heard Mr. Cornthwaite explain rapidly to Miss Biron as he shut himself out into the hall and waited.

Bram was divided between delight that he was to have the precious privilege of accompanying Miss Biron on her journey home, and a sense of humiliation caused by the shrewd suspicion that she would not like this arrangement.

But when a few minutes later Claire came out of the library all his thoughts were turned to compassion for the poor girl, who had evidently received a heavy blow, and who had difficulty in keeping back her tears. She dashed past him out of the house, and he followed at a distance, perceiving that she had forgotten him, and that his duty would be limited to seeing without her knowledge that she got safely home.

So when she got into a tram car at the bottom of the hill outside the park he got on the top. When she got out at St. Paul's Church, and darted away through the crowded streets in the direction of the Corn Exchange, he followed. Treading through the crowds of people who filled the roadway as well as the pavement, she fled along at such a pace that Bram had difficulty in keeping her little figure in view. She drew away at last from the heart of the town, and began the ascent of one of the stony streets, lined with squalid, cold-looking cottages, that fringe the smoke-wreathed city on its north-eastern side.

Bram followed.

Once out of the town, and still going upwards, Claire Biron fled like a hare up a steep lane, turned sharply to the left, and plunged into a narrow passage, with a broken stone wall on each side, which ran between two open fields. This passage gave place to a rough footpath, and at this point the girl stood still, her gaze arrested by a strange sight on the higher ground on the right.

It was dark by this time, and the outline of the hill above, broken by a few cottages, a solitary tall chimney at the mouth of a disused coal pit, and a group of irregular farm buildings, was soft and blurred.

But the windows of the farmhouse were all ablaze with light. A long, plain stone building very near the summit of the hill, and holding a commanding situation above a sudden dip into green pasture land, the unpretending homestead dominated the landscape and blinked fiery eyes at Claire, who uttered a low cry, and then dashed away from the footpath by a short cut across the fields, making straight for the house.

All the blinds were up, and groups of candles could be seen on the tables within, all flickering in the draught, while the muslin curtains in the lower rooms were blown by the evening wind into dangerous proximity to the lights.

And in all the house there was not a trace of a living creature to be seen, although from where Bram stood he could see into every room.

He followed still, uneasy and curious, as Claire climbed the garden wall with the agility of a boy, and ran up to the house door.

It was locked. Nothing daunted, she mounted on the ledge of the nearest window, which was open only at the top, threw up the sash, and got into the room.

A moment later she had blown out all the candles. Then she ran from room to room, extinguishing the lights, all in full view of the wondering Bram, who stood watching her movements from the lawn, until the whole front of the house was in complete darkness.

Then she disappeared, and for a few minutes Bram could see nothing, hear nothing.

But presently from the back part of the rooms, there came to his listening ears a long, shrill cry.

CHAPTER IV
CLAIRE'S APOLOGY

The effect of that cry upon Bram Elshaw was to set him tingling in every nerve.

The lawn which ran the length of the farmhouse was wide, and sloped down to a straggling hedge just inside the low stone wall which surrounded the garden and the orchard. Up and down this lawn Bram walked with hurried footsteps, uncertain what to do. For although he recognized Claire's voice, the cry she had uttered seemed to him to indicate surprise and horror rather than pain, so that he did not feel justified in entering the house by the way she had done until he felt more sure that his assistance was wanted, or that his intrusion would be welcome.

In a very few moments, however, he heard her cry—"Don't, don't; oh, don't! You frighten me!"

Bram, who was by this time close to the door, knocked at it loudly.

Waiting a few moments, on the alert for any fresh sounds, and hearing nothing, he then made his way round to the back of the house, leaping over the rough stone wall which divided the garden from the farmyard, and tried the handle of the back door.

This also was fastened on the inside.

But at the very moment that Bram lifted the latch and gave the door a rough shake he heard a sound like the clashing of steel upon stone, a scuffle, a suppressed cry, and upon that, without further hesitation, Bram put his sinewy knee against the old door, and at the second attempt burst the bolt off.

There was no light inside the house except that which came from the fire in an open range on the right; but by this Bram saw that he was in an enormous stone-paved kitchen, with open rafters above, a relic of the time when the farmer was not one of the gentlefolk, but dined with his family and his laborers at a huge deal table under the pendant hams and bunches of dried herbs which in the old days used to dangle from the rough-hewn beams.

Bram, however, noticed nothing but that a door on the opposite side of the kitchen was swinging back as if some one had just passed through, and he sprang across the stone flags and threw it open.

There was a little oil lamp on a bracket against the wall in the wide hall in which he found himself. Standing with his back to the solid oak panels of the front door, brandishing a naked cavalry sword of old-fashioned pattern, stood the airy Theodore Biron in dressing-gown and slippers, with his hair in disorder, his face very much flushed, and his little fair moustache twisted up into a fierce-looking point at each end.

On the lowest step of a wide oak staircase, which took up about twice the space it ought to have done in proportion to the size of the hall, stood little Claire, pale, trembling with fright, trying to keep her alarm out of her voice, as she coaxed her father to put down the sword and go to bed.

"Drunk! Mad drunk!" thought Bram as he took in the situation at a glance.

At sight of the intruder, whom she did not in the least recognize, Claire stopped short in the midst of her entreaties.

"What are you doing here? Who are you?" asked she, turning upon him fiercely.

The sudden appearance of the stranger, instead of further infuriating Mr. Biron, as might have been feared, struck him for an instant into decorum and quiescence. Lowering the point of the weapon he had been brandishing, he seemed for a moment to wait with curiosity for the answer to his daughter's question.

When, however, Bram answered, in a respectful and shame-faced manner, that he had heard her call out and feared she might be in need of help, Theodore's energy returned with full force, and he made a wild pass or two in the direction of the young man, with a recommendation to him to be prepared.

Claire's terrors returned with full force.

"Oh, father, don't, don't! You'll hurt him!" she cried piteously.

But the entreaty only served to whet Theodore's appetite for blood.

"Hurt him! I mean to! I mean to have his life!" shouted he, while his light eyes seemed to be starting from his head.

And, indeed, it seemed as if he would proceed to carry out this threat, when Bram, to the terror of Claire and the evident astonishment of her father, rushed upon Theodore, and, cleverly avoiding the thrust which the latter made at him, seized the hilt of the sword, and wrested it from his grasp.

It was a bold act, and one which needed some address. Mr Biron was for the moment sobered by his amazement.

"Give me back my sword, you impudent rascal!" cried he, making as he spoke a vain attempt to regain possession of the weapon.

But Bram, who was a good deal stronger than he looked, kept him off easily with his right hand, while he retained a tight hold on the sword with his left.

"You shall have it back to-morrow reeght enough," said Bram good-humoredly. "But maybe it'll be safer outside t'house till ye feel more yerself like. Miss Claire yonder knaws it's safe wi' me."

"Oh, yes; oh, yes," panted Claire eagerly, though in truth she had not the least idea who this mysterious knight-errant was. "Let him have it, father; it's perfectly safe with him."

But this action of his daughter's in siding with the enemy filled Mr Biron with disgust. With great dignity, supporting himself against the wall as he spoke, and gesticulating emphatically with his right hand, while with his left he fumbled about for his gold pince-nez, he said in solemn tones—

"I give this well-meaning but m-m-muddle-headed young man credit for the best intentions in the world. But same time I demand that he should give up my p-p-property, and that he should take himself off m-m-my premises without furth' delay."

"Certainly, sir. Good-evening," said Bram.

And without waiting to hear any more of Mr Biron's protests, or heeding his cries of "Stop thief!" Bram ran out as fast as he could by the way he had come, leaving the outer door, which he had damaged on his forcible entry, to slam behind him.

Once outside the farmyard, however, he found himself in a difficulty, being suddenly stopped by a farm laborer, in whom his rapid exit from the house had not unnaturally aroused suspicions, which were not allayed by the sight of the drawn sword in his hand.

"Eh, mon, who art ta? And where art agoin'?"

Bram pointed to the house.

"There's a mon in yonder has gotten t' jumps," explained he simply, "and he was wa-aving this abaht's head. So Ah took it away from 'un."

The other man grinned, and nodded.

"T' mester's took that way sometimes," said he. "But this sword's none o' tha property, anyway."

Bram looked back at the house. Nobody had followed him out; even the damaged door had been left gaping open.

"Ah want a word wi' t' young lady," said he. "She knaws me. I work for Mr. Cornthwaite down at t' works in t' town yonder."

"Oh, ay; Ah've heard of 'un. He's gotten t' coin, and," with a significant gesture in the direction of the farmhouse, "we haven't."

"You work on t' farm here?" asked Bram.

The man answered in a tone and with a look which implied that affairs on the farm were in anything but a flourishing condition—

"Ay, Ah work on t' farm."

And, apparently satisfied of the honesty of Bram's intentions, or else careless of the safety of his master's property, the laborer nodded good-night, and walked up the hill towards a straggling row of cottages which bordered the higher side of the road near the summit.

Bram got back into the farmyard, and waited for the appearance at the broken door of some occupant of the house to whom he could make his excuses for the damage he had done. He had a shrewd suspicion who that occupant would be. Since all the noise and commotion he and Theodore Biron had made had not brought a single servant upon the scene, it was natural to infer that Mr. Biron and his daughter had the house to themselves.

And this idea filled Bram with wonder and compassion. What a life for a young girl, who had seemed to rough Bram the epitome of all womanly beauty and grace and charm, was this which accident had revealed to him. A life full of humiliations, of terrors, of anxieties which would have broken the heart and the spirit of many an older woman. Instead of being a spoilt young beauty, with every wish forestalled, every caprice gratified, his goddess was only a poor little girl who lived in an atmosphere of petty cares, petty worries, under the shadow of a great trouble, her father's vice of drink.

And as he thought about the girl in this new aspect his new-born infatuation seemed to die away, the glamour and the glow faded, and he thought of her only as a poor little nestling which, deprived of its natural right of warmth and love and tenderness, lives a starved life, but bears its privations with a brave look.

And as he leaned against the yellow-washed wall he heard a slight noise, and started up.

Miss Biron, candlestick in hand, was examining the injuries done to her back door.

Bram opened his mouth to speak, but he stammered and uttered something unintelligible, taken aback as he was by the vast difference between the fancy picture he had been drawing of the young lady and the reality with which he was confronted.

For instead of the wan, white face, the streaming eyes, the anxious and weary look he had expected to see, he found himself face to face with a cheery little creature, brisk in movement, bright of eyes, who looked up with a start when he appeared before her, and said rather sharply—

"This is your doing, I suppose? And instead of being scolded for the mischief you have done you expect to be thanked and perhaps rewarded, no doubt?"

At first Bram could scarcely believe his ears.

"Ah'm sorry for t' damage Ah've done, miss," he said hurriedly. "And that's what Ah've waited for to tell yer, nowt but that. But it's not so bad as it looks. It's nobbut t' bolt sprung off and a scratch to the paint outside. If you can let me have a look into your tool-chest, Ah'll set it reght at once. And for t' paint, Ah'll come up for that to-morrow neght."

Miss Biron smiled graciously. The humble Bram had his sense of humor tickled by the airs she was giving herself now, as if she had forgotten altogether her helpless fright of only an hour before, and the relief with which she had hailed his disarming of her father.

"Well, that's only fair, isn't it?" said she with a bright smile, as she instantly acted upon his advice by disappearing into the house like a flash of lightning.

Bram heard the rattling of tools, and as it went on some time without apparent result, he stepped inside the door to see if he could be of any assistance.

Claire had thrown open the door of a cupboard to the left of the wide hearth, and was standing on a Windsor chair turning over the contents of a couple of biscuit tins on the top shelf. Bram, slow step by slow step, came nearer and nearer, fascinated by every rapid movement of this, the first feminine creature who had ever aroused his interest. How small her feet were! Bram looked at them, and then turned away his head, as if he had been guilty of something sacrilegious. And the movement of her arm as she turned over the odds and ends in the boxes, the bend of her dark head as she looked down, filled him afresh with that strange new sense of wonder and delight with which she had inspired him on his first sight of her at the works. Against the light of the candle, which she had placed on the shelf, he saw her profile in a new aspect, in which it looked prettier, more childlike than ever.

"Better give me t' box, miss," suggested Bram presently.

Miss Biron started, not knowing that he was so near.

"Very well," said she. "You can look, but I am afraid you won't find any proper tools here at all."

She was right. But Bram was clever with his hands as well as with his head, and he could "make things do." So that in a very few minutes he was at work upon the door, while Miss Biron held the light for him, and watched his nimble movements with interest.

And while she watched him it occurred to her, now that she felt quite sure he was no mere idler who had burst his way into the house from curiosity, that she had been by no means as grateful for his timely entrance as he had had a right to expect. And the candle began to shake in her hands as she glanced at him rather shyly, and wondered how, without casting blame upon her father, she could make amends to this methodical, quiet, and rather mysterious young Orson for the part he had taken in the whole affair.

"I'm really very much obliged to you," she said at last, with a very great change in her manner from the rather haughty airs she had previously assumed. "I—"

She hesitated, and stopped. Bram had glanced quickly up at her, and then his eyes had flashed rapidly back to his work again.

"I seem to know your face," said she with a manner in which sudden shyness struggled with a sense of the dignity it was necessary for her to maintain in these novel circumstances. "Where have I met you before? And what is your name?" she added quickly, as a fresh suspicion rushed into her mind.

"My name is Elshaw, miss. Bram Elshaw," he answered, as he sat back on his heels and hunted again in the biscuit tin. "And I've seen you. I saw you t' other day, last Tuesday, at Mr. Cornthwaite's works. It was me showed you round, miss."

"Oh!"

The bright little face of the girl was clouded with bewilderment.

"And then again Ah saw you to-neght up to Mr. Cornthwaite's house, up at t' Park. And he told me for to see you home, miss."

"Oh!"

This time the exclamation was one of confusion, annoyance, almost of horror.

"I remember! He said—he said—he would send some one to see me home. But—er—er—I was in such a hurry—that—that I forgot. And I ran off by myself. And—and so you followed; you must have followed me!"

And Claire's pretty face grew red as fire.

The truth was she had been angry with Mr. Cornthwaite for the manner of his reception, for the dry remarks he had made about her father, and for his manifest and most ungracious unwillingness to allow Christian to see her home. And she had made up her mind that no "respectable young man" of Mr. Cornthwaite's choosing should accompany her if Chris might not. And so, dashing off through the park in the dusk by a short cut, she had thought to escape the ignominy which Mr. Cornthwaite had designed for her.

Bram, with a long, rusty nail between his teeth, grew redder than she. In an instant he understood what he had not understood before, that the young lady had taken the offer of his escort as a humiliation. She had wanted to go back with Christian, and Mr. Cornthwaite had wished to put her off with one of his workmen! Bram felt that her indignation was just, although he was scarcely stoical enough not to feel a pang.

"You see, miss," he said apologetically, taking the nail out of his mouth, "Ah was bound to come this weay, and so Ah couldn't help but follow you. And—and when Ah heard you call aht—why Ah couldn't help but get in. Ah'm reght sorry if Ah seemed to be taking a liberty, miss."

Again Claire was struck as she had been that day at the works by the innate superiority of the man to his social position, of his tone to his accent.

"It was very lucky for me—I am very glad, very grateful," said she hurriedly, in evident distress, which was most touching to her hearer. "I don't know what I should have done—I—I must explain to you. You must not think my father would have done me any harm," she went on earnestly, with a great fear at her heart that Bram would report these occurrences to his employer, and furnish him with another excuse for slighting her father. "He gets like that sometimes, especially in the hot weather," she went on quickly, and with so much intensity that it was difficult to doubt her faith in the story. "He was in the army once, and he had a sword-cut on the head when he was out in India. And it makes him excitable, very excitable. But it never lasts long. Now he is fast asleep, and to-morrow morning he will be quite himself, quite himself again. You won't say anything about it to Mr. Cornthwaite, will you?" she wound up, with a sidelong look of entreaty, as Bram, having finished his task, rose to his feet and picked up the coat he had thrown off before setting to work.

"No, miss."

There was something in his tone, in his look, as he said just those two words which inspired Claire with absolute confidence.

"Thank you," she said. "Thank you very much."

And Bram understood that her gratitude covered the whole ground, and took in his forcible entrance, the time he had spent in mending the door, and his final promise.

"And Ah'll look in to-morrow neght, miss," said he as he turned in the doorway and noticed how sleepy her brown eyes were beginning to look, "and give a coat of paint to't."

"Oh, you need not. It's very good of you."

He touched his cap, and turned to go; but as he was turning, Claire, blushing very much, and conscious of this conflict between conventionality and her sense of what she owed to this dignified young workman, who could not be rewarded with a "tip," thrust out her little hand.

Then Bram's behavior was for the moment rather embarrassing. The privilege of touching her fingers, of holding the hand which had stirred in him so many strange reflections for a moment in his own, as if they had been friends, equals, was one which he could not accept with perfect equanimity. She saw that he started, and, blushing more than ever, she seemed in doubt as to whether she should withdraw her hand. But, seeing her hesitation, Bram mastered himself, took the hand she offered, wrung it in a strong grip, and walked quickly away towards the gate.

He felt as if he was in Heaven.

CHAPTER V
BRAM'S RISE IN LIFE

What was there about this little brown-eyed girl that she should bewitch him like this? Bram, who flattered himself that he had his wits about him, who had kept himself haughtily free from love entanglements up to now, could not understand it. And the most amazing part of it all was that his feelings about her seemed to undergo an entire change every half-hour or so. At least a dozen times since his infatuation began he fancied himself quite cured, and able to laugh at himself and look down upon her. And then some fresh aspect of the little creature would strike him into fresh ecstasies, and he would find himself as much under the spell as ever.

Thus the first sight of her that evening in Mr. Cornthwaite's study had thrilled him less than the announcement of her name. But, on the other hand, the touch of her hand so unexpectedly accorded, had quickened his feelings into a delicious frenzy, which lasted during the whole of his walk down into the town and out to the one small backroom in a grimy little red brick house where he lodged.

When Bram tried to think of Miss Biron soberly, to try to come to some sort of an estimate of her character, he was altogether at a loss. Her tears, her terrors, her smiles, her little airs, all seemed to succeed each other as rapidly as if she had been still a child. No emotion seemed to be able to endure in her volatile nature. He doubted, considering the matter in cold blood, whether this was a characteristic he admired; yet there it was, and his infatuation remained.

With all her limitations, whatever they might be; with all her faults, whatever they were, Miss Claire Biron had permanently taken her place in Bram's narrow life as the nearest thing he had ever seen to an ideal woman, as the representative, for the time being at least, of that feminine creature, the necessity for whom he now began to understand, and who was to come straight into his heart and into his arms some day.

For, with all his ambitions, his reasonable hopes, Bram was as yet too modest to say to himself that this white-handed lady herself, this pearl among pebbles, was the prize for which he must strive; no, she only stood for that prize in his mind, in his heart, or so at least Bram told himself.

Bram thought about Miss Biron and her bibulous papa all night, for he scarcely slept, but with the morning light came fresh cares to occupy his thoughts.

It was his first day at his new employment in the office, and Bram, though he managed to hide all traces of what he felt under a stolid and matter-of-fact demeanor, felt by no means at his ease on his first entrance among the young gentlemen in Mr. Cornthwaite's office.

He had put on his Sunday clothes, not without a pang at the extravagance in dress which his rise in life entailed. Nobody in the office seemed to have heard of his promotion, for the other clerks took no notice of him on his entrance, evidently supposing that he had been sent for, as was frequently the case, to take some message or to do some errand which required a trustworthy messenger.

When, after being called into the inner office, he came out again and took his place at a desk among the rest there was a burst of astonishment, amusement, and some contempt at his expense. And when the truth became known that he had come among them to stay, he straight from the coalyard and the mill and the shed outside, the feelings of all the young gentlemen found vent in "chaff" of a particularly merciless kind.

His accent, his speech, his dress, his look, his walk, his manner, all formed themes for the very easiest ridicule. Never before had they had such an opportunity, and they made the most of it. But if they thought to make life in the office unbearable for Bram they had reckoned without their host. Bram cased himself in an armor of stolid good humor, joined in the laugh against himself, and in affecting to try to assume their modes of speech and manner contrived to burlesque them at least as well as they had mimicked him.

And the end of it was that the fun languished all too soon for their wishes, and Bram when he left the office that afternoon, and wiped his face as he used to do after another sort of fiery ordeal, congratulated himself on having got through the day better than he had expected.

Christian Cornthwaite ran out after him, and slapped him on the back.

"Well, Elshaw," cried he, "and how do you feel after it?"

"Much t' same as Dan'l did when he'd come out of t' den o' lions, sir," replied Bram grimly. "T' young gentlemen in there," and he pointed with his thumb over his shoulder, "doan't find me grand enough for'em."

"And so you want to go back to the works, Bram?"

"No fear, sir," answered the new clerk dryly. "They'll get used to me, or else maybe I shall get used to them. Or wi' so many fine patterns round me maybe Ah shall be a polished gentleman myself presently."

"No doubt of it, Bram. But you've been rather roughly treated. It ought to have been managed gradually, bit by bit, and then at last, when you took your place in the office, I ought to have sent you to my own tailor first, and had you properly rigged out."

Bram looked down ruefully at his Sunday clothes.

"Ah felt a prince in these last evening," he expostulated.

Christian laughed heartily.

"Well, they couldn't beat you at the main things, Elshaw, at writing and spelling and calculating, eh?"

"No," answered Bram complacently. "Ah could beat most of 'em there."

As a matter of fact, Bram's self-teaching, with the additional help of the night school in the winter, had so developed his natural capacity that he was as far ahead of his new companions intellectually as he was behind them in externals. Christian, who knew this, felt proud of his protégé.

"There are some more hints I want to give you," said he, as he put his arm through that of his rough companion and walked with him up the street, with the good-natured familiarity which made him popular with everybody, but in the exercise of which he was very discriminating. "You will have to leave William Henry Street, or wherever it is you hang out, and take a room in a better neighborhood. And I will show you where you can go and dine. Look here," he went on, stopping abruptly, "come up to me this evening, and we'll have a talk over a pipe. You smoke, I suppose?"

"No, sir," said Bram. "Ah don't smoke. It's too expensive. And Ah thank you kindly, but Ah've got a job out Hessel way this evening, and—"

Christian interrupted him with sudden interest.

"Out Hessel way? Why, that's near Duke's Farm. Will you take a note up for me to Miss Biron? She lives there. You can find the house easy enough."

Bram, who had listened to these words with emotions he dared not express, agreed to take the note, but did not mention that it was to the farmhouse that his own errand took him.

All the happiness he had felt over the anticipated walk to Hessel evaporated as he watched Christian tear a leaf out of a note-book, scribble hastily on it in pencil, fold and addressed it to "Miss Claire Biron."

But what a poor fool he was to be jealous? Could there be a question but that Mr. Christian Cornthwaite, with his good looks and his gayety, his position and his fortune, would make her a splendid mate?

Something like this Bram carefully dinned into himself as he took the note, and went home to his tea.

But for all that, he felt restless, dissatisfied, and unhappy as he set out after tea on his walk up to Hessel with that note from Christian Cornthwaite to Miss Biron in his pocket.

Although it was a hot evening, and the walk was uphill all the way, Bram got to the farm by half-past six, and came up to the door just as a woman, whom he decided must be the servant, came out of it.

She was about forty years of age, a little under the middle height, thickset of figure, and sallow of skin. But in her light gray eyes there was a shrewd but kindly twinkle; there was a promise of humor about her mouth and her sharply-pointed nose which made the countenance a decidedly attractive one.

She made no remark to Bram, but she turned and watched him as he approached the back door, and did not resume her walk until he had knocked and been admitted by Claire herself.

Miss Biron seemed to feel some slight embarrassment at the sight of him, and received his explanation that he had come to repaint her door with an assumption of surprise. The shrewd young man decided that the young lady had repented her unconventional friendliness of the preceding evening, and was inclined to look upon his visit as an intrusion. His manner, therefore, was studiously distant and respectful as he raised his cap from his head, gave the reason for his coming, and then said that he had brought a note for her from Mr. Christian Cornthwaite.

Claire blushed as she took it. Bram, who had brought his paint can and his brush, took off his coat, and began his task in silence, with just a sidelong look at the girl as she began to read the note.

At that moment the inner door of the kitchen opened, and Mr. Biron entered with a jaunty step, arranging a rosebud in his button-hole in quite a light comedy manner. Catching sight at once of Bram at work on the door, that young man observed that a slight frown crossed his face. After a momentary pause in his walk, he came on, however, as gayly as ever, and peeping over his daughter's shoulder read the few words the note contained, and said at once—

"Well, you must go, dear; you must go."

Claire blushed hotly, and crumpled up the note.

"I—I don't want to. I would rather not," said she in a low voice.

"Oh, but that's nonsense," retorted he good-humoredly. "Chris is a good fellow, a capital fellow. Put on your hat, and don't be a goose. I'll see that the young man at the door has his beer."

Bram heard this, and his face tingled, but he said nothing. He perceived, indeed, from a certain somewhat feminine spitefulness in Mr. Biron's tone, that the words were said with the intention of annoying him.

Claire appeared to hesitate a moment, then quickly making up her mind she said—"All right, father, I'll go," and disappeared through the inner door.

Theodore, without any remark to Bram, followed her.

In a few moments Bram heard a movement in the straw of the farmyard behind him, and looking round saw that Claire was standing behind him with her hat and gloves on, and was apparently debating in her own mind whether she would utter something which was in her thoughts. He saluted her respectfully with a stolid face. Then she began to speak, reddened, stammered, and finally made a dash for it.

"Where do you live?" she asked suddenly. "I mean—is it far from here?"

"No, miss; it's over yon," answered Bram mendaciously, nodding in the direction of the cottages on the brow of the hill.

"Then would you very much mind—" and Bram could see that her breast was heaving under the influence of some strong emotion, "keeping your eye upon this place until I come back? You know all about it," she went on, with a burst of uneasy confidence, "so that it's no use my minding that. And when my father's left alone—well, well, you know," said she, blushing crimson, and keeping her eyes down. "And Joan has to go home to her husband and children at night. And—and I'm afraid when he gets excited, you know, that he'll set the place on fire. He nearly did last night. You see, my poor father has a great many worries, and a very little affects his head—since that sabre cut in India."

The humility, nay, the humiliation in her tone, touched Bram to the quick. He promised at once that he would take care that Mr. Biron did no harm either to himself or to the house while she was away, and received her grateful, breathless, little whisper of "Thank you; oh, thank you," with outward stolidity, but with considerable emotion.

Then she ran off, and he went quietly on with his work.

It took him a very short time to finish putting on the one coat of paint, which was all he could do that night; and then, as Mr. Biron had not appeared again, Bram thought he had better take a look round and see what that gentleman was doing. So he took up his paint-can, and, leaving the door open to dry, made his way round to the front of the house, and peeped cautiously in at the lower windows; and in one of them he saw a couple of empty champagne bottles, with the corks lying beside them, and an overturned glass on the table.

"T'owd rascal hasn't wasted much time," thought Bram to himself, as he stared at the evidences of Mr. Biron's solitary dissipation, and looked about for the toper himself. But Theodore was not in the room. Neither was he in the room on the other side of the front door, as Bram hastened to ascertain. Perhaps he had had sense enough to make his way upstairs to his own room to sleep off the effects of the wine.

This seeming to be a probable explanation of his disappearance, Bram was inclined to trouble himself no further on that head, when a faint noise, which seemed to proceed from the bowels of the earth, attracted his attention. There was a grating under the window of the room which appeared to be the dining-room, and in the cellar which was thus dimly lighted some one appeared to be moving about.

Bram, in his character of sworn guardian of the house, thought it best to investigate, so he ran round to the back, entered by the open door, and found a trap-door in the hall just outside the kitchen door.

A strong smell of paraffin was the first thing he noticed as he looked down the ladder; the next was the sight of Mr. Biron calmly emptying a can of the oil upon the loose straw and firewood which the cellar contained.

Startled by the sudden light and noise above, Mr. Biron dropped the can as the trap-door opened, and then Bram saw that in his left hand he held a box of matches.

"Tha fool, tha drunken fool, coom up wi' ye!" shouted Elshaw, as he stretched down a strong arm and pulled Theodore up by his coat collar.

Bram had expected his captive to stagger, and so he did. He had expected him to stammer and to stare; and he did these things also. But Bram had seen a good deal of drunkenness in his time, and he was not easy to deceive.

Suddenly holding the slender little man at arm's length from him, and looking steadily into his eyes with a black frown on his own face, he shouted in a voice which might have roused the village—

"Why, you d—d old rascal, what villainy have you been up to? You're as sober as I am!"

CHAPTER VI
MR. BIRON'S CONDESCENSION

When Mr. Theodore Biron found himself pulled up the steps of his cellar, and roughly shaken by the very person who had disarmed him on the previous evening, his rage was such that he lost his usual airy self-possession completely, and betrayed himself in the most unworthy manner.

"Who are you, sir? And how dare you interfere with me in this way?" stammered he, as he tried in vain to release himself from the determined grasp of the young clerk.

"Coom up to t' light, and then you'll see who Ah am," said Bram, as with a strong arm he dragged the little man up the steps, and, shutting the trap-door, folded his arms and turned to look at him.

"Do you dare to justify this outrage, this—this burglarious entry upon my premises? The second in two days? Do you dare to justify it?" said Theodore haughtily.

"Ay," said Bram surlily, "Ah'm going to give information to t' police. Ah'm goin' to tell them to keep an eye upon you, Mr. Biron, and not to be surprised if t' house is burnt down; since you've got odd ways of amusing yourself with matches and paraffin, and with candles left ablaze near light curtains. Ah suppose you're insured, Mr. Biron?"

"Whatever you suppose has nothing to do with the question," retorted Mr. Biron, whose little thin cheeks were pink with indignation, and whose light eyes were flashing with annoyance and malignity. "Nobody is likely to pay much attention to the statements of a man who is evidently a loafer and a thief."

"A thief!" shouted Bram with a menacing gesture, which had the effect of sending Theodore promptly into the little dining-room behind him. "Well, we'll see whether t' word of t' thief won't be taken against yours, Mr. Biron."

There was a pause. Theodore from behind the table in the little dining-room, where he was twirling his moustache with a trembling white hand, looked at him with apprehension, and presently laughed in an attempt to recover his usual light-hearted ease of manner.

"Come, come," said he, "this is carrying a joke too far, for I suppose it was intended for a joke—this intrusion upon my premises—and that you never had any real thought of carrying anything away. I remember your face now; you are one of the workmen at my cousin's place, Cornthwaite's Iron-Works."

Bram, who was not unwilling to make terms with Miss Biron's father, stared at him sullenly.

"Ah'm not one of t' workmen now. Ah'm in t' office," said he.

Mr. Biron raised his eyebrows; he did not seem pleased. It had in fact occurred to him that this young man was employed as a sort of spy by the Cornthwaites, with whom he himself was by no means an acceptable person.

He smiled disagreeably.

"One of the clerks, eh? One of the smart young men who nibble pens in the office?"

"Ay, but ma smartness isn't outside, Mr. Biron."

"I see. Great genius—disdains mere appearance and all that."

Bram said nothing. Theodore's sneers hurt him more than any he had ever been subjected to before. He felt, in spite of his contempt for the airy-mannered scoundrel, that he himself stood at a disadvantage, with his rough speech and awkward movements, with the dapper little man in front of him. The consciousness that he himself would be reckoned of no account compared to Theodore Biron by the very men who despised the latter and respected himself was the strongest spur he had ever felt towards self-improvement.

"And what brings a person of your intellectual calibre into our humble neighborhood?" pursued Theodore in the same tone.

"Ah'm looking for lodgings up this way," answered Bram shortly.

The idea had come to him that evening that, since he had been told to change his lodgings, he would settle in the neighborhood of Hessel.

As he had expected, Mr. Biron did not look pleased.

"And you are making yourself at home in advance!" suggested he dryly.

"Well, sir, you needn't see more of me than you feel inclined to," retorted Bram.

And, with a curt salutation, he turned on his heel and went out of the house by the back way, through the kitchen and the still open outer door.

He went up the hill towards the row of cottages on the summit, and made inquiries which resulted in his finding the two modest rooms he wanted in the end house of all, within a stone's throw of a ruin so strange-looking that Bram made a tour of inspection of the ramshackle old building before returning to the town.

This ruin had once been a country mansion of fair size and of some importance, but the traces of its architectural beauties were now few and far apart. Of the main building only one side wall retained enough of its old characteristics to claim attention; at the top of the massive stonework a Tudor chimney, of handsome proportions, rose in incongruous stateliness above the decaying roof which had been placed over a row of cottages, which, built up within the old wall, had grown ruinous in their turn, and were now shut up and deserted.

At the back of this heterogeneous pile and a little distance away from it, another long and massive stone wall, with a Tudor window out of which once Wolsey had looked, had now become the chief prop and mainstay of another row of buildings, one of which was a school, another a chapel, while a third was a now disused stable.

And in the shelter of these ruins and remains of greatness a tall chimney, a cluster of sheds, and a pile of grass-grown trucks marked the spot where a now disused coal mine added a touch of fantastic desolation to the scene.

Bram went all round the pit-mouth and surveyed the town of Sheffield, with its dead yellow lights and its patches of blackness, like an inky sea bearing a fleet of ill-lighted boats on its breast in a Stygian mist. He thought he should like this evening walk out of the smoke and the lick of the fiery tongues, even without the occasional peeps he should get at Miss Biron.

But he hardly knew, perhaps, how much the thought of her, of her dancing eyes, her rapid movements like the sweep of a bird's wing, had to do with his feeling.

He went back round the pit's mouth, making his way with some difficulty in the darkness over the rough stones with which the place was thickly strewn.

And as he came to the remains of the old mansion he heard the laugh of Christian Cornthwaite, a little subdued, but clearly recognizable, not very far from his ears.

Bram straightened himself with a nasty shock. By the direction from which the sound came, he knew that Christian was in the ruin itself; and that he was not there by himself was plain. Who then was with him? Bram did not want to find an answer to this question; at least he told himself that he did not. The dilapidated shell of the old mansion was not the place where a lady would meet her lover. Bram had peeped into one of the deserted cottages on his way to the pit's mouth, and had seen that, boarded up as doors and windows were, there were ruinous crannies and spaces through which a tramp or vagrant could creep to a precarious shelter.

Christian, who loved an adventure, amorous or otherwise, was evidently pursuing one now.

Bram walked down the hill, passed the cottage where he had engaged his new rooms, whistling to himself, and telling himself persistently that he was not wondering where Miss Biron had gone to that evening. And then he became suddenly mute, for, turning his head at the sound of a light footstep behind him, he saw Claire herself coming down the hill at a breathless rate.

She passed him without seeing him. Her head was bent low, and her feet seemed to fly. Bram's heart seemed to stop beating as he watched her.

But he would not allow that he suspected her of being the person who had been in the ruined building with Christian Cornthwaite. It was true that Christian had sent her a note in which he had evidently asked her to meet him; it was true that she had acceded to the request, at her father's instigation.

But although Bram clenched his teeth in thinking of Theodore, and felt a sudden impulse of fierce indignation against that gentleman, he would not acknowledge to himself that it was possible to connect her with an act inconsistent with the modesty of a gentlewoman.

He was not far behind when Theodore, lively, bright, and entirely recovered from the discomposure into which Bram's unseemly violence had thrown him, came forth from the farmyard to meet his daughter.

"My dear child, I was getting quite anxious about you. Where's Chris? I thought he would have seen you back home."

"I left him—at the top of the hill, papa," answered Claire in a demure voice.

And she ran past Theodore into the house.

Then Theodore, whose eyes were sharp, recognized Bram. And there flashed through his brain, always active on his own behalf, the suspicion that this presumptuous young man might be spying not so much on his employer's account, as upon his own. The idea struck Theodore as preposterously amusing; but at the same time he thought that something might be made out of the foolish fellow's infatuation, if it indeed existed.

"Well, and how about the lodgings?" said he with cheerful condescension, as Bram came nearer.

"Ah've found some," replied Bram shortly.

"And what brings you so far afield?" went on Theodore more urbanely than ever. "May I hazard the conjecture that there's a lady in the case?"

The young man was quick to seize this suggestion, which he saw might be used most usefully hereafter.

"Ay, sir, that's about reght," said he. "But she doan't live here," he went on, making up his story with great deliberation as he spoke. "She lives miles away in t' country; but Ah thought Ah'd better settle out of t' town myself, before Ah went courting."

Theodore was disappointed, but he did not show it.

"Well," said he, "we shall see something of you now and then, I daresay."

And he nodded good-bye in the most affable manner.

Bram saluted respectfully, but he was too shrewd to be much impressed, in the manner Theodore intended, by this change towards him.

Away from the glamour cast upon him by the fact of Claire's presence in his vicinity, Bram had sense enough to reflect that the less he saw of Miss Biron and her shifty father the better it would be for him. He did not say this to himself in so many words; but the knowledge was borne strongly in upon him all the same. There were forces in those two persons, differently as he esteemed them, against which he felt that he had no defence ready. Theodore was cunning and grasping; his daughter was, as Bram knew, used by her father as a tool in his unscrupulous hands. Deep as Bram's compassion for the charming girl was, and his admiration, he had the strength of mind to live for months in her neighborhood without making any attempt to speak to her.

He saw her, indeed, morning after morning, and evening after evening, on his way down to the works and on his way back. For the road from his lodgings lay past the farm, where Miss Biron was always busy with her poultry in the morning, and working in her garden at night.

It was not often that she saw Bram, but when she did she had always a smile and a nod for him; never more than that though, even when he lingered a little, in the hope that she would throw him a word.

Bram saw Theodore sometimes, lounging in a garden chair, with a cigarette in his mouth; and sometimes Chris Cornthwaite would be with him, or walking by Claire's side round the lawn, chattering to her while she pottered about her late autumn flowers.

This sight always sent a sharp pang through Bram's heart; for he had conceived the idea that Christian, nice fellow though he was, might be too volatile a person to value Claire's affection as she deserved.

Claire, on her side, seemed to be happy enough with Christian. Her pretty laugh rang out gayly; and Bram, even while he laughed at himself for a sentimental folly, found himself praying that the poor child might not be deceived in her hopes of happiness with her volatile lover.

For Christian, amiable and devoted as he might be with Claire, had not, as Bram knew, given up his amiability and devotion to other girls; and after the second or third time that Bram had seen him at Hessel Farm, he mentioned casually to the newly promoted clerk that he did not want his father to hear of his visits there.

Whereat Bram looked grave, and foresaw trouble in the near future.

The March winds had begun to blow fiercely on the high ground above Hessel, when Theodore Biron at last discovered a use to which to put his young neighbor. Would Bram do some marketing for him in the town? Bram was rather surprised at the request, for an excuse for going into the town was what Theodore liked to have. But when he found that the task he was expected to undertake was the purchase of one pound's worth of goods for the sum of five shillings, which was all the cash Theodore trusted him with, Bram, when Theodore had turned his back upon him, stood looking thoughtfully at the two half-crowns in his hand.

And while he was doing so Claire, who had seen the transaction from the window, ran out of the house and came up with him. As usual, the girl's presence threw a spell upon him, and put to flight all the saner ideas he had conceived as to the desirability of trying to conquer his own infatuation. She came up smiling, but there was anxiety in her face.

"What has papa been saying to you?" she asked imperiously.

"He wants me to get some things for him in the town," said Bram straightforwardly. "But Ah'm such a bad hand at marketing—that—that Ah'm afraid—"

Claire blushed, and interrupted him impatiently.

"He's not given you money enough, of course. He never does. He doesn't understand. Men never do. They think everything can be got for a few pence for the housekeeping, and that one is wasteful and extravagant. Give me the money; I'll see about the things."

"No, you won't, Miss Claire," said Bram composedly, as he put the two half-crowns in his pocket. "You've put me on my mettle. Ah'm going to see what Ah can do, and show you that the men can give the ladies a lesson in marketing, after all."

But Claire did not reply in the same light tone. She looked up in his face with an expression of shame and alarm in her eyes, which touched him keenly. With a little catch in her breath, she tried to protest, to forbid. Then she read something in Bram's eyes which stung her, some gleam of pity, of comprehension. She broke off short, burst into tears, and turned abruptly away.

Bram stood by the gate for a few seconds, with his head hung down, and a guilty, miserable look on his face. Then, as nobody came out to him, he slunk quietly away.

CHAPTER VII
BRAM'S DISMISSAL

It was with some diffidence that Bram presented himself at the farmhouse door that evening. He went through the farmyard to the back door, and gave a modest knock. It was Joan, the servant, who opened the door to him, and Bram, as his own eyes met those of the middle-aged Yorkshire woman, had a strong sense that she read him, as he would have expressed it, "like a book." Indeed Joan could read character in a face much more easily than she could read a printed page. Having been born long before the days of School Boards, she had been accustomed from her early youth to find her entertainment not in cheap fiction, but in the life around her; so that she was on the whole much better educated than women of her class are now, having stored her mind with the facts gained by experience and observation.

She looked at him not unkindly.

"Ah," she began, with a nod of recognition, as if she had known him well for a year instead of now speaking to him for the first time, "Ah thowt it was you. Mister Christian he comes in by t' front door."

Bram did not like this comparison. It suggested, in the first place, that Joan had an instinct that there was some sort of rivalry between himself and Mr. Christian. It suggested also the basis on which they respectively stood.

"I've brought some things Miss Biron wanted," he began, forgetting that he had been commissioned, not by the young lady, but by her father.

Joan smiled a broad smile of shrewd amusement. Bram wished she would mind her own business.

"Weel, here she be to see them hersen," said she, as the inner door of the kitchen opened, and Claire came in.

"Oh, Joan, papa wants you to—" began she.

Then she saw Bram, and stopped.

"I've brought the things, Miss Claire," said he in a shy voice.

Miss Biron had stopped short and changed color. She now came forward slowly, and passing Joan, held open the door for him to enter.

"Oh, please come in," she said in a very demure voice, from which it was impossible to tell whether she was pleased or annoyed, grateful or the reverse, for his good offices.

Bram entered, and proceeded to place his enormous parcel on the deal table, and to cut the string. He was passing through the refining process very rapidly; and, already, in the clothes which he had chosen under Chris Cornthwaite's eye, he looked too dignified a person to engage in the duties of a light porter.

Claire, more demure than ever, spoke as if she was much shocked.

"Oh, have you carried that heavy parcel? Oh, I'm so sorry. It is very, very kind of you, but—"

She stopped, stammering a little. Joan, who was standing with her hands on her hips, admiring the scene, laughed scornfully.

"Eh, but it's a grand thing to be yoong! Ah can't get no smart yoong gen'lemen to carry my parcels for me, not if they was to see me breakin' ma back."

"Why, you've got a husband to carry them for you," said Claire quickly, and not very happily; for Joan laughed again.

"Ay, Miss Claire, but they doan't do it after they're married; so do you make t' moast o' your time."

And Joan, with an easy nod which was meant to include both the young people, went through into the hall with leisurely steps.

As she had left behind her a slight feeling of awkward reserve, Claire felt bound to begin with an apology for her.

"She's rather rough, but, oh, so good," said she.

"Then if she's good to you, I can forgive all her roughness," said Bram.

And the next minute he wished he had not said it.

There was a momentary pause, during which Bram busied himself with the strings of his parcels. With a rapid eye, Miss Biron ran over the various things which the outer wrapper had contained. Then, with a bright flush in her face, she took her purse from her pocket.

"How much do I owe you?" she asked quickly. "Three boxes of candles, eighteenpence. Two boxes of sardines, two and sixpence. Box of figs, half-a-crown—"

Bram interrupted her hotly. "One and ninepence, the figs," cried he, "and the sardines were only ninepence a tin."

"Then they are not the best."

"Yes, they are."

This colloquy, short and simple as it was, had left the combatants, for such they seemed, panting with excitement. Miss Biron looked at the young man narrowly and proceeded in a tone of much haughtiness—

"I must beg you to tell me really what they cost, whatever my father said. He knows nothing about the price of things, but"—and the young lady gave him a look which was meant to impress him with her vast experience in these matters—"I do."

Bram, afraid of offending her still further, and conscious of the delicate ground upon which he stood, began submissively to add up the various items, deducting a few pence where he dared, until the total of nineteen shillings and fourpence was reached. Miss Biron opened her purse rather nervously, and took out a small handful of silver, a very small handful, alas!

"Let me see. Papa gave you five shillings—"

"And then the ten he gave me as I went out by the gate after you'd gone up," pursued Bram, imperturbably.

"Ten!" echoed Claire, sharply. "Papa gave you ten shillings more!"

"Half-a-sovereign, yes," replied Bram, mendaciously. "You said he hadn't given me enough, you know, so he gave me the ten shillings. You ask him."

Claire shook her head.

"It's no use asking papa anything," she said with a sigh. Then she added, suddenly raising her head and flashing her eyes, "I must trust to your honor, Mr. Elshaw."

The sound of his name uttered by her lips gave Bram a ridiculous thrill of pleasure. He had supposed she only knew him as "Bram," and the thought that she had taken the trouble to inquire his name was a delicious one.

"Yes," said he simply, in no wise troubled by the doubt she expressed. "Well, that's fifteen shillings, and you owe me four shillings and fourpence."

She gave him a quick glance of suspicion, and then counted out her poor little hoard of sixpences and coppers. She had only three shillings and sevenpence.

"I owe you," said she, as she put the money into his hand, "ninepence, which I must pay you next week. But, please, I want you to promise," she earnestly went on, "not to do any more shopping for papa. He is so extravagant," and she tried to laugh merrily, "that I have to keep some check upon him, or we should soon be ruined."

"All right, Miss Claire, I'll do just as you wish, of course. But it's a great pleasure to me to be able to do any little thing for you. You know, for one thing," he added quickly, fancying that she might think this presumptuous, "that Mr. Christian was the person who got me moved up out of the works, so I am doubly glad to do anything for—for anybody he takes an interest in."

Over Claire's sensitive face there passed a shadow at the mention of Christian's name.

"Christian Cornthwaite is my cousin, you know," said she. "He often talks of you. He says you are very clever, and he is very proud of having discovered you, as he calls it."

"It was very good of him," said Bram. "I'm afraid I don't do him much credit; I'm such a rough sort of chap."

Miss Biron looked at him rather shyly, and laughed.

"Well, you were, just a little. But you are—are—"

"A little bit better now?" suggested Bram modestly.

"Well, I was going to say a great deal better, only I was afraid it sounded rather rude. What I meant was that—that—"

"Well, I should like to hear what it was you meant."

"Well, that you speak differently, for one thing."

"But I slip back sometimes," said Bram, laughing and blushing, just as she laughed and blushed. "It's so hard not to say 'Ah' when I ought to say 'I.' I'm getting on, I know, but it's like walking on eggs all the time."

Then they both laughed again, and at this point the door opened and Mr. Biron came in.

He was very amiable, and insisted on Bram's coming into the dining-room with him. As Bram neither smoked nor drank, however, Theodore's offer of whisky and cigars was thrown away. But Bram sat down and made a very good audience, laughing at his host's stories and jokes, so that he found himself forced into accepting an invitation to come in again on the following evening.

By Theodore's wish it became Bram's frequent custom to spend an hour at the farmhouse in the evening; and the young man soon availed himself of the intimacy thus begun to make himself useful to Claire in a hundred ways. He would chop wood in the yard, mend broken furniture, fetch things from the town, and bargain for her for her poultry, suggest and help to carry out reformations in her management of the dairy—doing everything unobtrusively, but making his shrewd common sense manifest in a hundred practical ways.

And Claire was grateful, rather shy of taking advantage of his kindness, but giving him such reward of smiles and thanks as more than repaid him for labor which was pleasure indeed.

Sometimes Christian Cornthwaite would be at the farm, and on these occasions Bram saw little of Claire, who was always monopolized by her cousin. Christian was as devoted as Bram could have wished; but, if Theodore thought that the young man delayed his coming, he did not scruple to send his daughter on some excuse to call at Holme Park, always refusing Bram's humble offers to take the message or to escort Claire.

The one thing Bram could have wished about Claire was that she should be less submissive to her unscrupulous father in matters like this. He would have had her refuse to go up to Holme Park, where she was always received, as Bram knew, with the coldness which ought to have been reserved for Theodore. And especially did Bram feel this now that he knew, from Theodore's own lips, that the notes he sent by his daughter's hand to Josiah Cornthwaite were seldom answered. It made Bram's blood boil to know this, and that in the face of this fact Theodore continued to send his daughter up to his rich cousin's house on begging errands.

Bram was in the big farm kitchen by himself one cool September evening, busily engaged in making a new dressing-table for Claire out of some old boxes. He had his coat off, and was sawing away, humming to himself as he did so, when, turning to look for something he wanted, he found, to his surprise, that Claire, whom he had not seen that evening, was sitting in the room.

She had taken her hat off, and was sitting with it in her lap, so silently, so sadly, that Bram, who was not used to this mood in the volatile girl, was struck with astonishment.

For a moment he stood, saw in hand, looking at her without speaking.

"Miss Claire!" exclaimed he at last.

"Well?"

"When did you come in? I never saw you come in!"

"No. I didn't want you to see me. I don't want any one to see me. So I can't go in because papa has the door open, and he would catch me on the way upstairs."

"What's wrong with you, Miss Claire?"

Bram had come over to her and was leaning on the table and speaking with so much kindness in his voice that the girl's eyes, after glancing up quickly and meeting his, filled with tears.

"Oh, everything. One feels like that sometimes. Everybody does, I suppose."

Bram's heart ached for the girl. He guessed that she had been to Holme Park on the usual errand, and that she had been coldly received. He could hear Theodore strumming on the piano in the drawing-room. The piano was so placed that the player had a good view of the open door, and Bram knew that Theodore had chosen this method of filling up the time till his daughter's return. Apparently he had now caught with his sharp ears the sound of voices in the kitchen, for the playing ceased, and a moment later he presented himself at the door with a smiling face.

"Good-evening, Elshaw. Heard you sawing away, but didn't like to disturb you till I heard another voice, and guessed that I might. Any answer to my note, Claire?"

For a moment he stood, saw in hand, looking at her without speaking.

"No, papa."

Claire had risen from her chair, and was standing with her back turned to her father, pretending to be busy sticking the long, black-headed pins into her hat.

"No answer. Oh, well, there was hardly an answer needed. That's all right."

From his tone nobody would have guessed that Theodore cared more than his words implied; but Bram, who saw most things, noticed a frown of disappointment and anger on the airy Mr. Biron's face. After a pause Theodore said—

"I think I shall go down the hill and have a game of billiards. That will fill up the time till you've finished your carpentering, Elshaw, and then we'll finish up with a game of chess."

And Theodore disappeared. A few moments later they heard him shut himself out by the front door.

Bram after a glance at Claire went on with his sawing, judging it wiser not to attempt to offer the sympathy with which his heart was bursting.

When he had been going on with his work for some minutes, however, Claire came and stood silently beside him. He looked up and smiled.

"Go on with your work," said she gravely, "just for a few minutes. Then I'm going to send you away."

"Send me away, Miss Claire? What for?"

"For your own good, Mr. Elshaw."

Bram suddenly pulled himself upright, and then looked down at her in dismay.

"Mr. Elshaw! I'm getting on in the world then! I used to be only Bram."

"That's it," said Claire in a low voice, looking at the fire. "You used to be only Bram; but you've got beyond that now."

"But I don't want to get beyond that with you, Miss Claire," protested he.

"What you want doesn't matter," said she decidedly. "You can't help yourself. I've heard something about you to-night. Oh, don't look like that; it was nothing to your discredit, nothing at all. But you've got to give up your carpentering and wood chopping for us, Bram, and you're not to come here again." She spoke with much decision, but her sensitive face showed some strange conflict going on within her, in which some of the softer emotions were evidently engaged. Whatever it was that made her turn her humble and useful old friend away, the cause was not ingratitude.

Before he could put another question, being indeed too much moved to be able to frame one speedily, Bram was startled by a tapping at the door. Miss Biron started; Bram almost thought he saw her shiver. She pointed quickly to the inner door.

"Go at once," said she in an imperious whisper, "and remember you are not to come back; you are never to come back."

Bram took up his coat, slipped his arms into it, and obeyed without a word. But the look on his face, as Claire caught a glimpse of it, was one which cut her to the quick. She drew a deep breath, and threw out her hands towards him with a piteous cry. Bram stopped, shivered, made one step towards her, when the tap at the door was repeated more sharply.

Claire recovered herself at once, made a gesture to him to go, and opened the one door as he let himself out by the other.

Bram heard the voice of the newcomer. It was Christian Cornthwaite.

CHAPTER VIII
ANOTHER STEP UPWARD

Bram left the farmhouse in a tumult of feeling. Why had he been dismissed so abruptly? Why had he been dismissed at all?

It was on Christian's account apparently. But what objection could Christian have to his visits to the farm?

On the many occasions when the two young men had met there Bram had always been shunted into the background for Christian, and had been left at his modest occupations unheeded, while Claire gave all her attention to her cousin. Bram had looked upon this arrangement as quite natural, and had never so much as winced at it. The idea that Christian Cornthwaite might look upon him as a possible rival being out of the question, again Bram asked himself—What could be the reason of his dismissal?

He did not mean to take it quietly; he had conceit enough to think that Claire would be sorry if he did. He could flatter himself honestly that during the past six months he had become the young lady's trusted friend, never obtrusive, never demonstrative, but trusted, perhaps appreciated, none the less on that account.

Bram had the excuse of Theodore's invitation for hanging about the neighborhood until that gentleman's return. But at the very moment when Mr. Biron's gay voice, humming to himself as he came up the hill, struck upon Bram's ear, Christian Cornthwaite came out through the farmyard gate.

"Hallo, Elshaw, is that you?" he asked, as he came out and passed his arm through Bram's. "I wondered what had become of you when I did not find you in the house this evening. I'd begun to look upon you as one of the fixtures."

"I was there this evening, Mr. Christian," replied Bram soberly. "But I got turned out without much ceremony just before you came."

"Turned out, eh? I didn't think you ever did anything to deserve such treatment from any one." And Chris looked curious. "You are what I call a model young man, if anything a little too much like the hero of a religious story for young ladies, written by a young lady."

Bram was quite acute enough to understand that this was a sneer.

"You mean that I'm what you and your friends call a prig, Mr. Christian?" he said quite unaffectedly, and without any sign of shame or regret. "Well, I suppose I am. But you don't allow for the difference between us at starting. To get up to where you stand from where I used to be, one must be a bit of a prig, don't you think?"

"Perhaps so. I think you may be trusted to know your own business, Elshaw. You're one of the men that get on. It won't do you any harm on the way up if you leave off chopping firewood in your shirt-sleeves for people who don't think any the better of you for it."

Bram, who had let himself be led up the hill, stopped short.

"She doesn't think any the worse of me for doing any little thing I can to help her," said he in a muffled voice.

Christian began to laugh.

"She? You mean Claire. Oh, no, no, she does justice to everybody, bless her dear little heart! I was thinking of our rascally friend, her father. You know very well that he uses his daughter as a means for getting all he can out of everybody. I hope you've not been had by the old ruffian, Elshaw?"

"No, Mr. Christian; no, I haven't," answered Bram hastily. "That is, not to an extent that matters."

"Ah, ha! That means you have been had for half-crowns, for instance?" As Bram moved uneasily, Chris laughed again. "Of course, it is no affair of mine; I'm quite sure you can see through our frivolous friend as well as anybody else. But if, as you say, you have been dismissed, why, I advise you not to try to get reinstated."

Now, this advice troubled Bram exceedingly. It was excellent of its kind, no doubt; but he asked himself whether the man who was so keenly alive to the disadvantages of even an acquaintance with the Birons could really be ready to form an alliance which must bring the burden of the needy elderly gentleman upon him for life. His feelings upon the subject were so keen that they would not permit him to temporize and to choose his words and his opportunity. Quite suddenly he blurted out—

"You're going to marry Miss Claire, aren't you?"

Christian, who always took things more easily than his deeper-natured companion, looked at the earnest, strongly-cut face with something like amusement. Luckily, it was too dark for Bram to see the full significance of his companion's expression.

"Marry her? Why, yes, to be sure I hope so. My father is very anxious for me 'to settle down,' as he calls it, though I would rather, for my own part, not settle down quite so far as matrimony just yet."

There was a pause. Then Bram said in a dry voice—

"I can't understand you, Mr. Christian. You seem just as nigh what a man ought to be as a man can be in lots of ways. And I can't understand how a man like that, that is a man like you, shouldn't be all on fire to make the girl he loves his wife as quick as he can. Is that a part of my priggishness, Mr. Christian, to wonder at that?"

Christian did not answer at once. They had reached the top of the hill, and were standing by the ruined cottages, which looked more desolate than ever in the darkness of the winter evening. The wind whistled through the broken walls and the decaying rafters.

Bram remembered the evening when he had heard Christian's laugh in that very pile.

"I suppose it is, Bram," said Chris at last. "But I rather like it in you, all the same. I can't help laughing at you, but I think you're rather a fine fellow. Now, listen to me. You may go on wondering at my behavior as much as you like, but you mustn't yourself have anything more to do with the Birons. We'll say I'm jealous, Bram, if you like. I really think it's true, too," he added with a flippancy which belied his words.

But Bram shook his head solemnly.

"No, Mr. Christian," he answered; and in the excitement he felt the strong Yorkshire accent was heard again in his voice. "You've no call to be jealous of me, and you know that right well. If I were a gentleman born, like you—"

"Don't use that expression,'gentleman born,' Elshaw," interrupted Chris lightly. "It means nothing, for one thing. My great-grandfather was a mill hand, or something of that sort, and so were the great-grandfathers of half the men in the House of Lords. And it sounds odd from a man like you, who will be a big pot one of these days."

"Well, Mr. Christian, if I'd been brought up in a big house, like you, and had had my face kept clean and my hair curled instead of being allowed to make mud-pies in the gutter—"

"I *wanted* to make mud-pies in the gutter!" interpolated Christian cheerfully.

"Well, you know what I mean, anyhow. If we'd stood just on the same ground—"

"We never should have stood on the same ground, Elshaw," said Chris with a shrewd smile.

"—And if I hadn't been beholden to you for the rise I've got, I'd have fought you for the place you've got with her very likely. But, as it is, I'm nowhere; I don't count. And you know that, Mr. Christian."

"Indeed, I'm very glad to hear it, for if there's one man in the world I should less like to have for a rival than another, in love or in anything else, it's you, Bram. I know you're a lamb outside; but I can't help suspecting that there's a creature more like a tiger underneath."

"I'm inclined to think myself, Mr. Christian, that the creature underneath's more like an ass," said Bram good-humoredly.

They were standing at the top of the hill; it was a damp, cold night, and Christian shivered.

"You mustn't stand here talking, Mr. Christian," said Bram. "You are not so used to strong breezes as me."

"Well, good-night; I won't take you any further. You live somewhere about here, I know. But, I say." He called after Bram, who was turning back. "There's one thing I want to tell you. Don't say anything to the guv'nor about meeting me at the farm."

Bram stared blankly, and Christian laughed.

"My dear fellow, don't you know that these matters require to be conducted with a little diplomacy? When a man is dependent upon his father, as he always is if he's a lazy beggar like me, that father has to be humored a little. I must prepare him gradually for the shock, if I'm ever to marry Claire."

"All right, Mr. Christian. I'll say nothing, of course. But I shall be glad to hear that matters are straight. It seems hard on the young lady, doesn't it?"

"Ah, well, life isn't all beer and skittles for any of us."

Christian called out these words, turning his head as he walked rapidly away on the road to Holme Park.

Bram had made such astonishing progress in the office since his promotion, not much more than a year before, that nobody but himself was astonished when he was called into the private office of the elder Mr. Cornthwaite, about a fortnight after his talk with Christian, and was formally invited by that gentleman to dine at Holme Park in the course of the following week. Bram's first impulse was to apologize for declining the invitation, but Mr. Cornthwaite insisted, and with such an air of authority that Bram felt there was no escape for him.

But, meeting Christian later in the day, Bram related the incident rather as if it were a grievance.

"You know, Mr. Christian, it's not in my line, that sort of thing. Ah shall make a fool o' myself, Ah know Ah shall."

And, either accidentally or on purpose, he dropped again into the strong Yorkshire dialect, which since his elevation he had worked successfully to overcome.

But Christian only laughed at his excuses.

"You'd be a fool to refuse," he said shortly. "I'll take you round to my tailor's again, and he'll measure you for your war-paint."

Bram's face fell.

"No, Mr. Christian, no. I'm not going to dress myself up. Mr. Cornthwaite won't expect it, and what would be the good of my wasting all that money on clothes you'll never catch me wearing again? And the oaf I should look in 'em too! Why, you'd all be laughin' at me, an' not more than I should be laughin' at myself."

"Elshaw," returned Chris gravely, "the one thing which distinguishes you above all the self-made men and born geniuses I've ever heard about is that you've got too broad a mind to despise trifles. While Sir George Milbrook, who began as a factory hand, and Jeremiah Montcombe of Gray's Hall, and a lot of other men who've got on like them, make a point of dropping their H's and clipping their words just as they used to do forty years ago, you've thought it worth your while to drop your Ah's and your tha's, till there's very little trace of them left already, and there'll be none in another year. Well, now, there are some more trifles to be mastered, and dressing for dinner is one of them. So buck up, old man, and come along. And by-the-by, as you'll always take a hint from me, couldn't you let yourself drop into slang sometimes? Your language is so dreadfully precise, and you use so many words that I have to look out in the dictionary."

"Do I, Mr. Christian?" asked Bram, surprised. Then he laughed and shook his head. "No, I can't trust myself as far as the slang yet. It wouldn't come out right perhaps. I shouldn't have discrimination enough to choose between the slang that was all right and the slang which would make the ladies look at each other."

"Well, I suppose I must let you have a few months' grace. But it's only on condition that you smoke an occasional cigarette, and that you don't stick so persistently to soda water and lemonade, when you're asked to have a drink."

"But, Mr. Christian, I'm not used to wine and spirits, not even to beer, and if I was to drink them they would get into my head. And as it takes me all my time to speak properly and behave so as to pass muster, as it is, you'd better leave pretty well alone, and let me keep to the soda water."

"Oh, well, as long as you're not moved by conscientious scruples I don't so much mind. But teetotalism savors rather too much of the Sunday-school and the Anti-Tobacco League. Mind, I don't want to make you an habitual drunkard, but I should like to feel sure that you understand there is a happy medium."

"Oh, yes, I understand that," said Bram with a comical look; "but I wish I hadn't to go up to the Park Thursday week all the same."

Chris looked at him steadily, and played with his long, tawny moustache for a few moments in silence.

"So do I. I wish you hadn't got to go too," said he at last.

But he would not explain why; he turned the subject by remarking that they mustn't forget the visit to the tailor's.

CHAPTER IX
A CALL AND A DINNER PARTY

It is not to be supposed that Bram had forgotten all about Claire Biron, or that he had not been tempted to break through the command she had imposed upon him. At first he had intended to present himself as usual at the farm on the evening after his summary dismissal, and to brave her possible displeasure. He felt so sure of her kind feeling toward himself that he had very little doubt of overcoming her scruples from whatever cause they arose.

On the very next morning, however, he had come suddenly upon her as he went down the hill towards the town; and Claire had cut him, actually cut him, passing him with her eyes on the ground, at a rapid pace.

Bram was so utterly overwhelmed by this action on her part that he stood stupidly staring at her figure as it went quickly upwards, uncertain what to do, until she turned into the farmyard and disappeared.

He went on to the office with a dull weight at his heart, hoping against hope that she would relent, that she would smile at him with her old friendliness when next they met, but unable to stifle the fear that the pleasant friendship which had been so much to him was now over.

As to her reasons for this new course of treatment he could make no guess which seemed to him at all likely to be the right one. She had heard something about him, that was her excuse, something not to his discredit, but which was, nevertheless, the cause of her sending him away. Now, Bram could think of nobody who was likely to be able to tell Claire the one fact which might have brought about his banishment conceivably, the fact that he loved her. He had kept his secret so well that he might well feel sure it was in his own power, so well that he sometimes honestly doubted whether it was a fact at all.

Besides, even if it had been possible for her to find this out, she would not have dismissed him in this curt, almost brutal, fashion.

The more Bram thought about his banishment, the farther he seemed to get from a sane conclusion; but he could not rest. He could not dismiss the matter from his mind. Full as his new life was of work, of interest, of ambitions, of hopes, the thought of Claire haunted him. He wondered how she was getting on without him, knowing that he had made himself useful to her in a hundred ways, and that if she did not miss him, she must at least miss the work he did for her.

And Christian—he had told Bram in so many words that he meant to marry his cousin; yet his visits had fallen off in frequency, and Bram had an idea that Claire looked unhappy and anxious.

Bram knew very well that he could get an invitation back to the farm at any moment by putting himself in the way of Theodore. But he would not do this; he would not go back without the invitation, or at least the consent of Claire herself.

So he avoided Theodore, and went up and down the hill with an outward air of placid unconcern until the evening before the day when he was to dine at Mr Cornthwaite's.

It was a pleasant October evening; there was a touch of frost in the air, which was bracing and pleasant after the heavy atmosphere of the town. When he got close to the farmhouse, he saw Claire crossing the farmyard on her way to the kitchen door, with a heavy load of wood in her arms. It seemed to him that her face looked sad and worn, that odd little face which had so little prettiness in repose except for those who knew the possibilities for fun, for tenderness, that lay dormant in her bright brown eyes.

He hesitated a moment, and then went quickly through the gate.

"May I help you, Miss Claire?"

She did not start or pretend to be surprised. She had seen him coming.

She stopped.

"You know what I told you, that you were not to come here again," she said severely.

But it was severity which did not frighten him.

"Well," he began humbly, "I've kept away nearly a fortnight."

"But I said you were never to come again."

"I don't think you can have meant it though. You would have given me some reason if you had."

Claire frowned and tapped her little foot impatiently on the ground.

"Oh, you know, you must know. You are not stupid, Mr. Elshaw."

"I'm beginning to think I am," said Bram, as he began to take her load from her with gentle insistence.

It amused and touched him to note how glad she was, in spite of her assumed displeasure, to give her work up to him in the old way. He opened the kitchen door, and took the wood into the scullery, where Joan was at work, just as he used to do for her, and then went through the kitchen slowly on his way out again.

Claire was standing by the big deal table.

"Thank you, thank you very much," said she.

But her tone was not so bright as usual; she was more subdued altogether—a quiet, demure, downcast little girl. Bram, making his way with leaden feet to the outer door, wanted to say something, but hardly knew what. He hoped that she would stop him before he reached the door, but he was disappointed. He put his hand upon the latch and paused. Still she said nothing. He opened the door, and glanced back at her. Although the look she gave him in return had nothing of invitation in it, he felt that there was something in her sad little face which made it impossible to leave her like that.

"Miss Claire," said he, and he was surprised to find that his voice was husky and not so loud as he expected, "mayn't I finish the dressing-table?"

"If you like."

Her voice was as husky as his own.

Without another word he set about the work, found the saw, which, by-the-bye, was his own, the wood, and the rest of the things he wanted, and in less than ten minutes was at work in the old way, and Claire, fetching her needlework, was busy by the fire, just as she used to be. She was too proud to own it; but Bram saw quite plainly that this quiet re-establishment of the old situation made her almost as happy as it did him.

"Things going all right, Miss Claire?" asked he as he took up his plane.

"No, of course they're not. They're going all wrong, as usual. More wrong than usual. Johnson takes more advantage than ever of there being nobody to look after him properly."

Johnson was the farm bailiff, and he had worked all the better for the suggestions sharp-sighted Bram had made to Claire. Since Bram's banishment Johnson had been rampant again. Claire was quite conscious of this, and she turned to another subject, to allow him no opportunity of applying her comments.

"And you—at least I needn't ask. You always get on all right, don't you?"

"I shall come to grief to-morrow," answered Bram soberly. "I've got to go up to the Park to dinner. What do you think of that, Miss Claire? And to wear a black coat and a stiff shirt-front, just like a gentleman! Won't they all laugh at me when my back's turned, and talk about daws' and peacocks' feathers? It's all Mr. Christian's fault, so I suppose you will say it's all right?"

"It is all right, Bram," said Claire gravely; "and they won't laugh at you. They can't. You're too modest. And too clever besides." She paused, dropped her work in her lap, and looked intently at the fire. "Is it true that you're going to be married, Bram?" she presently asked abruptly.

"Married! Me! Lord, no. Who told you such a thing as that?" And Bram stood up and looked at her, letting his plane lie idle.

"Papa said he thought you were. He said you were engaged to a girl who lived in the country. You never told me about her."

"And is that why you sent me away?"

At his tone of dismay Claire burst out laughing with her old hilarity.

"Oh, no, oh, no. I sent you away, if you must know, because I had heard that you were to go up and dine at Holme Park, and because I knew that it would be better for you to be able to say there that you didn't visit us."

"Is *that* what you call a reason?" asked Bram scornfully, angrily.

"Yes, that's one reason."

"Well, well, haven't you any better ones?"

"Perhaps. But I shan't tell you any more, so you need not ask me for them. I want to know something about this girl you're engaged to."

"Not engaged," said Bram stolidly.

"Well, in love with then? I want to know something about her. I think it very strange that I never heard anything about her before. What is she like?"

"Well, she's like other girls," said Bram. "She is much like nine out of every ten girls you meet."

"Really? I shouldn't have thought you'd care for a girl like that, Bram."

"You must care for what you can get in this world," said Bram sententiously.

"Well, tell me something more. Is she tall or short, fair or dark? Has she blue eyes, or gray ones, or brown?"

Bram looked thoughtful.

"Well, she's neither tall nor short. She's not very dark, nor yet very fair. And her eyes are a sort of drab color, I think."

"You don't mean it, Bram? I suppose you think it's no business of mine?"

"That's it, Miss Claire."

"I don't believe in the existence of this girl with the drab-colored eyes, Bram."

Claire had jumped up, and darted across to the table in her old impulsive way; and now she stood, her eyes dancing with suppressed mirth, just as she used to stand in the good old days before the rupture of her own making.

Bram was delighted at the change.

"Well, I won't say whether she exists or not," replied he with a smile lurking about his own mouth; "and I don't choose to have my love affairs pried into by anybody, I don't care who. How would you like people to pry into yours?"

She grew suddenly grave, and he wished he had not said it.

"There's no concealment about mine, Bram," she said quietly.

"You're going to marry Mr. Christian?"

"I suppose so."

Why did she speak so quietly, so wistfully? The question troubled Bram, who did not dare to say any more upon a subject which she seemed anxious to avoid as much as she could. And the talk languished until Claire heard her father's footsteps coming down the stairs.

"Now go," said she imperiously. "I don't want you to meet papa. And you mustn't come again. And you mustn't tell them up at Holme Park that you were here this evening."

Bram frowned.

"Miss Claire," said he, "I am a deal prouder of coming here than I am of going up to t' Park. And if I'm to choose between here and t' Park, I choose to come here. But I shall be let to do as I please, I can promise you. But, of course, if you don't want me here, I won't come."

"Good-night," said she for answer.

And she hurried him out of the house, and shut the door upon him in time to prevent her father, who was in the passage outside, from meeting him.

Bram went up to the Park on the following evening in much better spirits than if he had not had that reassuring interview with Claire. He still felt rather troubled as to the prospects of the marriage between her and her cousin, but he hoped that he might hear something about it in the family circle at Holme Park.

The ordeal of the evening proved less trying than the promoted clerk had expected—up to the certain point.

With the ladies of the family he had already become acquainted. Mrs. Cornthwaite was a tiresome elderly lady of small mental capacity and extremely conservative notions, who alternately patronized Bram and betrayed her horror at the recollection of his former station. The good lady was a perpetual thorn in the side of her husband, whom she irritated by silly interruptions and sillier comments on his remarks, and to her daughter, who had to be ever on the alert to ward off the effects of her mother's imbecility.

The daughter, Hester, was a thoroughly good creature, who had been worried into a pessimistic view of life, and into a belief that much "good" could be done in the world by speaking her mind with frank rudeness upon all occasions. The consequence of these peculiarities in the ladies of the household was that to spend an evening in their society was a torture from which all but the bravest shrank, although every one acknowledged that they were the best-intentioned people in the world.

The only guests besides Bram were Mr. and Mrs. Hibbs and their only daughter, whom Bram knew already by name and by sight.

Mr. Hibbs was a coal-owner, a man of large means, and a great light in evangelical circles. He was a tall, sallow man, with thin whiskers and a deliberate manner of speaking, as if he were always in the reading-desk, where on Sundays he often read the lessons for the day. His wife was a comfortable-looking creature, with a round face and a round figure, and a habit of gently nodding her head after any remark of her husband's, as if to emphasize its wisdom.

As for Minnie, it struck Bram, as he made her the bow he had been practising, that she exactly answered to the description he had given Claire of the supposed lady of his heart. There was only this difference, that she was distinguished from most young women of her age by the exceedingly light color of her eyebrows and eyelashes. She appeared to have none until you had the opportunity for a very close inspection.

She had quite a reputation for saintliness, which had reached even Bram's ears. Her whole delight was in Sunday-school work and in district visiting, and the dissipations connected with these occupations.

She was, however, very cheerful and talkative during dinner; and Bram was surprised to see how very attentive Christian, who sat by her side, was to this particularly unattractive young person, who was the antithesis of all he admired.

For Christian's good nature did not generally go the length of making him more than barely civil to plain women.

Bram found Miss Cornthwaite kind and easy to get on with. She was a straightforward, practical woman, on the far side of thirty, and this grave, simple-mannered young man, with the observant gray eyes, interested and pleased her. She tried to intercept the glances of horror which Mrs. Cornthwaite occasionally threw at him, and the terrible explanations with which the elder lady condescendingly favored him.

Thus, when the Riviera was mentioned, Mrs. Cornthwaite threw him the good-natured aside, audible all over the room—

"The shore of the Mediterranean, you know, the sea that lies between France and Italy, and—and those places!"

And when some one used the word "bizarre," Mrs. Cornthwaite smiled at Bram again, and again whispered loudly—

"Quaint, odd, you know. It's a French word."

"Mamma, you needn't explain. Mr. Elshaw speaks better French than we do, I'm quite sure," said Hester good-naturedly enough, though she had better have made no comment.

But Bram said at once, as if grateful to the old lady—

"No, Miss Cornthwaite, I can read and write French pretty well, but I can't speak it. And when I hear a French word spoken I don't at once catch its meaning."

"There, you see, Hester, I was right. I knew Mr. Elshaw would be glad of a little help," said Mrs. Cornthwaite triumphantly.

"Very glad, indeed," assented Bram, quickly interposing as Hester was about to continue the argument with her mother.

It was not until the ladies had left the room, and Bram, with an amused glance at Christian, had taken a cigarette, that the real ordeal of the evening came for the young clerk in a shape he had never expected.

"I suppose you hardly know, Elshaw," said Mr. Cornthwaite with a preliminary cough, as if to show that he was about to make an announcement of importance, "why I was so particularly anxious for you to dine with us this evening?" Bram looked interested, as, indeed, he felt. "You are aware, Elshaw, of the enormously high opinion of your talents which my son has always held. He now proposes that you should go to London to represent us in a rather delicate negotiation, in place of himself. And as the reason is that he will himself be occupied with pleasanter matters than those of dry business, I thought it would interest you to be present on the occasion of the first announcement of the pleasanter matter in question. It is not less than a wedding—"

"A wedding, sir?" Bram's face clouded with perplexity.

"Yes, Elshaw. You have had the honor of being introduced to the young lady this evening. My son has been fortunate enough to obtain the heart and a promise of the hand of Miss Minnie Hibbs."

Bram looked steadily at Christian. He dared not speak.

CHAPTER X
THE FINE EYES OF HER CASH-BOX

Christian Cornthwaite pretended to be occupied in conversation with his future father-in-law, while Mr. Cornthwaite, senior, in his blandest and most good-humored tones, made the announcement of his son's intended marriage to the astonished Bram.

But Christian's attention was not so deeply engaged that he could not take note of what was happening, and he noticed the dead silence with which Bram received the announcement, and presently stole a furtive look at the face of the young clerk.

Bram caught the look, and replied to it with a steady stare. Chris turned his eyes away, but that look of Bram's fascinated him, worried him. In truth, it had been his fear of what Elshaw would say, even more than his own disinclination, which had kept him hovering on the brink of his engagement with Miss Hibbs for so long.

And now he felt that he would have preferred some outbreak on Bram's part to this stony silence.

"A wedding, Sir?" Bram's face clouded with perplexity.

Even Josiah Cornthwaite was puzzled by Bram's reception of the news. The young man seemed absolutely unmoved by the fresh proof of his employer's confidence given in the information that he was to be sent to London on important business. He grew even uneasy as Bram's silence continued, or was broken only by the briefest and coldest of answers. He looked from his son to Bram, and perceived that there was some understanding between them. And his fears grew apace. He shortened the stay in the dining-room, therefore, and letting Mr. Hibbs and Chris enter the drawing-room together, he took Bram up the stairs, with the excuse of showing him the view of the town from one of the windows.

Bram was shrewd enough to guess that he was to be "pumped."

"This news about my son's intended marriage seems to have taken you by surprise, Elshaw," said Mr. Cornthwaite as they stood together looking out on the blurred lights of the town below.

"Well, sir, it has," admitted Bram briefly.

"But you know he is twenty-six, an age at which a young man who can afford it ought to be thinking of marrying."

"Oh, yes."

"You thought, perhaps, that such a volatile fellow would be scarcely likely to make such a sensible choice as he has done?" went on Josiah with an air of bland indulgence, but with some anxiety in his eyes.

There was a pause.

"That was what you thought, eh?" repeated Mr. Cornthwaite more sharply.

Bram Elshaw frowned.

"Sir, may I speak out?" asked he bluntly.

"Certainly."

"Well, then, sir, I don't think it is a wise choice—if it was his choice at all, and not yours, sir?"

Now, Mr. Cornthwaite, while giving his permission to speak out, had not expected such uncompromising frankness as this. He was taken aback. He stammered as he began to answer—

"Why, why, what do you mean? Could there be a more sensible choice than such a lady as Miss Hibbs? A good daughter, not frivolous, or vain, or flighty; a sensible, affectionate girl, devoted to her parents and to good works. Just such a girl, in fact, as can be depended upon to make a thoroughly good, devoted wife."

"For some sort of men, sir. But not for a man like Mr. Christian," returned Bram with decision.

His blood was up, and he spoke with as much firmness as, and with more fire than, he had ever before shown to his employer.

Mr. Cornthwaite, who had grounds for feeling uneasy, was lenient, patient, attentive, curious.

"Why, don't you know, Elshaw," said he sharply, "that a man should mate with his opposite if he wants to be happy? That grave and serious men like frivolous wives; but that your lively young fellow likes a sober-minded wife to keep his house in order?"

"Sir, if it's Mr. Christian's choice, there's an end of it," said Bram brusquely.

"Of course it's his choice, none the less, but rather the more, that it meets not only with my approval, but with that of the ladies of my family," said Mr. Cornthwaite pompously.

Yet still he was curious, still unsatisfied. And still Bram said nothing.

"Believe me," Mr. Cornthwaite went on impressively, "a man is none the less amenable to the influence of a good wife for having sown his wild oats first. With a wife like the one I—no, I mean he has chosen," a faint smile flickered over Bram's mouth at this correction, "my son will settle down into a model husband and father. You want the two elements, seriousness on the one side, good-humored gayety on the other, to make a happy marriage. Why, I ought to know, for these are exactly the principles on which I married myself."

Mr. Cornthwaite uttered these words with an air of bland assurance, which, he thought, must carry conviction. But his young hearer, unfortunately, had heard enough about the domestic life at Holme Park to know that the "sensible marriage" on which Mr. Cornthwaite prided himself had by no means resulted in domestic peace. The bickerings of the ill-matched pair were, in fact, a constant source of misery to all the household, and were used freely by Chris as an excuse for his neglect of home.

Bram, therefore, received this information with courtesy, but without comment. Mr. Cornthwaite kept his eyes steadily fixed upon the young man, and found himself at last obliged to put a direct question.

"You had, I suppose, expected him to make a different sort of choice?"

"Very different, sir."

"Some one, perhaps, whom you would have considered better suited to him?"

"Much better suited, sir."

Mr. Cornthwaite's face clouded.

"Whom do you mean?"

Bram only hesitated a moment. He could do Christian no harm now by telling the truth; and he had a lingering hope that he might bring old Mr. Cornthwaite to see the matter with his own eyes.

"Sir," said he, "have you never suspected your son of any attachment, any serious attachment, to a lady as good as Miss Hibbs is said to be, and a great deal more attractive?"

Bram felt as he said this that he had lapsed into the copybook style of conversation which Chris had pointed out as one of his besetting sins. But he could not help it. He felt the need of some dignity in speaking words which he felt to be momentous.

Mr. Cornthwaite looked deeply annoyed.

"I have not," said he shortly. And again he asked—"Whom do you mean?"

"Miss Claire Biron, sir," answered Bram.

Mr. Cornthwaite's face darkened still more.

"What!" cried he in agitation which belied his words. "You believe that my son ever gave that girl a serious thought? And that the daughter of such a father could be a proper match for my son? Absurd! Absurd! Of course, you are a very young man; you have no knowledge of the world. But I should have thought your native shrewdness would have prevented your falling into such a mistake as that."

Bram said nothing. Mr. Cornthwaite, in spite of the scornful tone he had used, was evidently more anxious than ever to learn whatever Bram had to tell on the subject. After a short silence, therefore, he asked in a quieter tone—

"How came you to get such a notion into your head, Elshaw?"

"I knew that they were fond of each other, sir; and I knew that Miss Biron was a young lady of character, and what you call tact."

"Tact! Humbug!" said Mr. Cornthwaite shortly. "She is an artful, designing girl, and she and her father have done all in their power to entangle my son. But I foresaw his danger, and now I flatter myself I have saved him. You, I see, have been taken in by the girl's little mincing ways, just as my son was in danger of being. But I warn you not to have anything to do with them. They are an artful, scheming pair, both father and daughter, and it would be ruin for any man to become connected with them—ruin, I say."

And he stared anxiously into Bram's face.

"Has she led you on too?" he asked presently, with great abruptness.

Bram's face flushed.

"No, sir. She has forbidden me to come to her father's house."

"Ah! A ruse, a trick to encourage my son!" cried the old gentleman fiercely. "I wish he were safely married. I shall do all in my power to hurry it on. How often have you seen him about there? You live near, I believe?" said he curtly.

"I have seen him now and then, not so very often lately," answered Bram.

"Ah, well, you won't see him there much longer. Miss Hibbs will see to that."

"Sir, you are wrong," cried Bram, whose head and heart were on fire at these accusations against Claire. "Miss Hibbs may be a good girl, as girls go. I don't know" (Bram's English gave way here) "nothing against her. But I do know you don't give your son a chance when you make him marry a sack o' meal like that, and him loving a flesh-and-blood woman like Miss Biron! Why, sir, ask yourself whether it's in nature that he should settle down to the psalm-singing that would suit her, so as to be happy and satisfied to give up his wild ways? Put it to him point blank, sir, which he'd do of his own free will, and see what answer you'll get from him!"

"I shall do nothing of the kind," said Mr. Cornthwaite hastily, "and I'm exceedingly sorry to find you so much more gullible than I had expected, Elshaw. Is it possible you didn't observe how this young woman ran after my son? Coming to this house on every possible occasion with some excuse or other?"

"That was her father's fault, sir," retorted Bram hotly.

"Probably he had something to do with it; but she fell in with his wishes with remarkable readiness, readiness which no modest girl would have shown in the circumstances. She must have seen she was not welcomed with any warmth by the heads of the household at least."

The blood rushed to Bram's forehead. The idea of poor little Claire creeping unwillingly to the great house on one of her father's miserable errands, only to be snubbed and coldly received by every one, struck him like a stab.

"Surely, sir, there was no place in the world where she had so good a right to expect to be well received as here?" said he, with difficulty controlling the emotion he felt. "A young girl, doing her best to fulfil every duty, with no friends, no mother, no father worthy of the name. And you are her relations; here there were women, ladies, who knew all about her, and who might be expected to sympathize with her difficulties and her troubles!"

Bram, who spoke slowly, deliberately, choosing his words with nice care, but uttering them with deep feeling, paused, and looked straight into Mr. Cornthwaite's face. But there was no mercy in the fiery black eyes, or about the cold, handsome mouth.

"They would have shown her every sympathy," said he coldly, "if she had not abused the privilege of intimacy by trying to ensnare my son."

"Mr. Cornthwaite," interrupted Bram scornfully, "do you really think Mr. Christian ever waited for a girl to run after him? Why, for every time Miss Biron's been up here—sent here by her father, mind—he's been three or four or five times down at the farm!"

Mr. Cornthwaite's eyes blazed. By a quick movement he betrayed that this was just what he had wanted to know. His face clouded more than before.

"Ah!" said he shortly, "that's what I've been told. Well, it's the girl's own doing. If she's got herself into a scrape, she has no one but herself to thank for it, no one. Shall we join the ladies in the drawing-room?"

He led the way downstairs, and Bram followed in dead silence.

A horrible, sickly fear had seized his heart; he could not but understand the imputation Mr. Cornthwaite had made, accompanied as it was by a look, the significance of which there was no mistaking.

Claire, poor little helpless Claire, the cherished idol of his imagination and of his heart, lay under the most cruel suspicion which can assail a woman, the suspicion of having held her honor too lightly.

Bram, shocked beyond measure, recoiled at the bare mention of this suspicion in connection with the girl he worshipped. The next moment he cast the thought behind him as utterly base, and felt that he had disgraced himself and her by the momentary harboring of it.

But as for Mr. Cornthwaite, Bram felt that he hated the smug, elderly gentleman, who troubled himself not in the least about the helpless, friendless girl who loved his son, and whose only thought was to hurry his son into a heartless marriage in order to "save him from" the danger of his repairing his supposed error.

In these circumstances, Bram lost all self-consciousness, all remembrance of his unaccustomed dress, of his attitudes, of his awkwardness, and entered the drawing-room utterly absorbed in thoughts of Claire. Old Mrs. Cornthwaite, who was fumbling about with a lapful of feminine trifles, smelling-bottle, handkerchief, spectacle-case, dropped one of them, and he hastened to pick it up.

"Thank you," said she, with a gracious, good-humored smile, "you are more attentive than any of the grand folk."

"Mamma," cried Hester in fidgety exasperation. And good-naturedly fearing that he might have been hurt by her mother's lack of tact, she opened the old-fashioned, but not unhelpful, album of photographs, which lay on a table near her, and asked him if he cared for pictures of Swiss scenery.

"Not much, Miss Hester," said Bram.

But he went up to the table, encouraged by her kind manners, by the honest look in her eyes, in the hope that he might find a supporter in her of the cause he had at heart.

"But I should like to see some photographs of you and Mr. Christian, if you have any."

She opened another album, smiling as she did so, and offering him a chair near her, which he immediately took.

"I never show these unless I am asked," she said. "Family photographs I always think uninteresting, except to the family."

"And to those interested in the family," amended Bram. "You see, Miss Hester, there's hardly another thing in the world I care about so much. That's only natural, isn't it, after what I've been treated like at their hands."

He was conscious that his English was getting doubtful under the influence of the emotion which he could not master. But Miss Cornthwaite seemed, of course, not to notice this. She was extremely well disposed towards this frank young man with the earnest eyes, the heavy, obstinate mouth, and the long, straight chin, which gave so much character to his pale face.

"Christian always speaks of you with such boyish delight, as if he had discovered you bound hand and foot in the midst of cannibals who wanted to eat you," said she laughing.

"So he did, Miss Hester," answered Bram gravely, almost harshly.

He could not speak, could not think of Chris just now without betraying something of the emotion the name aroused in him. And he glanced angrily across to the corner where Chris was sitting beside prim little Miss Hibbs, who was giggling gently at his remarks, but clasping her hands tightly together, and keeping her arms pinned closely to her sides, as if she felt that she was unbending more than was meet, and that she must atone for a little surface hilarity by this penitential attitude.

Hester Cornthwaite noticed the glance thrown by Bram, and felt curious.

"I am very glad he is going to be married," she said quickly, with an intuition that he would not agree with her. Bram looked her full in the face in a sudden and aggressive manner.

"Why are you glad?" he asked abruptly.

She was rather disconcerted for a moment.

"Why? Oh, because I think it will be good for him, that he will be happier, that he will settle down," she answered with a little confusion.

Surely he must know as well as she did that there were many reasons for wishing Chris to grow more steady. A little prim suggestion of this feeling was noticeable in her tone.

"I don't think he would settle down, if so he was to marry a girl he didn't care for," said Bram bluntly. "And I should have thought you would agree with me, understanding Mr. Christian as you do, Miss Hester."

Miss Cornthwaite drew her lips rather primly together.

"He does care for her, of course," said she rather tartly, "else why should he marry her?"

Bram smiled, and gave her a glance of something like scorn.

"There are a good many reasons why he should marry to please Mr. Cornthwaite, your father, when he can't marry to please himself."

"Why can't he? Who does he want to marry?" asked Miss Cornthwaite quickly.

"Why, Miss Biron, Miss Claire Biron, of Duke's Farm," replied honest Bram promptly.

Hester's thin and rather wizened face flushed. She frowned; she looked annoyed. "Dear me! I never heard anything about it," she said testily. "And I can hardly think he would wish to do anything so very unwise. Christian isn't stupid, though he's rather volatile."

"Stupid! No, indeed. That he should want to marry Miss Biron is no proof of stupidity. Where could he find a nicer wife? How could you expect him to sit and look contentedly at Miss Hibbs when there is such a girl as Miss Biron within ten miles?"

Hester looked more prim than ever.

"You seem very enthusiastic, Mr. Elshaw. Pray, what have you to say about Mr. Biron?"

"Well, Mr. Christian wouldn't have to marry him."

"That is just what he would have to do," retorted she quickly. "Mr. Biron would take good care of that. Christian would never be able to shake him off."

"Well," said Bram, "he can't shake him off now, can he? So he would be no worse off."

"Now, seriously, Mr. Elshaw, would you like to have such a father-in-law yourself?"

Bram's heart leapt up. But he did not tell the young lady that he only wished he had the chance. Instead of that, he answered in a particularly grave and judicial tone—

"If I had, I'd soon bring him to reason. He's not stupid either, you see. I'd make an arrangement with him, and I'd make him keep to it. And if he didn't keep to it—"

"And he certainly wouldn't. What then?"

"Well, then perhaps I'd get rid of him some way, Miss Hester."

"I certainly shouldn't advise my brother to run the risk of having to do that, and all for a girl much too volatile to make him a good wife. Why, she is nearly half French."

Bram looked at her quickly.

"Surely, Miss Hester, you who have travelled and been about the world, don't think the worse of a lady for that?"

Miss Cornthwaite reddened, but she stuck to her guns.

"I hope I am above any silly insular prejudice," she said coldly. "But I certainly think the French character too frivolous for an Englishman's wife. Why, when Claire comes here, though she will sob as if her heart was breaking one moment at the humiliations her father exposes her to, she will be laughing heartily the next."

"Poor child, poor child! Thank heaven she can," said Bram with solemn tenderness which made Miss Cornthwaite just a little ashamed of herself. "And don't you think a temper like that would come in handy for Mr. Christian's wife, as well as for Mr. Biron's daughter?"

"Oh, perhaps," said Miss Cornthwaite very frigidly, as she stretched out her hand quickly for a fresh book to show him.

Poor Claire had no partisan here.

CHAPTER XI
BRAM SHOWS HIMSELF IN A NEW LIGHT

Now, Christian felt throughout the evening that Bram was avoiding his eyes, saving himself up, as it were, for an attack of eye and tongue, a combat in which Chris would have all he could do to hold his own.

Christian was fond of Bram, fonder even, perhaps, than Bram, with his honest admiration and indulgence, was of him. The steady, earnest character of the sturdy man of the people, with his straightforward simplicity, his shrewdness, and his blunt outspokenness when his opinion was asked, had constant attraction for the less simple, but more amiable, son of the owner of the works. He wanted to put himself right with Bram, and to do it in such a way as to put Bram in the wrong.

He tried to get an opportunity of a chat with the sullen-looking young clerk, who, however, avoided this chance more cleverly than Chris sought it.

At the close of the evening, when Bram had reeled off without a mistake the elaborate speech of thanks to Mrs. Cornthwaite which he had prepared beforehand, he contrived very cleverly to slip out of the house while Chris was occupied with the perfunctory attentions demanded by his *fiancée*. And with the start he thus obtained, he contrived to reach the foot of Hassel Hill before he became aware that he was being followed.

"Hallo!" cried out a bright voice, which he knew to be that of Chris. "Hallo!"

Bram did not answer, did not slacken his pace, but went straight on up the hill, leaving Chris to follow or not as he pleased.

He had reached the outer gate of Duke's Farm before Chris came in sight, toiling up the steep road in silence after him. Then the pursuer called out again. Somebody besides Bram recognized the voice, for a minute later Bram saw a light struck in an upper window of the farm. The window was thrown up, and somebody looked out. Bram, however, stalked upwards in silence still.

He had reached the first of the row of cottages on the top of the hill, when Chris, making a last spurt, overtook him, and seized him by the arm.

"Bram, Bram, what's the matter with you? I've been panting and puffing after you for a thousand miles, and I can't get you to turn that wooden head of yours. Come, I know what's wrong with you, and I mean to have it out with you at once, and have done with it. So come along."

He had already hooked his arm within that of the unwilling Bram, who held himself stiffly, stubbornly, with an air which seemed to say—"Well, if you want it, you can have it."

And so, the one eager, defiant, impetuous, the other stolid and taciturn, the two men walked past the rows of mean cottages, past Bram's own lodgings, and up to the very summit of the hill, where the ruined, patched-up, and re-ruined mansion was, and the disused coal shaft with its towering chimney.

"And now," cried Chris, suddenly stopping and swinging Bram round to face him in the darkness, "we are coming to an understanding."

"Very well, sir."

"Now, don't 'sir' me, but tell me if you're not ashamed of yourself—"

"Me ashamed of myself! I like that!" cried Bram with a short laugh. "But that's the way with you gentlemen. If you please, we'll not have any talk about this, because honor and honesty don't mean the same thing to you as to me."

"That's a nasty one," retorted Chris in his usual airy tone. "Now, look here, Bram, although you're so entirely unreasonable that you don't deserve it, I'm going to condescend to argue with you, and to prove to you the absurdity of your conduct in treating me like this."

"Like what, Mr Christian?"

"Oh, you know. Don't let's waste time. You are angry because I'm marrying Miss Hibbs—"

"No," said Bram obstinately. "I'm not angry with you for marrying Miss Hibbs. I'm angry because you're not marrying the girl you love, the girl you've taught to love you."

"Same thing, Bram. I can't marry them both, you know."

Bram shook his arm free angrily.

"Mr. Christian, we won't talk about this no more," said he in a voice which was hoarse, and strained, and unlike his own. "I might say things I shouldn't like to. Let me go, sir; let me go home, and do you go home and leave me alone."

"No, I won't leave you till we've threshed the matter out. Be reasonable, Bram. You know as well as I do that I'm dependent on my father—"

"You knew that all along. But you said, you told me—"

"I told you that I wanted to marry my cousin Claire. Well, so I did. But my father wouldn't hear of it; apart from the objection he has to the marriage of cousins—"

"That's new, that is," put in Bram shortly.

"Apart from that, I say, he wouldn't have anything to say to the match for a dozen reasons. You know that. And, knowing how I'm placed, it is highly ridiculous of you to make all this fuss, especially as you, no doubt, intend to use the opportunity to cut in yourself."

His tone changed, and Bram detected real pique, real jealousy in these last words.

Bram heard this in dead silence.

"You do, eh?" went on Chris more sharply.

"No, Mr. Christian, I do not. I couldn't come after you in a girl's heart."

"Why not? You are too modest, Bram."

Perhaps Chris flattered himself that he spoke in his usual tone; but an unpleasant, jeering note was clearly discernible to Bram Elshaw's ears. Christian went on in a more jarring tone than ever.

"Or have you been so far penetrated with the maxims of the Sunday-school that you would not allow a girl a little harmless flirtation?"

"Flirtation!" echoed Bram angrily. "It was more than that, Mr. Christian, more than that—to her!"

"It was nothing more than that," said Chris emphatically. "I have done the girl no harm."

Before the words were out of his mouth Bram had sprung forward with the savagery of a wild animal. In the obscurity of the cloudy night his eyes gleamed, and with set teeth and clenched fists he came close to Christian, staring into his eyes, stammering in his vehemence.

"If you had," whispered he almost inaudibly, but with passion which infected Christian and awed him into silence, "If you had done her—any—harm, I'd ha' strangled you, Mr. Christian. I'd ha' gone down to t' works, when you was there, and I'd ha' taken one o' t' leather bands o' t' wheels, and I'd ha' twisted it round your neck, Mr. Christian, and I'd ha' pulled, and pulled, till I saw t' eyes start out o' your head, and t' blood come bursting out o' your mouth. And I'd ha' held you, and tightened it, and tightened it till the breath was out o' your body!"

When he had finished, Bram still stood close to Christian, glaring at him with wild, bloodshot eyes. Christian tried to laugh, but he turned suddenly away, almost staggering. He felt sick and faint. It was Bram who recovered himself first. He confronted Chris quickly, looking ashamed, penitent, abashed.

"Ah shouldn't ha' said what Ah did," said he, just in his old voice, as if he had been again a mere hand at the works. "It was not for me to say it, owing what Ah do to you, Mr. Christian. But—by—I meant it all the same." And again the strange new Bram flashed out for a moment. "And I'm thinking, Mr. Christian," he went on, resuming the more refined tones of his later development, "that it will be best for me to leave the works altogether, for it can never be the same for you and me after to-night. You can't forgive me for what I've said, and—well, I feel I should be more comfortable away, if it's the same to you."

There was a pause, hardly lasting more than a few seconds, and then Chris spoke, with a hoarse and altered voice, but in nearly his ordinary tones—

"But it's not the same to me or to us, not at all the same, Bram. My delinquencies, real or imaginary, cannot be allowed to come between my father and the best clerk he ever had, the man who is to make up for my business shortcomings. So—so if you please, Elshaw, I'll take my chance of the strangling, though, mind you, I should have thought you might have discovered some more refined mode of making away with me, something just as effective, and—and nicer to look at."

His voice was tremulous, and he did not look at Bram, though he succeeded pretty well in maintaining a light tone. Bram laughed shortly.

"My refinement's only skin deep, you see, Mr. Christian. I told you so. The raw Sheffielder's very near the top. And in these fine clothes, too!"

He glanced down rather scornfully at the brand-new overcoat, and at the glazed expanse of unaccustomed shirt-front which showed underneath.

There was another pause. Both the young men were trembling violently, and found it pretty hard to keep up talk at this placid level of commonplace. Quite suddenly Chris said—"Well, good-night, Elshaw," and started on his way back to Holme Park at a good pace.

Bram drew a long breath. He had just gone through an experience so hideous, so horrible, that he felt as if he had been seared, branded with a hot iron. For the first time he realized now what he had been simple enough not to suspect before, that Christian had never for a moment seriously entertained the idea of marrying Claire.

And yet he was in love with her! Bram, loving Claire himself, was clear-sighted and not to be deceived on this point. Christian loved her still enough to be jealous of any other man's feelings for her. He had betrayed this fact in every word, in every tone. If, then, he loved her and did not mean to marry her, he, the irresistible, the spoilt child of the sex, what right had he to love her, to make her love him? What motive had he in passing so much of his time at Duke's Farm?

And there darted into poor Bram's heart a jealous, mad fear that was like a poison in his blood. He clenched his teeth, he shook his fists in the air; again the wild, fierce passion which had swept over him at Christian's stabbing words seized him and possessed him.

He turned quickly, as if to start in pursuit of Chris, when a low sound, a cry, stopped him, turned him as if into stone.

For, at a little distance from him, between where he stood and the retreating figure half-way down the hill, stood Claire.

An exclamation escaped his lips. She ran panting towards him.

CHAPTER XII
A MODEL FATHER

Dark as the night was, the moon being so thickly obscured by clouds that she never showed her face except through a flying film of vapor, Claire seemed to detect something alarming in Bram's attitude, something which caused her to pause as she was running up the hill towards him.

At last she stopped altogether, and they stood looking each at the figure of the other, motionless, and without speaking.

As for Bram, he felt that if he tried to utter a single word he should choke. He could not understand or analyze his own feeling; he did not well know whether his faith in her innocence and purity remained intact. All he knew, all he felt, as he looked at the little creature who seemed so pitifully small and slight as she stood alone on the hillside, wrapt tightly in a long cloak, but shivering in the night air, was that his whole heart was sore for her, that he ached for pity and distress, that he did not know what he should say, what he could do, to comfort and console her.

At last she seemed to take courage, and came a few steps nearer.

"Mr. Elshaw!"

"Yes, Miss Claire."

She started, and no wonder. For his voice was as much changed as were the sentiments he felt for her.

An exclamation escaped his lips. She ran panting towards him.

She came a little nearer still, with hesitating feet, before she spoke again.

"Was that—wasn't that my cousin, Christian Cornthwaite, who went away when he saw me?"

It was Bram's turn to start. So that was the reason of the sudden flight of Chris! He had seen and recognized the figure of Claire as she came up the hill behind Bram.

"Yes, Miss Claire."

Another pause. She was near enough now to peer up into his face with some chance of discerning the expression he wore. It was one of anxiety, of tenderness. She drew back a little.

"I—I heard him call—I heard a voice call out 'Hallo!'" she explained, "and I jumped up, and looked out of the window, and I saw you, and I saw my cousin following you. And you would not answer him. But he still went on. And—and I was frightened; I thought something dreadful had happened, that you had quarrelled; so I got up and came up after you. And I saw—"

She stopped. Bram said nothing. But he turned his head away, unable to look at her. Her voice, now that she spoke under the influence of some strong emotion, played upon his heartstrings like the wind upon an Æolian harp. He made a movement as if to bid her go on with her story.

"I saw," she added in a lower voice, "I saw you spring upon him as if you were going to knock him down. You had been quarrelling. I'm sure you had. And I was frightened. I screamed out, but you didn't hear me, either of you; you were too full of what you were saying to each other. And it was about me; I know it was about me. Now, wasn't it?"

Bram was astonished.

"What makes you think that, Miss Claire? Did you hear anything?"

"Ah!" cried she quickly. "That's a confession. It was about me you were quarreling. Can't you tell me all about it at once?"

But Bram did not dare. He moved restlessly from the one foot to the other, and suddenly said—

"You're cold; you're shivering. You'll catch an awful chill if you stay up here. Just go down back to the farm, Miss Claire, like a good girl"—and unconsciously his tone assumed the caressing accents one uses to a favorite child—"and you shall hear all you want to know in the morning."

But she stood her ground, making an impatient movement with one foot.

"No, Bram, you must tell me now. What was it all about?"

He hesitated. Even if he were able to put her off now, which seemed unlikely, she must hear the truth some day. It was only selfishness, the horror of himself giving her pain, which urged him to be reticent now. So he said to himself, doggedly preparing for his avowal. His anger against the Cornthwaites, his fear of hurting her, combined to make his tone sullen and almost fierce as he answered—

"Well, Miss Claire, I was angry wi' him because I thought he hadn't behaved as he ought."

There was a pause. It seemed to Bram that she guessed, with feminine quickness, what was coming. She spoke, after another of the short pauses with which their conversation was broken up, in a very low and studiously-restrained tone—

"How? To whom, Bram?"

"To—to you, Miss Claire," answered Bram with blunt desperation.

Another silence.

"Why, what has he done to me?" asked she at last.

"He has gone and got engaged—to be married—to somebody else; that's what he's done, there!"

Bram was fiercer than ever.

"Well, and what of that?"

He could not see her face, and her tone was one of careless bravado. But Bram was not deceived. He clenched his fists till the nails went deep into his flesh. It cut him in the heart to have to tell her this news, to feel what she must be suffering. He answered as quietly as he could.

"Nothing, but that I think he ought—he ought—"

"You think he ought to have told me. Oh, I guessed, I guessed what was going to happen," replied Claire rapidly in an off-hand tone. "I should have heard it from himself to-morrow. Who—who is it?"

"A Miss Hibbs."

"Oh, yes, of course. I might have known."

But her voice trembled, and Bram, turning quickly, saw that the tears were running down her cheeks. She was angry at being thus caught, and she dashed them away impatiently.

"D— him!" roared Bram, clenching his fists and his teeth.

"Hush, Bram, hush! I'm surprised. I'm ashamed of you! And, besides, what does it matter to you or to me either whom Mr. Cornthwaite marries?"

"It does matter. He ought to have married you, and taken you away out of the place, and away from the life you have to live with that old rascal—"

Bram was beside himself; he did not know what he was saying. Claire stopped him, but very gently, saying—

"Hush, Bram. He's my father."

"Well, I know that, but he's a rascal all the same," said Bram bluntly. "And Mr. Christian knows it, and he had ought to be glad to have the chance of taking you away, and making you happier. He's behaved like a fool, too, for the girl his father's found for him will never get on with him, never make him happy, like you would have done, Miss Claire. He is just made a rod for his own back, and it serves him jolly well right!"

Claire did not interrupt him; she was crying quietly, every tear she let fall increasing Bram's rage, and throwing fuel on the fire of his indignation. Perhaps his anger soothed her a little, for it was in a very subdued little voice that she presently said—

"Oh, Bram, I don't think that! I do wish him to be happy! Indeed, indeed I do. And if it wasn't for one thing I should be very, very glad he's going to marry somebody else—very, very glad, really!"

Bram had come a little nearer to her; he spoke earnestly, tenderly, with a voice that trembled.

"You're fond of him?" said he, quickly, imperiously.

"Yes, I'm very fond of him. He's my cousin, and he's always been kind to me. But I didn't want to marry him. Oh, I didn't want to marry him!"

Bram was astonished, incredulous. He spoke brusquely, almost harshly.

"He thought you did. He thought you cared for him. So did I, so did everybody."

"Yes. I know that. He's so popular that people take it for granted one must care for him. But I didn't—in the way you mean."

Bram was still dubious.

"Then, why," said he suddenly, "do you take this so much to heart?"

Claire made a valiant attempt to dry her eyes and steady her voice.

"Because," said she in a hesitating voice, "because of—of—because of papa! He wanted me to marry him; he counted on it; and now—oh, dear, I don't know what he will do, what he will say. Well, it can't be helped. I must go back; I must go home. Good-bye; good-night!"

Before Bram could do more than babble out "Good-night, Miss Claire," she had flown like the wind down the hill towards the farm.

Bram went back to his lodging in a sort of delirium. Was it possible that Claire had spoken the truth to him? That she really cared not a straw for her cousin except in a cousinly way; that all she was troubled about was her father's displeasure at having missed such a chance of a connection with the family of the long purse.

Bram understood very little about the nature of women. But he had, of course, acquired the usual vague notions concerning the reticence, the ruses of girls in love, and he could not help feeling that in Claire's denial there was matter for distrust. How, indeed, should she, this little friendless girl who had no other lovers, fail to respond to the affection of a man as attractive, both to men and women, as Chris Cornthwaite? And did not the behavior of Chris himself confirm this view? If Claire had not cared for him, why should he have received Bram's frowns, his angry reproaches, with something which was almost meekness, if he had felt them to be absolutely undeserved? The more he considered this, the more impossible it seemed that Claire's lame explanation of her tears, of her distress, could be the true one. It seemed to Bram that Theo Biron, with his shrewdness and his cunning, must have been the very person to feel most sure that Josiah Cornthwaite would never allow the marriage of Chris with Claire.

Again, why, if she had not felt a most deep interest in Chris had she taken such a bold step as to follow him up the hill that night? Surely it must have been in the hope of speaking with him, perhaps of reassuring herself from his own lips on the subject of the rumors of his approaching marriage, which must have reached her? If, too, Chris had had nothing to reproach himself with on her account, why had he fled so quickly, so abruptly, at the first sight of her?

More and more gloomy grew Bram Elshaw's thoughts as he approached the cottage where he lodged, passed through the little bit of cramped garden, and let himself in. Entering his little sitting-room, and striking a light, he found a note addressed to himself lying on the table. The writing of the envelope was unknown to him, and he opened it with some curiosity. The letter was stamped with this heading—"The Vicarage, East Grindley."

"Grindley! East Grindley!" thought Bram to himself. "Why, that's where my father's people came from!"

And he read the letter with some interest. It was this:

> "Dear Sir,—I am sorry to inform you that Mr. Abraham Elshaw, who is some relation of yours, though he hardly seems himself to know in what degree, is very ill, and not expected to live many days. He has desired me to write and ask you if you will make an effort to come and see him without delay. I may tell you that I understand Mr. Elshaw has heard of the rapid manner in which you are getting on in the world; he has, in fact, often spoken of you to us with much pride, and he is anxious to see you about the disposal of the little property of which he is possessed. I need not ask you under the circumstances to come with as little delay as possible.—Yours very truly,
>
> "Bernard G. Thorpe.
>
> "P.S.—Mr Elshaw has been a member of my congregation for many years, and he chose me rather than one of his own relations to open communication with you. I should have preferred his choosing one of them, but he refused, saying they were unknown to you, so that I could not refuse to fulfil his wishes."

Bram put down the letter with a rather grim smile. He had never seen this namesake of his, but he had heard a good deal about him. An eccentric old fellow, not a rich man by any means, he had saved a few hundred pounds in trade of the smallest and most pettifogging kind, on the strength of which he had given himself great airs for the last quarter of a century among the pit hands and mill hands and grinders who formed his family and acquaintance. A sturdy, stubborn, miserly old man, of whose hard-fistedness and petty money-grabbing Bram had heard many tales. But the family was proud of him, though it loved him not. Bram remembered clearly how, when he was a very small child, his father had gone out on a strike with his mates, and his poor mother, at her wits' end for a meal, had applied to the great Abraham for a small loan, and how it had been curtly and contemptuously refused.

This was just the man, this hard-fisted, self-helping old saver of halfpence, to bestow upon the successful and prosperous young relation the money of which he would not have lent him a cent if he had been starving. Bram told himself that he must go, of course: and he resolved to do his best with the old man for those unknown relations who might be more in want of the money than he himself was. For he was shrewd enough to foresee that old Abraham's intention was to make his prosperous young relation heir to what little he possessed. He resolved to ask next morning for a day off, and to go at once to East Grindley.

Bram got the required permission easily enough, and went on the very next day to see his reputed wealthy namesake. East Grindley was a good many miles north of Sheffield and it was late in the day before he returned.

Throughout the whole of the day he had been haunted by thoughts of Claire; and no sooner had he had his tea than he determined to go to the farm, with the excuse of asking if she had caught cold the night before.

He was in a fever of doubt, anxiety, and only half-acknowledged hope. He had wished, honestly wished, when he believed Claire to be as fond of Chris as Chris was of her, that the cousins should marry, that little Claire should be taken right out of her troubles and her difficulties, and set down in a palace of peace and content, of luxury and beauty, with the man of her heart. But if those words of Claire's uttered to him the night before were really true, might there not be a chance that he might win her himself? That he might be the lucky man who should build her a palace, and lift her from misery into happiness?

Bram knew that Claire liked him; knew that the distance between himself and her, which had seemed immeasurable thirteen months before, had diminished, and was every day diminishing. If, indeed she did not care, had never cared for her cousin with the love Bram wanted, who had a better chance with her than himself, whom she knew so well, and trusted so completely?

Bram with all his humility, was proud in his own way, and exceedingly jealous. If Claire had loved her cousin passionately, and had been jilted by him, as Bram had believed to be the case, he did not feel that he should even have wished to take the vacant place in her heart. No doubt the wish would have come in time, but not at once. If, however, it were true that she had not cared for Chris in the only way of which Bram would have been jealous, why, then, indeed, there was hope of the most brilliant kind.

Bram, on his way to the farm, began to see in his heart such visions as love only can build and paint, love, too, that has not taken the edge off itself, frittered itself away, on the innumerable flirtations with which his daily companions at the office beguiled the dead monotony of existence.

In his new life, as in his old, it was Bram's lot to be "chaffed" daily on his unimpressionability, on the stolid, matter-of-fact way in which he went about his daily work, "as if," as the other clerks said, "his eyes could see nothing better in the world than paper and ink, print and figures."

Bram on these occasions was accustomed to put on an air of extra stolidity, and to shake his head, and declare that he had no time to think of anything but his work. And all the time he wondered to himself at the ease with which they could chatter of their affection for this girl and that, and enjoy the jokes which were levelled at them, and wear their heart upon their sleeve with ill-concealed delight.

And he smiled to himself at their mistake, and went on nourishing his heart with its own chosen food in secret, with raptures that nobody guessed.

And now the thought that his dreamy hopes might grow into realities brought the color to his pale cheeks and new lustre to his steady gray eyes, as he walked soberly down the hill, and entered the farmyard in the yellow sunlight of the end of a fine day in September.

He knocked at the kitchen door, and nobody answered. He knocked more loudly, fancying that he heard voices inside the house. But again without result. So he opened the door, and peeped in. A small fire was burning in the big grate, but there was nobody in the room. With the door open, however, the voices he had faintly heard became louder, and he became aware that an altercation was going on between Claire and her father in the front part of the house.

He was on the point of retiring, therefore, with a sigh for the poor little girl, when a cry, uttered by her in a wailing tone, reached his ears, and acted upon his startled senses like flaming pitch on tow.

"Oh, papa, don't, don't hurt me!"

The next moment Bram had burst the opposite door open, and saw Theodore, his little, mean face wrinkled up with malice, strike Claire's face sharply with his open hand. This was in the hall, outside the dining-room door.

No sooner was the blow given than Bram seized Theodore, lifted him into the air, and flung him down against the door of the dining-room with such force that it burst open, and Mr. Biron lay sprawling just inside the room.

Claire, her cheek still white from the blow, her eyes full of tears of shame, rushed forward, ready to champion her father.

"Go away," she said in a strangled, breathless voice. "Go away. How dare you hurt my father? You have no right to come here. Go away."

She tried to speak severely, harshly, but the tears were running down her face; she was heart-broken, miserable, full of such deep humiliation that she could scarcely meet his eyes. But Bram did not heed her, did not hear her perhaps. He was himself trembling with emotion, and his eyes shone with that liquid lustre, that yearning of long-repressed passion, which no words can explain away, no eyewitness can mistake.

He stretched out his hand, without a single word, and took both hers in one strong clasp. And the moment she felt his touch her voice failed, died away; she bent down her head, and burst into a fit of weeping more passionate than ever.

"Hush, my dear; hush! Don't cry. Remember, it's only me; it's only Bram."

He had bent his head too, and was leaning over her with such tender yearning, such undisguised affection, in look, manner, voice, that no girl could have doubted what feeling it was which animated him. With his disengaged hand he softly touched her hair, every nerve in his own body thrilling with a sensation he had never known before.

"Hush, hush!"

The whisper was a confession. It seemed to tell what love he had cherished for her during all these months; a love which gave him now not only the duty, but the right of comforting her, of soothing the poor little bruised heart, of calming the weary spirit.

"Hush, dear, hush!"

Whether it was a minute, whether it was an hour, that they stood like this in the little stone-flagged hall in the cool light of the dying September evening, Bram did not know. He was intoxicated, mad. It was only by strong self-control that he refrained from pressing her to his breast. He had to tell himself that he must not take advantage of her weakness, he must not extort from her while she was crushed, broken, a word, a promise, an assurance, which her stronger, her real self would shudder at or regret. She must feel, she must know, that he, Bram, was her comforter, the tender guardian who asked no price, who was ready to soothe, to champion, and to wait.

Meanwhile the strong man found in his own sensation reward enough and to spare. Here, with her heart beating very near his, was the only woman who had ever lit in him the fiery light of passion; her little hands trembled in his, the tender flesh pressing his own hard palm with a convulsive touch which set his veins tingling. The scent of her hair was an intoxicating perfume in his nostrils. Every sobbing breath she drew seemed to sound a new note of sweetest music in his heart.

At last, when he had been silent for some seconds, she suddenly drew herself back, with a face red with shame; with eyes which dared not meet his. Reluctantly he let her drag her hands away from him, and watched her wipe her wet eyes.

"Papa! Where is he?" asked she quickly.

Staggering, unsteady, hardly knowing where he went, or what he did, Bram crossed the hall, and looked into the dining-room. But the lively Theodore was not there. He turned and came face to face with Claire, who was redder than ever, the place where her father had struck her glowing with vivid crimson which put the other cheek to shame.

She moved back a step, looking about also. Then she went quickly out of the room, and recrossed the hall to the drawing-room. But her father was not there either. Back in the hall again, she met Bram, and they glanced shyly each into the face of the other.

Both felt that the fact of their having let Mr. Biron disappear without having noticed him was a mutual confession. Claire looked troubled, frightened.

"I wonder," said she in a low voice, "where he has gone?"

But Bram did not share her anxiety. There was no fear that Mr. Biron would let either rage or despair carry him to the point of doing anything rash or dangerous to himself.

"He'll turn up presently," said he, with a scornful movement of the head, "never fear, Miss Claire. Have you got anything for me to do this evening? You're running short of wood, I think."

He walked back into the kitchen, which, being the least frequented by the fastidious Theodore, was Bram's favorite part of the house. In a few moments Claire came softly in after him. She seemed rather constrained, rather stiff, and this made Bram very careful, very subdued. But there was a delicious peace, a new hope in his own heart; she had rested within the shelter of his arms; she had been comforted there.

"You ought not to have come this evening, Bram," she said with studied primness. "You know, I told you that before. It only makes things worse for me, it does really."

"Now, how can you make that out?" asked Bram bluntly.

"Why, papa will be all the angrier with me afterwards. As for—for what you saw him do, I don't care a bit. It makes me angry for the time, and just gives me spirit enough to hold out when he wants me to do anything I won't do, I can't do."

"What was it he wanted you to do?" asked Bram, grinding his teeth.

Claire hesitated. She grew crimson again, and the tears rushed once more to her eyes.

"I'd rather not tell you." Then as she noticed the expression on Bram's face grow darker and more menacing, she went on quickly—"Well, it was only that he wanted me to go up to Holme Park again to-night—with a note—the usual note. And that I can't—*now!*"

Bram's heart sank. Of course, she meant that it was the engagement of Chris which made this difference. But why should this be, if she did not care for him? Bram came nearer to her, leaned on the table, and looked into her face. What an endless fascination the little features had for him. When she looked down, as she did now, he never knew what would be the expression of her brown eyes when she looked up, whether they would dance with fun, or touch him by a queer, dreamy, expression, or whether there would be in them such infinite sadness that he would be forced into silent sympathy. Bram waited impatiently for her to look up.

As he came nearer and nearer, she still looking down, but conscious of his approach, a new thought came into his mind, a cruel, a bitter thought. Suddenly he stood up, still leaning over the corner of the table.

"Are you what they call a coquette, Miss Claire?" he asked with blunt earnestness.

She looked up quickly then, with a restless, defiant sparkle in her eyes.

"Perhaps I am. French people, French women, are all supposed to be, aren't they? And my grandmother was French. Why do you ask me?"

"Because I don't understand you," answered Bram in a low, thick voice. "Because you tell me you don't care for Mr. Christian, and I should like to believe you. But you tell me to keep away, and yet—and yet—whenever I come you make me think you want me to come again, though you tell me to go. But surely, surely, you wouldn't play with me; you wouldn't condescend to do that, would you? Now, would you?"

She looked up again, stepping back a little as she did so; and there was in her eyes such a look of beautiful confidence, of kindness, of sweet, girlish affection, that Bram's heart leapt up. He had promptly sat down again on the table, and was bending towards her with passion in his eyes, when there stole round the half-open door the little, mean, fair face of Theodore.

Bram sprang up, and stood at once in an attitude of angry defiance.

But Theodore, quite unabashed, was in the room in half a second, holding out his pretty white hand with a smile which was meant to be frankness itself.

"Mr. Elshaw," said he, "we must shake hands. I won't allow you to refuse. I owe you no grudge for the way you treated me a short time ago; on the contrary, I thank you for it. I thank you—"

"Papa!" cried poor Claire.

He waved her into silence.

"I thank you," he persisted obstinately, "for reminding me that I was treating my darling daughter too harshly, much too harshly. Claire, I am sorry. You will forgive me, won't you?"

And he put his hand on her shoulder, and imprinted delicately on her forehead a butterfly kiss. Claire said nothing at all. She had become quite pale, and stood with a face of cold gravity, with her eyes cast down, while her father talked.

Bram felt that he should have liked to kick him. Instead of that he had to give his reluctant hand to the airy Mr. Biron, an act which he performed with the worst possible grace.

"You must stay to supper," said Theodore. "Oh, yes; I want a talk with you. About this marriage of my young kinsman, Chris Cornthwaite. Frankly, I think the match a most ill-chosen one. He would have done much better to marry my little girl here—"

"Papa!" cried Claire angrily, impatiently.

"Only, unfortunately for *him*, she didn't care enough about him."

Claire drew a long breath. Bram looked up. Theodore, in his hurry to secure for his daughter another eligible suitor whom he saw to be well disposed for the position, was showing his hand a trifle too plainly. Bram grew restless. Claire said sharply that they could not ask Mr. Elshaw to supper, as she had nothing to offer him. She was almost rude; but Bram, whose heart ached for the poor child, gave her a glance which was forgiveness, tenderness itself. He said he could not stay, and explained that he had been out all day on an errand, which had tired him. To fill up a pause, he told the story of his eccentric kinsman.

"And he means to leave me all his money, whatever it is," went on Bram. "He showed me the box he keeps it in, and told me in so many words that it would be mine within a few days. And all because he thinks I've got on. If I'd been still a hand at the works down there, and hard up for the price of a pair of boots, I shouldn't have had a penny."

"Ah, well, it will be none the less welcome when it comes," said Mr. Biron brightly. "What is the amount of your fortune? Something handsome, I hope."

"I don't know yet, Mr. Biron. Not enough to call a fortune, I expect."

"Well, you must come and tell us about it when it's all settled. There's nobody who takes more interest in you and your affairs than my daughter and I—eh, Claire?"

But Claire affected to be too busy to hear; she was engaged in making the fire burn up, and at the first opportunity she stole out of the room, unseen by her father. So that Bram, who soon after took his departure, did not see her again.

He went back to his lodging in a fever. This new turn of affairs, this anxiety of Theodore's to make him come forward in the place of Christian, filled him with dismay. On the very first signs of this disposition in her father Claire had shrunk back into herself and had refused to give him so much as another look. But then that was only the natural resentment of a modest girl; it proved, it disproved nothing but that she refused to be thrown at any man's head. That look she had given him just before her father's entrance, on the other hand, had been eloquent enough to set him on fire with something more definite than dreamy hope. If it had not betrayed the very love and trust for which he was longing, it had expressed something very near akin to that feeling. Bram lived that night in alternate states of fever and frost.

He dared not, however, for fear of giving pain to Claire, go to the farm again for the next fortnight. He would linger about the farmyard gate, and sometimes he would catch sight of Claire. But on these occasions she turned her back upon him with so cold and decided a snub that it was impossible for him to advance in face of a repulse so marked. And even when Theodore lay in wait for him, and tried to induce him to go home with him, Bram had to refuse for the sake of the very girl he was longing to see.

Meanwhile the date of Christian's marriage with Miss Hibbs was rapidly approaching. Chris maintained an easy demeanor with Bram, but that young man was stiff, reserved, and shy, and received the confidences, real or pretended, of the other without comment or sympathy. When Chris lamented that he could not make a match to please himself, Bram looked in front of him, and said nothing. When he made attempts to sound Bram on the subject of Claire, the young clerk parried his questions with perfect stolidity.

The day of the wedding was a holiday at the works, and Bram, who dared not spend the day at the farm, as he would have liked to do, and who had refused to take any part in the festivities, paid another visit to old Abraham Elshaw at East Grindley as an excuse for staying away.

He returned, however, early in the evening, and was on his way up the hill by way of the fields, when, to his unbounded amazement, he saw a side-gate in the wall of the farmhouse garden open quickly, and a man steal out, and run hurriedly down across the grass in the direction of the town.

Bram felt sure that there was something wrong, but he had hardly gone a few steps with the intention of intercepting the man, when he stopped short. Something in the man's walk, even at this distance, struck him. In another moment, in spite of the fact that the stealthy visitor wore a travelling cap well over his eyes, Bram recognized Chris Cornthwaite.

Stupefied with dread, Bram glanced back, and saw Claire standing at the little gate, watching Chris as he ran. Shading her eyes with her hand, for the glare of the setting sun came full upon her face, she waited until he was out of sight behind a stone wall which separated the last of the fields he crossed from the road. Then she shut the gate, locked it, and went indoors.

Bram stared at the farmhouse, the windows of which were shining like jewels in the setting sun. He felt sick and cold.

What was the meaning of this secret visit of Chris Cornthwaite to Claire on his wedding day?

CHAPTER XIII
AN ILL-MATCHED PAIR

Nobody but simple-hearted Bram Elshaw, perhaps, would have been able to doubt any longer after what he had seen that there was something stronger than cousinly affection between Christian Cornthwaite and Claire. But even this wild visit of Chris to his cousin on his very wedding day did not create more than a momentary doubt, a flying suspicion, in the heart of the devoted Bram.

Had he not looked into her dark eyes not many days before, and read there every virtue and every quality which can make womanhood sweet and noble and dear?

Unluckily, Chris had been seen on this mysterious visit by others besides Bram.

It was not long after the wedding day that Josiah Cornthwaite found occasion, when Bram was alone with him in his office, to break out into invective against the girl who, so he said, was trying to destroy every chance of happiness for his son. Bram, who could not help knowing to what girl he referred, made no comment, but waited stolidly for the information which he saw that Mr. Cornthwaite was anxious to impart.

"I think even you, Elshaw, who advocated this young woman so warmly a little while ago, will have to alter your opinion now." As Bram still looked blank, he went on impatiently—"Don't pretend to misunderstand. You know very well whom I mean—Claire Biron, of Duke's Farm.

"It has come to my ears that my son had a meeting with her on his wedding day—"

Bram's countenance looked more blank than ever. Mr. Cornthwaite went on—

"I know what I am talking about, and I speak from the fullest information. She sent him a note that very morning; everybody knows about it; my daughter heard her say it was to be given to Mr. Christian at once, and that it was from his cousin Miss Biron. Is that evidence enough for you?"

Bram trembled.

"There must be some other explanation than the one you have put upon it, sir," said he quietly but decidedly. "Miss Biron often had to write notes on behalf of her father," he suggested respectfully.

"Pshaw! Would any message of that sort, a mere begging letter, an attempt to borrow money, have induced my son to take the singular, the unprecedented action that he did? Surprising, nay, insulting, his wife before she had been his wife two hours."

Bram heard the story with tingling ears and downcast eyes. That there was some truth in it no one knew better than he. Had he not the confirmatory evidence of his own eyes? Yet still he persisted in doggedly doubting the inference Mr. Cornthwaite would have forced upon him. His employer was waiting in stony silence for some answer, some comment. So at last he looked up, and spoke out bravely the thoughts that were in his mind.

"Sir," said he steadily, "the one thing this visit of Mr. Christian's proves beyond any doubt is that he was in love with her at the time you made him marry another woman. It doesn't prove anything against Miss Biron, until you have heard a great deal more than you have done so far, at least. You must excuse me, sir, for speaking so frankly, but you insisted on my telling you what I thought."

Mr. Cornthwaite was displeased. But as he had, indeed, forced the young man to speak, he could not very well reproach him for obeying. Besides, he was used to Bram's uncompromising bluntness, and was prepared to hear what he really thought from his lips.

"I can't understand the young men of the present generation," he said crossly, with a wave of the hand to intimate to Bram that he had done with him. "When I was between twenty and thirty, I looked for good looks in a girl, for a pair of fine eyes, for a fine figure, for a pair of rosy cheeks. Now it seems that women can dispense with all those attributes, and bowl the men over like ninepins with nothing but a little thread of a lisping voice and a trick of casting down a pair of eyes which are anything but what I should call fine. But I suppose I am old-fashioned."

Bram retired respectfully without offering any suggestion as to the reason of this surprising change of taste.

He was in a tumult of secret anxiety. He felt that he could no longer keep away from the farm, that he must risk everything to try to get an explanation from Claire. If she would trust him with the truth, and he believed her confidence in himself to be great enough for this, he could, he thought, clear her name in the eyes of the angry Josiah. It was intolerable to him that the girl he worshipped as devotedly as ever should lie under a foul suspicion.

So that very evening, as soon as he had left the office, he went straight to the farm. It was his last day before starting on the mission with which he was to be intrusted in the place of Chris, who was on his honeymoon. This was an excellent excuse for a visit, which might not, he feared, be well received.

He was more struck than ever as he approached the farmyard gate with a fact which had been patent to all eyes of late. The tenants of Duke's Farm had fallen on evil days. Everything about the place betrayed the fact that a guiding hand was wanting; while Bram had kept an eye on the farm bailiff things had gone pretty smoothly, fences had been repaired, the stock had been well looked after. Now there were signs of neglect upon everything. The wheat was still unstacked; the thatch at one end of the big barn was broken and defective; a couple of pigs had strayed from the farmyard into the garden, and were rooting up whatever took their fancy.

Bram leaned on the gate, and looked sorrowfully around.

Was it by chance that the back door opened, and Joan, the good-humored Yorkshire servant, peeped out? She looked at him for a few minutes very steadily, and then she beckoned him with a brawny arm. He came across the yard at once.

"Look here, mister," said she in her broadly familiar manner, "what have ye been away so long for? Do ye think there's nought to be done here now? Or have ye grown too grand for us poor folks?"

He laughed rather bitterly.

"No, Joan, I've only kept away because I'm not wanted."

"Hark to him!" she cried ironically, as she planted her hands on her hips, and glanced up at him with a shrewd look in her gray-green clever eyes. "He wants to be pressed now, when he used to be glad enoof to sneak in and take his chance of a welcome! Well, Ah could tell a tale if Ah liked, and put the poor, modest fellow at his ease, that Ah could!"

Bram's face flushed.

"Do you mean she wants me?" he asked so simply that Joan burst into a good-humored laugh.

"Go ye in and see," said she with a stupendous nod. "And if ye get the chuck aht, blame it on to me!"

Bram took the hint, and went in. Joan followed, and pointed to a chair by the table, where Claire sat bending over some work by the light of a candle. The evening was a gray one, and the light was already dim in the big farm kitchen.

"Here's a friend coom to see ye who doan't coom so often as he might," cried Joan, following close on the visitor's heels. Claire was looking up with eyes in which Bram, with a pang, noted a new look of fear and dismay. For the first time within his recent memory she did not seem glad to see him. He stopped.

"I've only come, Miss Claire," said he in a very modest voice, "to tell you I'm going to London to-morrow on business for the firm. I shall be away ten days or a fortnight; and I came to know whether there was anything I could do for you, either before I go or while I'm there. But if there's nothing, or if I'm in the way—"

"You're never in anybody's way, Mr. Elshaw," said she quite cordially, but without the hearty ring there used to be in her welcome. "Please, sit down."

She offered him a chair, and he took it, while Joan, round about whose wide mouth a malicious smile was playing, disappeared into her own precincts of scullery and back-kitchen.

For some minutes there was dead silence, not the happy silence of two friends so secure in their friendship that they need not talk—the old-time silence which they had both loved, but a constrained, uncomfortable taciturnity, a leaden, speechless pause, during which Bram watched with feverish eyes the little face as it bent over her work, and noted that the outline of her cheek had grown sharper.

He tried to speak, to break the horrid silence which weighed upon them both. But he could not. It seemed to him that there was something different about this meeting from any they had ever had, that the air was heavy with impending disaster.

He spoke suddenly at last in a husky voice.

"Miss Claire, I want you to tell me something."

She looked up quickly, with anxiety in her eyes. But she said nothing.

"I want you to tell me," he went on, assuming a tone which was almost bullying in his excitement, "why Mr. Christian came to see you the day he was married?"

To his horror she stood up, pushing back her chair, moving as if with no other object than to hide the frantic emotion she was seized with at these words. There passed over her face a look of anguish which he never forgot as she answered in a low, breathless voice.

"Hush, I cannot tell you. You must not ask. You must never ask. And you must never speak about it again, never, never!"

Bram leaned over the table, and looked straight into her eyes. In every line of her face he read the truth.

"He asked you to—to go away with him!" he growled, hardly above his breath.

"Hush!" cried she. "Hush! I don't know how you know; I hope, oh, I pray that nobody else knows. I want to forget it! I will forget it! If I had to go through it again it would kill me!"

And, dry-eyed, she fell into a violent fit of shuddering, and sank down in her chair with her head in her hands.

"The scoundrel!" said Bram in a terrible whisper.

And there came into his face that look, that fierce peep out of the primitive north country savage, which had startled Chris himself one memorable night.

Claire saw it, and she grew white as the dead.

"Bram," cried she hoarsely, "don't look like that; don't speak like that. You frighten me!"

But he looked at her with eyes which did not see. This fulfilment of his fears, of his doubts of Chris, was a shock she could not understand.

There was a pause before he was able to speak. Then he repeated vaguely—

"Frightened you, Miss Claire! I didn't mean to do that!"

But the look on his face had not changed. Claire leaned across the table, touched his sleeve impatiently, timidly.

"Bram," said she in a shrill voice, sharpened by alarm, "you are to forget it too! Do you hear?"

He turned upon her suddenly.

"No," said he, "you can't make me do that!"

"But I say you must, you shall. Oh, Bram, if you had been here, if you had heard him, you would have been sorry for him, you would have pitied him, as I did!"

Bram leaped up from his chair. All the fury in his eyes seemed now to be concentrated upon her.

"You pitied him! You were sorry for him! For a black-hearted rascal like that!"

"Oh, Bram, Bram, don't you know that those are only words! When you see a man you've always liked, been fond of, who has always been happy and bright, and full of fun and liveliness, quite suddenly changed, and broken down, and wretched, you don't stop to ask yourself whether he's a good man or a bad one. Now, do you, Bram?"

"You ought to!" rejoined Bram in fierce Puritanism militant. "You ought to have used your chance of showing him what a wicked thing he was doing to his poor wife as well as you!"

"Oh, Bram, I did. I said what I could!"

"Not half enough, I'll warrant!" retorted he, clenching his fist. "You didn't tell him he was a blackguard who ought to be kicked from one end of the county to the other! And that you'd never speak to him again as long as you lived!"

"No, I certainly didn't."

"Then," almost shouted Bram, bringing his fist down on the table with a threatening, sounding thump, "you ought to be ashamed of yourself! You good women do as much harm as the bad ones, for you are just as tender and sweet to men when they do wrong as when they do right. You encourage them in their wicked ways, when you should be stand-off and proud. I do believe, God forgive me for saying so, you care more for Mr. Chris now than you did before!"

Claire, who was very white, waited a moment when he had come to the end of his accusation. Then she said in a weak, timid, little voice, but with steadiness—

"It is true, I believe, that I like him better than I did before. You are too hard, Bram; you make no allowance for anything."

"There are some things no allowance should be made for."

"Well, there's one thing you forget, and that is that I've not been used to good people, so that I am not so hard as you are. I've never known a good man except you, Bram, but then I've never known one so severe upon others either."

"You shouldn't say that, Miss Claire; I'm not hard."

"Oh!"

"Or if I am, it's only so as I shouldn't be too soft!" cried he, suddenly breaking down into gentleness, and forgetting his grammar at the same time. "It's only because you've got nobody to take care of you, nobody to keep harm away from you, that I want you to be harder yourself!"

There was a pause. Claire was evidently touched by his solicitude. Presently she spoke, persuasively, affectionately, but with caution.

"Bram, if I promise to be hard, very hard, will you give me a promise back?"

"What's that?"

"Will you promise me that you will forget"—Bram shook his head, and at once began a fierce, angry protest—"well, that you will say nothing about this. Come, you are bound in honor, because I told you in confidence—"

"No, you didn't; I found out!"

"You can't deny that I have told you some things in confidence. Now, listen. You can do no good, and you may do harm by speaking about this. You must behave to Christian as if you knew nothing. It is of no use for you to shake your head. I insist. And remember, it is the only way you have of proving to me that you are not hard. Why, what about the poor wife you pretended to be so anxious about just now? Isn't it for her advantage as well as mine that this awful, dreadful mistake should be forgotten?"

There was no denying this. Bram hung his head. At last he looked up, and said shortly—

"If I promise to behave as if I hadn't heard will you promise me not to see Mr. Christian again?"

Claire flushed proudly. But when she answered it was in a gentle, kind voice.

"You won't trust me, Bram?"

"I think it will be better for the wife, for you, for him, for everybody, if you promise."

"Very well. I promise to do my best not to see him again."

She was looking very grave. Bram stared at her anxiously. She got up suddenly, and looked at him as if in dismissal. He held out his hand.

"Good-bye, Miss Claire. You forgive my rough manners, don't you? If only you had somebody better than me to take care of you, I wouldn't be so meddlesome. Good-bye. God bless you!"

He wanted to say a great deal more; he wanted to know a great deal more; but he dared not risk another word. Giving her hand a quick, firm pressure, which she returned without looking up, and with a restraint and reserve which warned him to be careful, he hurried out of the house.

CHAPTER XIV
THE DELUGE

Bram was away much longer than the ten days he had expected. Difficulties arose in the transaction of the affair which had called him to London; he had to take a trip to Brussels, to return to London, and then to visit Brussels again. It was two months after his departure from Sheffield before he came back.

In the meantime old Abraham Elshaw, his namesake, had died. A letter was forwarded to Bram informing him of the fact, and also that by the direction of the deceased the precious box in which the old man had kept his property had been sent to Bram's address at Hessel.

Bram acknowledged the letter, and sent directions to his landlady for the safe keeping of the box containing his legacy.

When he got back home to his lodging, one cold night at the end of November, Bram received the box, and set about examining its contents. It was a strong oak miniature chest, hinged and padlocked. As there was no key, Bram had to force the padlock. The contents were varied and curious. On the top was a Post Office Savings Bank book, proving the depositor to have had two hundred and thirty-five pounds to his credit. Next came a packet of papers relating to old Elshaw's transactions with a building society, by the failure of which he appeared to have lost some ninety-six pounds. Then there were some gas shares and some deeds which proved him to have been the owner of certain small house property in the village where he had lived. Next came a silver teapot, containing nothing but some scraps of tissue paper and a button. And at the bottom of the box was a very old-fashioned man's gold watch, with a chased case, a large oval brooch containing a woman's hair arranged in a pattern on a white ground, and a broken gold sleeve-link.

Bram, who, from inquiries he had made, considered himself at liberty to apply all the money to his own uses, the other relations of old Abraham not being near enough or dear enough to have a right to a share, looked thoughtfully at the papers, and then put them carefully away. He knew what the old man had apparently not known, that there were formalities to be gone through before he could claim the house property. He should have to consult a solicitor. There was no doubt that his windfall would prove more valuable than he had expected, and again his thoughts flew to Claire, and he asked himself whether there was a chance that he might be able to devote his little fortune to the building of that palace which his love had already planned—in the air.

He told himself that he was a fool to be so diffident, but he could not drive the feeling away. The truth was that there was still at the bottom of his heart some jealousy left of the lively Chris, some proud doubt whether Claire's heart was as free as she had declared it to be.

But if, on the one hand, she had spoken compassionately of her erring cousin, there was to be remembered, as a set-off against that, the delicious moment when she had stood contented in the shelter of Bram's own arms on that memorable evening when he had, for the second time, protected her from the violence of her father.

On the whole, Bram felt that it was time to make the plunge; now, when he had money at his command, when he was in a position to take her right out of her dangers and her difficulties. With Theodore, who was not without intelligence, a bargain could be made, and Bram could not doubt that this moment, when the supplies had been cut off at Holme Park, and the farm was going to ruin, would be a favorable one for his purpose.

He resolved to go boldly to Claire the very next day.

When the morning broke, a bright, clear morning, with a touch of frost in the air, Bram sprung out of bed with the feeling that there were great things to be done. The sun was bright on the hill when he started, though down far below his feet the town lay buried in a smoky mist. Just before he reached the farmyard gate he paused, looking eagerly for the figure which was generally to be seen busily engaged about the place at this hour of the morning.

But he was disappointed. Claire was nowhere to be seen.

Reluctantly Bram went on his way down the hill, when the chirpy, light voice of Theodore Biron, calling to him from the front of the house, made him stop and turn round. Mr. Biron was in riding costume, with a hunting crop in his hand. He was very neat, very smart, and far more prosperous-looking than he had been for some time. He played with his moustache with one hand, while with the other he jauntily beckoned Bram to come back.

"Hallo!" said Bram, returning readily enough on the chance of seeing Claire. "Where are you off to so early, Mr. Biron? I didn't think you ever tried to pick up the worm."

"Going to have a day with the hounds," replied Theodore cheerfully. "They meet at Clinker's Cross to-day. I picked up a clever little mare the other day—bought her for a mere song, and I am going to try her at a fence or two. Come round and see her. Do you know anything about hunters, Elshaw?"

"No," replied the astonished Bram, who knew that Mr. Biron's purse had not lately allowed him to know much about hunters either.

"Ah!" said Theodore, as he opened the garden gate for Bram to enter, and led him into the house. "All the better for you. When you've once got to think you know something about horse-flesh, you can't sit down quietly without a decent nag or two in your stable."

And Mr. Biron, whose every word caused Bram fresh astonishment, flung back the door of the kitchen with a jaunty hand.

Bram followed him, but stopped short at the sight which met his eyes.

Springing up with a low cry from a stool by the fire on Bram's entrance, Claire, with a face so white, so drawn that he hardly knew her, stared at him with a fixed look of horror which seemed to freeze his blood.

"Miss Claire!" he said hoarsely.

She said nothing. With her arms held tightly down by her sides, she continued to stare at him as if at some creature the sight of whom had seized her with unspeakable terror. He came forward, much disturbed, holding out his hand.

"Come, come, Claire, what's the matter with you? Aren't you glad to see Bram Elshaw back among us?" said Theodore impatiently.

Still she did not move. Bram, chilled, frightened, did not know what to do. Mr. Biron left the outer door, by which he stood, and advanced petulantly towards his daughter. But before he could reach her she staggered, drew away from him, and with a frightened glance from Bram to him, fled across the room and disappeared.

Bram was thrown into the utmost consternation by this behavior. He had turned to watch the door by which she had made her escape, when Theodore seized him by the arm, and dragged him impatiently towards the outer door.

"Come, come," said he, "don't trouble your head about her. She's not been well lately; she's been out of sorts. I've talked of leaving the place, and she doesn't like the idea. She'll soon be herself again. Her cousin Chris has been round two or three times since his return from his honeymoon trying to cheer her up. But she won't be cheered; I suppose she enjoys being miserable sometimes. Most ladies do."

Bram, who had followed Mr. Biron with leaden feet across the farmyard towards the stables, felt that a black cloud had suddenly fallen upon his horizon. The mention of Chris filled him with poignant mistrust, with cruel alarm. He felt that calamity was hanging over them all, and that the terrible look he had seen in Claire's eyes was prophetic of coming evil. He hardly saw the mare of which Theodore was so proud; hardly heard the babble, airily ostentatious, cheerily condescending, which Claire's father dinned into his dull ears. He was filled with one thought. These new extravagances of Theodore's, the look in Claire's face, were all connected with Chris, and with his renewed visits. Bram felt as if he should go mad.

When he reached the office he watched for an opportunity to get speech alone with Christian. But he was unsuccessful. Bram did not even see him until late in the day.

Long before that Bram had had an interview with the elder Mr. Cornthwaite, which only confirmed his fears. He had to give an account to the head of the firm of the business he had transacted while away. He had carried it through with great ability, and Mr. Cornthwaite complimented him highly upon the promptitude, judgment, and energy he had shown in a rather difficult matter.

"My son Christian was perfectly right," Mr. Cornthwaite went on, "in recommending me to send you away on this affair, Elshaw. You seem to have an old head upon young shoulders. I only hope he may do half as well on the mission with which he himself is to be entrusted."

Bram looked curious.

"Is Mr. Christian going away again so soon, sir?" asked he.

Mr. Cornthwaite, whose face bore traces of some unaccustomed anxiety, frowned.

"Yes," he answered shortly. "I am sorry to say that he and his wife don't yet rub on so well as one could wish together. You see I tell you frankly what the matter is, and you can take what credit you please to yourself for having predicted it. No doubt they will shake down in time, but on all accounts I think it is as well, as there happens to be some business to be done down south, to send him away upon it. He will only be absent a few weeks, and in the meantime any little irritation there may be on both sides will have had time to rub off."

Bram looked blank indeed.

He was more anxious than ever for a few words alone with Chris, but he was unable to obtain them. When his employer's son appeared at the office, which was not till late in the day, he carefully avoided the opportunity Bram sought. After shaking hands with him with a dash and an effusion which made it impossible for the other to draw back, even if he had been so inclined, Chris, with a promise of "seeing him presently," went straight into his father's private office, and did not reappear in the clerks' office at all.

In spite of the boisterous warmth of his greeting, Bram had noticed in Christian two things. The first was a certain underlying coldness and reserve, which put off, under an assumption of affectionate familiarity, the confidences which had been the rule between them. The other was the fact that Christian looked thin and worried.

Bram lingered about the office till long after his usual hour of leaving in the hope of catching Christian. And it was at last only by chance that he learnt that Chris had gone some two hours before, and, further, that he was to start for London that very evening.

Now, this discovery worried Bram, and set him thinking. The intercourse between him and Christian had been of so familiar a kind that this abrupt departure, without any sort of leave-taking, could only be the result of some great change in Christian's feeling towards himself. So strong, although vague, were his fears that Bram when he left the office went straight to the new house in a pretty suburb some distance out of Sheffield, where Christian had settled with his bride. Here, however, he was met with the information that Mr. Christian had already started on his journey, and that he had gone, not from his own, but from his father's house.

As Bram left the house he saw the face of young Mrs. Christian Cornthwaite at one of the windows. She looked pale, drawn, unhappy, and seemed altogether to have lost the smug look of self-satisfaction which he had disliked in her face on his first meeting with her.

Much disturbed, Bram went away, and returned to his lodging, passing by the farm, where there was no sign of life to induce him to pause. It was nine o'clock, and as there was no light in any of the windows, he concluded that Mr. Biron had gone to bed, tired out with his day's hunting, and that Claire had followed his example.

He felt so restless, so uneasy, however, that instead of passing on he lingered about, walking up and down, watching the blank, dark windows, almost praying for a flicker of light in any one of them for a sign of the life inside.

After an hour of this unprofitable occupation, he took himself to task for his folly, and went home to bed.

On the following morning, before he was up, there was a loud knocking at the outer door of the cottage where he lived. Bram, with a sense of something wrong, something which concerned himself, ran down himself to open it.

In the middle of the little path stood Theodore Biron, with the same clothes that he had worn on the morning of the previous day, but without the hunting-crop.

He was white, with livid lips, and his limbs trembled.

"What's the matter?" asked Bram in a muffled voice.

"Claire, my daughter Claire!" stammered Theodore in a voice which sounded shrill with real feeling. All the jauntiness, all the vivacity, had gone out of him. He shivered with something which was keener than cold.

"Well?" said Bram, with a horrible chill at his heart.

"She's—she's gone, gone!" said Theodore, reeling back against the fence of the little garden. "She's run away. She's run right away. She's left me, left her poor old father! Don't you understand? She is gone, man, gone!"

And Mr. Biron, for once roused to genuine emotion, broke into sobs.

Bram stood like a stone.

CHAPTER XV
PARENT AND LOVER

For some minutes after he had made the announcement of his daughter's flight Mr. Biron gave himself up openly and without restraint to the expression of a sorrow which, while it might be selfish, was certainly profound.

"My daughter! My daughter!" he sobbed. "My little Claire! My little, bright-faced darling! Oh, I can't believe it! It must be a dream, a nightmare! Do you think, Elshaw," and he suddenly drew himself up, with a quick change to bright hope, in the midst of his distress, "that she can have gone up to the Park to stay at her uncle's for the night?"

But Bram shook his head.

"I don't think it's likely," he said in a hollow voice. "They were none so kind to her that she should do that." A pause. "When did you miss her?"

"This morning when I got back," replied Theodore, who looked blue with cold and misery. "I went out with the hounds yesterday as you know. And we got such a long way out that I couldn't get back, and I put up at an inn for the night. Don't you think," and again his face brightened with one of those volatile changes from misery to hope which made him seem so womanish, "that she may have been afraid to spend a night in the house by herself, and that she may have gone down to Joan's place to sleep? I'll go there and see. Will you come? Yes, yes, you'd better come. I don't care for Joan; she's a rough, unfeeling sort of person. I should like you to come with me."

"I'll come—in a minute," said Bram shortly.

He knew very well that there was nothing in Mr. Biron's idea. He spoke as if this were the first time that Claire had been left to spend the night alone in the farmhouse; but, as a matter of fact, Bram knew very well that it had been Theodore's frequent custom to spend the night away from home, and that his daughter was too much used to his vagaries to trouble herself seriously about his absence.

He went upstairs, finished dressing, came out of the house, and rejoined Mr. Biron; and that gentleman noticed no change in him, thought, indeed, that he was taking the matter with heartless coolness. Certainly, if behavior which contrasted strongly with that of the injured father gave proof of heartlessness, then Bram was a very stone.

All the way down the hill Mr. Biron lamented and moaned, sobbed, and even snivelled, loudly cursed the wretches at Holme Park who had made an outcast of his daughter, and, above all, Chris himself, who had stolen and ruined his daughter.

But Bram cut him short.

"Hush, Mr. Biron," said he sternly. "Don't say words like that till you are sure. For her sake hold your tongue. It's not for you to cast the first stone at her, or even at him."

Even in his most sincere grief Mr. Biron resented being taken to task like this; and by Bram, of all people, whom he secretly disliked, as well as feared, although the young man's strong character attracted him instinctively when he was in want of help. He drew himself up with all his old airy arrogance.

"Do you think I would doubt her for a single moment if I were not cruelly sure?" cried he indignantly. "My own child, my own darling little Claire! But I understand it all now. I see how thoroughly I was deceived in Chris. But he shall smart for it! I'll thrash him within an inch of his life! I won't leave a whole bone in his body! I'll strangle him! I'll tear him limb from limb!"

And Mr. Biron made a gesture more violent with every threat, until at last it seemed as if his frantic gesticulations must dislocate the bones in his own slim and fragile little body.

As for Bram, he seemed to be past the stage of acute feeling of any sort. He was benumbed with the great blow that had fallen upon him; overwhelmed, in spite of the foreshadowings which had of late broken his peace. With the fall of his ideal there seemed to have crumbled away all that was best in his life, leaving only a cold automaton to do his daily work of head and hand. He was astonished himself, if the pale feeling could be called astonishment, to find that he could laugh at the antics of his companion; not openly, of course, but with secret and bitter gibes at the careless, selfish father, and the frantic gestures by which he sought to impress his companion.

When Theodore's energies were exhausted they walked on in silence. And then Theodore felt hurt at Bram's blunt, stolid apathy.

"I thought I should find you more sympathetic, Elshaw," he said in an offended tone. "You always pretended to think so much of my daughter!"

"It wasn't pretence," said Bram shortly. "But I'm thinking, Mr. Biron, though I don't like to say it now, that she must have been very unhappy before she went away like that."

Quite suddenly his voice broke. Mr. Biron, surprised in the midst of his theatrical display of emotion into a momentary pang of real compunction and of real remorse, was for a few moments entirely silent. Then he said in a quiet voice, more dignified and more touching than any of his loud outbursts—

"It's true, I've not been a good father to her. But she was such a good girl—I never guessed it would come to this."

Bram said nothing. He felt as hard as nails. Theodore was really suffering now; but it served him right. What had the poor little creature's life been but a long and terrible struggle between temptation on the one side, worry and difficulty on the other? She had held out long and bravely. She had struggled with a bright face, bearing her father's burdens for him, and her own as well. What wonder that human nature had been too weak to hold out forever?

Bram's heart was like a great open sore. He dared not look within himself, he dared not think, he dared not even feel. He tried to stupefy himself to the work of the moment, to stifle all sense but that of sight, and to fix his eyes upon Joan's cottage, which they were now approaching, as if upon the mere reaching of it all his hopes depended.

But if Theodore had found Bram unsympathetic, what must he have thought of Joan? She heard his inquiries with coldness, and after saying that Claire had not been with her since she left the farmhouse on the previous evening, she asked shortly whether she had gone away.

"I—I am afraid so. Oh, my child, my poor child!" cried Theodore.

Joan grew very red, and clapping her hands on her hips, nodded with compressed lips.

"You've got no one but yourself to thank for this, Mr. Biron," she said. "T' poor young lady's had a cruel time these many months through yer wicked ways! God help her, poor little lady!"

And the good woman turned sharply away from him, and slamming the door in his face, disappeared, sobbing bitterly.

Theodore was very white; he trembled from head to foot, and was even for a little while too angry and too much perturbed to speak.

At last, when Bram had put a hand within his arm to lead him away, he stammered out—

"You heard that, Elshaw! You heard the woman! That's what these — North country — are like; they haven't a scrap of feeling, even for the sacred grief of a father! But I don't care a hang for the whole ---- lot of them! I'll go up to the Park, and I'll tell Mr Cornthwaite, the purse-proud old humbug, who thinks money can buy anything—I'll tell him what I think of him and his scoundrel of a son! And then I'll go up to town, and I'll find him out, I'll hunt out Christian himself, and I'll avenge my child."

Bram said nothing.

"And I'll make him provide for her. I'll bring out an action against him, and make him shell out, him and his skinflint of a father. Chris is nothing but a chip off the old block, and I'll make them suffer together, in the only way they can suffer—through the money-bags."

Bram was disgusted, sickened. He scented through this new turn of Mr. Biron's thoughts that feeling for the main chance which was such a prominent feature of that gentleman's character. And quite unexpectedly he stopped short, and said bluntly—

"That may comfort you, Mr. Biron, but it will never do aught for her! If—if," he had to clear his throat to make himself heard at all, "if she—comes back, she'll never touch their money! Poor, poor child!"

"You think she'll come back?" asked Theodore almost wistfully.

But Bram could not answer. He did not know what to think, what to wish. He shrugged his shoulders without speaking, and with a gesture of abrupt farewell turned from his companion, who had now nearly reached his own door, and walked rapidly back in the direction of his lodging.

He could not bear to come near the farm, the place which had been hallowed in his eyes by thoughts of her who had been his idol.

Theodore called out to him.

"You'll give me a look in to-night, won't you, when you come back from the office? Think how lonely I shall be."

Bram, without turning round, made a gesture of assent. He felt with surprise to himself that he was half-drawn to this contemptible creature by the fact that, underneath all his theatrical demonstrations of regret and grief, there was some very strong and genuine feeling. It was chiefly a selfish feeling, as Bram knew; indeed, a resentful feeling, that Claire had treated him shabbily and ungratefully in leaving him to shift for himself without any warning, after so many years of patient slavery, of tender care for him.

But still Bram felt that he had at last some emotion in common with this man, whom he had so far only despised. Theodore even felt the disgrace, the moral shame of this awful disaster to his daughter more keenly than any one would have given him credit for.

As for Bram himself, he went home, he ate his breakfast, he started for the town almost in his usual manner. No one who passed him detected any sign in his look or in his manner of the blow which had fallen upon him. But, for all that, he was suffering so keenly, so bitterly, that the very intensity of his pain had a numbing effect, reducing him to the level of a brute which can see, and hear, and taste, and smell, but in which all sense of anything higher is dead and cold.

It was not until he had nearly passed the garden of the farm, keeping his eyes carefully turned in the opposite direction, that a bend in the road caught his eye, where not many evenings before he had seen Claire standing with a letter in her hand, waiting for some one to pass who would take it to the post for her.

And his face twitched; from between his closed teeth there came a sort of strangled sob, the sound which in Theodore had roused his contempt. He remembered the smile which had come into her eyes when he came by, the word of thanks with which she had slipped the letter into his hand, and run indoors. He remembered that a scent of lavender had come to him as she passed, that he had felt a thrill at the sound, the sight of her flying skirts as she fled into the house.

Oh! it was not possible that she could have done this thing, she who was so proud, so pure, so tender to her friends!

And Bram stopped in the middle of the road, with an upward bound of the heart, and told himself that the thing was a lie.

What a base wretch he was to have harbored such a thought of her! She was gone; but what proof had they but their own mean and base suspicions that she had not gone alone?

And Bram by a strong effort threw off the dark cloud which was pressing down upon his soul, or at least lifted one corner of it, and strode down towards the office resolved to trust, to hope, in spite of everything.

At the office everything was reassuringly normal in the daily routine. And, by a great and unceasing effort, Bram had really got himself to hold his opinions on the one great subject in suspense, when a carriage drove up to the door, and a few minutes later young Mrs. Christian, with a face which betrayed that she was suffering from acute distress, came into the office.

As soon as she saw Bram, she stopped on her way through.

"No," she said quickly to the clerk who was leading her through to the private office of Mr. Cornthwaite, "it is Mr. Elshaw I want to see. Please, can I speak to you?"

Bram felt the heavy weight settling at once on his heart again. He followed her in silence into the office. Mr. Cornthwaite had not yet arrived.

As soon as the door was shut, and they were alone, she broke out in a tremulous voice, not free from pettishness—

"Mr. Elshaw, I wanted to see you because I feel sure you will not deceive me. And all the rest try to. Mr. and Mrs. Cornthwaite, and my sister-in-law, and my own people, and everybody. You live near Duke's Farm? Tell me, is Miss Claire Biron at home with her father, or—or has she gone away?"

"I believe, Mrs. Christian, she has gone away."

The young wife did not cry; she frowned.

"I knew it!" she said sharply. "They pretended they did not know; but I knew it, I felt sure of it. Mr. Elshaw, she has gone away with my husband!"

"Oh, but how can you be sure? How—"

"Mr. Elshaw, don't trifle with me. You know the truth as well as I do. Not one day has passed since our marriage without Christian's flaunting this girl and her perfections in my face; not one day has passed since our return from abroad without his either seeing her or making an effort to see her. Oh, I daresay you will say it was mean; but I have had him watched, and he has been at the farm at Hessel every day!"

"But what of that? He is her cousin, you know. He has always been used to see a great deal of her and of her father."

"Oh, I know all about her father!" snapped Minnie. "And I know how likely any of the family are to go out to Hessel to see him! Don't prevaricate, Mr. Elshaw. I had understood you never did anything of the kind. Can you pretend to doubt that they have gone away together?"

Bram was silent. He hung his head as if he had been the guilty person.

"Of course, you cannot," went on the lady triumphantly. "Where has she got to go to? What friends has she to stay with? Who would she leave her father for except Christian? It seems she has never had the decency to hide that she was fond of him!"

"Don't say that," protested Bram gently. "Why should she hide it in the old days before he was married? There was no reason why she should. They were cousins; they were believed to be engaged. They would have been married if Mr. Cornthwaite had allowed it. Didn't you know that?"

"Not in the way I've known it since, of course," said Minnie bitterly. "Everything was kept from me. I heard of a boy-and-girl affection; that was all. The whole family are deceitful and untrustworthy. And Christian is the worst of them all. He doesn't care for me a bit; he never, never did!"

And here at last she broke down, and began to cry piteously.

Bram, usually so tender-hearted, felt as if his heart was scorched up within him. He looked at her; he tried to speak kindly, tried to say reassuring things, to express a doubt, a hope, which he did not feel.

But she stopped him imperiously, snappishly.

"Don't talk nonsense, Mr. Elshaw, please. And don't say you are sorry. For I know you are sorry for nobody but her. Miss Biron is one of those persons who attract sympathy; I am not. But you can spare yourself the trouble of pretending." She drew herself up, and hastily wiped her eyes. "I know what to do. I shall go back to my father's house, and I shall have nothing more to do with him. I am not going to break my heart over an unprincipled man, or over a creature like this Claire Biron."

Bram offered no remonstrance. He knew that he ought to be sorry for this poor little woman, whose only and most venial fault had been a conviction that she possessed the power to "reform" the man she married. Unhappily, it was true, as she said, that she was not one of those persons who attract sympathy. Her hard, dry, snappish manner, the shrewish light in her blue eyes, repelled him as they had repelled Christian himself. And Bram, though far from excusing or forgiving Christian, felt that he understood how impossible it would have been for a man of his easy, genial temperament to be even fairly, conventionally happy with a nature so antipathetic to his own.

In silence, in sorrow, he withdrew, with an added burden to bear, the burden of what was near to absolute certainty, of extinguished hope.

CHAPTER XVI
THE PANGS OF DESPISED LOVE

The farmhouse looked desolate in the dusk of the November evening when Bram, in fulfilment of his promise to Theodore, crossed the farmyard to the back door and tapped at it lightly.

It was opened by Joan, who looked as if she had been interrupted in the middle of "a good cry."

"Ay, coom in, sir," said she, "coom in. But you'll find no company here now."

"Isn't Mr. Biron back yet?"

"No, sir," she answered with a sudden change to aggressive sullenness, "and he's welcome to stay away, he is! If it hadn't been for that miserable auld rascal, poor Miss Claire 'ud never been took away from us. Ah wouldn't have on my conscience what yon chap has, no, not for a kingdom."

Bram, sombre and stern, sat down by the fire, staring at the little wooden stool on which he had so often seen Claire sitting in the opposite corner, with her sewing in her hand. The big chimney-corner which they had both loved—how bare it looked without her! Joan, alone of all the people he had met that day, seemed to understand what had taken place in him, to realize the sudden death, the total, irremediable decay, of what had been the joy of his life. She put down the plate she had been wiping, and she came over to look at him in the firelight. There was no other light in the room.

"Poor lad! Poor chap!" she murmured in accents so tender, so motherly, that her rough voice sounded like most sweet, most touching music in his dull ears.

For the first time since the horrible shock he had received that morning his features quivered, became convulsed, and a look of desperate anguish came into his calm gray eyes.

Her strong right hand came down upon his shoulder with a blow which was meant to be inspiriting in its violent energy.

"Well, lad, ye must bear oop; ye must forget her! Ay, there's no two ways about it. It's a sad business, an' Ah'm broken oop abaht it mysen, but she's chosen to go, an' there's no help for it, an' no grieving can mend it! It was only you, an' her liking for you, that stopped her from going before,

I reckon. Look at yon auld spend-t'-brass and the life she's led wi' him, always having to beg, beg, beg for him from folks as didn't pity her as they should!"

Bram moved impatiently.

"Yes, that's what I cannot forgive him!" growled he.

Joan stared at him in the dusk.

"Have you heard," said she, peering mysteriously into his face, "if anything 'as happened while you were away?"

Bram shook his head.

"Well, summat did happen. Mr. Biron got money from some one, an' began to spend it loike one o'clock. You must have heard o' that?"

Bram nodded, remembering the new hunter and Theodore's smart appearance.

"Well," went on Joan, leaning forward, and dropping her voice, "it was summat to do wi' that as broke oop poor Miss Claire. Ay, lad, don't shiver an' start; it's best you should know all, and forget all if you can. Well, it was after that, after t' auld man had gotten t' brass, that I saw a change coom over her. She went abaht loike one as warn't right, an' she says to 'im one day—Ah were in t' kitchen yonder an' Ah heard her—'Papa,' says she, 'Ah can never look Bram Elshaw in t' face again.' That's what she said, my lad; Ah heard her."

Bram got up, and began to pace up and down the tiled floor without a word. Joan went on, quickening her pace, a little anxious to get the story over and done with.

"You know his way. But there was summat in her voice told me it were no laughin' matter wi' her. An'," went on the good woman in a voice lower still, "when Mr. Christian coom that evening, says she, says Miss Claire—'Ah mun see 'im to-neght.' An' he came in, an' they went in through to the best parlor, and they had a long talk together. That were t' day before yesterday. She must have gone last neght, as soon as Ah left t' house."

Still Bram said nothing, pacing up and down, up and down, on the red tiles which he had trodden so often with something like ecstasy in his heart.

Joan was shrewd enough and sympathetic enough to understand why he did not speak. She finished her plate-washing, disappeared silently into the outhouse, and presently returned with her bonnet on.

"Are ye going to stay here, sir?" she asked, as she laid her hands on the door to go out.

"Yes; I promised I'd look in."

"Friendly loike? You aren't going for to do him any hurt?"

"No, oh, no."

"Well," said Joan, as she turned the handle and took her portly person slowly round the door, "if so be you had, you might ha' done it an' welcome! Ah wouldn't have stopped ye. Good-neght, sir."

"Good-night, Joan."

She went out, and Bram was left alone. The sound of her footsteps died away, until he felt as if he was the only living thing about the farm. Even the noises that usually came across from the sheds and the stables where the animals were kept seemed to be hushed that evening. No sound reached his ears but the moaning of the rising wind, and the scratching of the mice in the old wainscotting.

Never before had he felt so utterly, hopelessly miserable and castdown. In the old days, when he had lived one of a wretched, poverty-stricken family in a squalid mean way, ill-kept, half-starved, he had had his daydreams, his vague ambitions, to gild the sorry present. Now, on the very high-road to the fulfilment of those ambitions, he was suddenly left without a ray of hope, without a rag of comfort, to bear the most unutterable wretchedness, that of shattered ideals.

Not Claire alone, but Chris also had fallen from the place each had held in his imagination, in his heart, and Bram, who hid a spirit-world of his own under a matter-of-fact manner and a blunt directness of speech, suffered untold anguish.

While he watched the embers of the fire in profound melancholy, with his hands on his knees, and his eyes staring dully into the red heart of the dying fire, he heard something moving outside. He raised his head, expecting to hear the sound of Mr. Biron's voice.

But a shadow passed before the window in the faint daylight that was left; and with a wild hope Bram sat up, his heart seeming to cease to beat.

The shadow, the step were those of a woman.

The next moment the door was softly, stealthily opened, and away like a dream went joy and hope again.

The woman was not Claire.

He could see that the visitor was tall, broad-shouldered, of well-developed figure, and that she was of the class that wear shawls round their heads, and clogs on their feet in the daytime.

She stood in the room, just inside the door, and seemed to listen. Then she said in a voice which was coarse and uncultivated, but which was purposely subdued to a pitch of insincere civility, as Bram instantly felt sure—

"Miss Biron! Is Miss Claire Biron here?"

Now, Bram had never, as far as he knew, met this girl before; he did not even know her name. But, with his sense of hearing made sharper, perhaps, by the darkness, he guessed at once something which was very near the truth. He knew that this woman came with hostile intent of some kind or other.

He at once rose from his seat, and said—"No; Miss Biron is not in."

And he put his hand up to the high chimney-piece, found a box of matches, and lit a candle which was beside it. Meanwhile the visitor stood motionless, and was so standing when the light had grown bright enough for him to see her by. She was a handsome girl, black-haired, blacked-eyed, with cheeks which ought to have been red, but which were now pale and thin, showing a sharp outline of rather high cheek-bone and big jaw. Bram recognized her as a girl whom he had often seen about Hessel, and who lived at a little farm about a mile and a half away. Her name was Meg Tyzack. She was neatly dressed, without any of the flaunting, shabby finery which the factory girls usually affect when they leave their shawl and clogs. Her lips were tightly closed, and in her eyes there was an expression of ferocious sullenness which confirmed the idea Bram had conceived at the first sound of her voice. Her black cloth jacket was buttoned only at the throat, and her right hand was thrust underneath it as if she was hiding something.

"Not in, eh?" she asked scoffingly, as she measured Bram from head to foot with a look of ineffable scorn. Then, with a sudden, sharp change of tone to one of passionate anxiety, she asked, "Where's she gone to then?"

Bram hesitated. This woman's appearance at the farm, her look, her manner, betrayed to him within a few seconds a fact he had not guessed before, though now a dozen circumstances flashed into his mind to confirm it. This was one of the many girls with whom Chris had had relations of a more or less questionable character. Bram had seen her with him in the lane leading to her home, and on the hill above Holme Park; had seen her waiting about in the town near the works. But to see Chris talking to a good-looking girl was too common a thing for Bram to have given this particular young woman much attention. Now, however, he divined in an instant that it was jealousy which had brought her to the farmhouse, and a feeling of sickening repulsion came over him at the thought of the words which he might have to hear directed by this virago at Claire. If the idol was broken, it was an idol still.

As he did not reply at once, Meg Tyzack stepped quickly across the floor, and glared into his eyes with a look terrible in its fierce eagerness, its deadly anxiety.

"Where has she gone? Ye can't keep t' truth from me." Then, as he was still silent, she burst out with an overwhelming torrent of passion. "Ah know what they say! Ah know they say he's taken her away wi' him, Mr.

Christian of t' works, Cornthwaite's works. But it's a lie. Ah know it's a lie. He'd never take her wi' him; he'd never dare take any one but me. He care for her? Not enoof for that! She's here, Ah know she is; only she's afraid to coom out, afraid to meet me! But Ah'll find her; Ah'll have her aht. What 'ud you be doin' here if she wasn't here? Oh, Ah know who Christian was jealous of; Ah know she was artful enough to keep the two of ye on. Ah know it was her fault he used to coom here and—" Her eyes flashed, and her voice suddenly dropped to a fierce whisper. "Ah mean to have her aht."

As she suddenly swung round and made for the inner door leading into the hall, Bram saw that she held under her jacket a bottle. There was mischief in the woman's eyes, worse mischief even than was boded by her tongue. For one moment, as he sprang after her, Bram felt glad that Claire was not there. Meg laughed hoarsely in his face as she eluded him, and disappeared into the hall, slamming the door.

Bram did not follow her. Claire being gone, she could do little harm. He opened the outer door, and went out into the farmyard. In a few minutes he saw a light flickering in room after room upstairs. Meg Tyzack was searching, hunting in every nook and every corner, searching for her rival with savage, despairing eagerness. Bram shivered. It was a relief to him when he heard footsteps approaching the farm, and a few moments later the voice of Theodore calling to him.

"Yes, Mr. Biron, it's me."

"Then who's that in the house? Is it Joan?" asked Theodore fretfully, testily.

He was dispirited, dejected; evidently he had met with neither comfort nor sympathy at Holme Park. He had been trying to comfort himself on the way back, as Bram discovered by his unsteady gait and husky utterance.

"It's a girl, Meg Tyzack," answered Bram.

Mr. Biron started.

"That vixen!" cried he. "That horrible virago! Why did you let her get in?"

"I couldn't help it," replied Bram simply.

"What is she up to?"

"She's looking for Miss Claire," said Bram in a low voice.

Theodore made no answer. But he shuddered, and leaning against the wall of the farmyard began to cry.

"Come, Mr. Biron," said Bram impatiently, "it's no use giving way like that. It's just something to be thankful for that this mad woman can't get hold of her."

Mr. Biron did not answer. A moment later, attracted probably by the voices, Meg came rushing out of the house like a fury, and made straight for the two men.

"Ah!" cried she shrilly, when she made out who the newcomer was, thrusting her angry face close to his in the gloom. "So it's you, is it? You, the father of that—"

"Hold your tongue."

"Hush!" cried Bram, seizing her arm.

There was a sound so impressive in his voice, short and blunt as his speech was, that the woman turned upon him sharply, but for a moment was silent. Then she said with coarse bravado—

"And who are you to talk to me? Why, t' very mon as ought to take my part, if you had any spirit? But you leave it to me to pay out t' pair on 'em. An' Ah'll do it. Ah'll made 'em both smart for it, if Ah swing for it! Ah'll show him the price he has to pay for treatin' a woman like me the way he's done. When Ah loved him so! Ay, ten times more'n than that little hussy could! Oh, my God, my God!"

Bram, child of the people that he was, was moved in the utmost depths of his heart by the woman's mad, passionate despair. He felt for her as he could never feel for the cool, prim, little wife Christian had served so ill. He would have comforted her if he could. But as no words strong enough or suitable enough to the occasion came to his lips, he just put a gentle hand upon the woman's shoulder as she bowed herself down and sobbed.

But Mr. Biron's refinement was shocked by this scene. Seeing the woman less ferocious, now that she was more absorbed in her grief, he ventured to come a little nearer, and to say snappishly—

"But, my good woman, though we may be sorry for you, you have no right to force yourself into my house. Nor have you any right to speak in such terms of my daughter."

Meg was erect in a moment, her eyes flashing, her nostrils quivering. With a wild, ironical laugh, she faced about, pointing at his mean little face a scornful finger.

"You!" cried she in a very passion of contempt. "You dare to speak to me! You as would have sold your daughter a dozen times over if t' price had been good enoof! Why, mon, your hussy of a daughter's a pearl to you! You're a rat, a cur! Ah could almost forgive her when Ah look at you! It's you Ah've got to blame for it all, wi' your black heart an' your mean, white face! You more'n her, more'n him!"

With a sudden impulse of indomitable rage, she stepped back, and raising her right hand quickly, flung something at his face.

With a sudden impulse of indomitable rage, she stepped back, and raising her right hand quickly, flung something at his face.

Mr. Biron uttered a piercing shriek, as shrill as a woman's.

"Fiend! She-devil! She's killed me! Help! Oh, I'm on fire!"

Bram, who hardly knew what had happened, caught Theodore as the latter fell shrieking into his arms. Meg, with a wild laugh, picked up the remains of her broken bottle, and ran out of the farmyard.

CHAPTER XVII
BRAM SPEAKS HIS MIND

Meg Tyzack had hardly left the farmyard before Bram knew what she had done, and realized the full extent of the danger Claire had escaped. The bottle Meg had carried, and which she had thrown at the head of Theodore Biron, had contained vitriol. Luckily for Mr. Biron, he had moved aside just in time to escape having the bottle broken on his face, but part of the contents had fallen on his head, on the side of his face, and on his left hand before the bottle itself was dashed into two pieces as it fell on the ground.

Bram wiped Theodore's face and hands as quickly as he could, but the effeminate man had so entirely lost his self-control that he could not keep still; and by his own restlessness he hindered the full effect of Bram's good offices.

The young man saw that his best chance with the hysterical creature was to get him into the house as quickly as he could. But Theodore objected to this. He wanted Bram to go in pursuit of the woman, to bring her back, to have her taken up. And as his cries had by this time caused a little crowd to assemble from the cottages round about, he began to harangue them on the subject of his wrongs, and to try to stir them up to resent the outrage to which he had been subjected.

It is needless to say that his efforts were ineffectual. Mr. Biron had succeeded in establishing a thoroughly bad reputation among his neighbors, who knew all about his selfish treatment of his daughter. He found not one sympathizer, and at last he was fain to allow himself to be led indoors by Bram, who was very urgent in his persuasions, being indeed afraid that Theodore's curses upon the bystanders for their supineness would bring upon him some further chastisement. He prevailed upon a lad in the crowd to go for a doctor, assuring him that it was the pain from which the gentleman was suffering that made him so irritable.

Once inside the house, Bram found that his difficulties with his unsympathetic patient had only just begun. Mr. Biron was not used to pain, and had no idea of suffering in silence. He raved and he moaned, he cursed and he swore, and Bram was amazed and disgusted to find that this little, well-preserved, middle-aged gentleman was quite as much concerned by the injury which he should suffer in appearance as by the pain he had to bear.

"Do you think, Elshaw, that the marks will ever go away? Oh, good heavens, I know they won't," he cried, as with his uninjured eye he surveyed himself in the glass over the dining-room sideboard by the light of a couple of candles. "Oh, oh, the wretch! The hag! I'll get her six months for this!"

And the little man, trembling with rage, shook his fist and gnashed his teeth, presenting in his anger and disfigurement a hideous spectacle.

The left side of his face was already one long patch of inflammation. His left eye was shut up; the hair on that side of his head had already begun to come away in tufts from the burnt skin.

Bram was disgusted. Mr. Biron's grief over the loss of his daughter, keen as it had been, could not be compared to that which he felt now at the loss of his remaining good looks. There was a note of absolute sincerity in his every lament which had been conspicuously lacking in his grief of the morning. The young man could scarcely listen to him with patience. He tried, however, out of humanity, to remain silent, since he could give no comfort. But silence would not do for his garrulous companion, who insisted on having an answer.

"Do you think, Elshaw, that I shall be disfigured for life?" he asked with tremulous anxiety.

"I'm afraid so," answered Bram rather gruffly. "But I don't think I'd worry about that when you have worse things than that to trouble you."

Unluckily, Mr. Biron was so much absorbed in the loss of his own beauty that he fell into the mistake of being absolutely sincere for once.

"Worse troubles than that! Worse than to go about like a scarecrow, a repulsive object, all the years of one's life! What can be worse?" groaned he.

Bram, who was standing solemnly erect, answered at once, in a deep voice, out of the fulness of his heart—

"Well, Mr. Biron, if you don't know of anything worse, I suppose there is nothing worse—for you!"

But Mr. Biron was impervious to sneers. He walked up and down the room in feverish anxiety until the arrival of the doctor, whom he interrogated at once with as much solicitude as if he had been a young beauty on the eve of her first ball.

The doctor, a stolid, hard-working country practitioner, with a dull red face and dull black eyes, showed Theodore much less mercy than Bram had done. He knew his patient well, having been called in to him on several occasions when that gentleman's excesses had brought on the attacks of dyspepsia to which he was subject; and the more he saw of him the less he liked him. Theodore's anxiety about his appearance he treated with cruel bluntness.

"No, you'll never be the same man again to look at, Mr. Biron," he said quite cheerfully. "And you may be thankful if we can save you the sight of the left eye."

"You think the scar will never go away? Nor the hair grow again?" asked Theodore piteously.

"The scar won't go away certainly. But that's not much to trouble about at your time of life, I should think," returned the doctor bluntly. "There's a greater danger than that to concern ourselves with. Unless you are very careful, you will have erysipelas. You must get that little daughter of yours to nurse you very carefully. Where is she?"

Theodore burst out fretfully with a new grievance—

"My daughter! She's not here to nurse me. I've no one to nurse me now. She's gone away, gone away and left me all by myself!"

The doctor stared at him with the unpleasant fixity of eyes which have to look hard before they see much.

"You told her to go, I suppose?" said he at last, abruptly.

Taken by surprise, Theodore, to the horror of Bram, who was standing in the background, confessed—

"Well, I told her she could go if she liked; but I never meant her to take me at my word."

Bram was thunderstruck. Such a simple solution of the mystery of the disappearance of the dutiful daughter had never entered his mind. In a fit of passion, perhaps of partial intoxication, Theodore had bade his daughter get out of the house. And the long-suffering girl had taken him at his word.

The doctor nodded.

"I thought so," said he. "I thought there was no end to what the child would put up with at your hands. So you have driven her away? Well, then you'll have to suffer for it, I'm afraid. I don't know of anybody else who would come to nurse you."

"I'll do what I can," said Bram in a hollow voice from the background.

It needed an effort on his part to make this offer. He felt that he loathed the little wretch who had himself driven his daughter into the arms of her untrustworthy lover. Only the thought that Claire would wish him to do so enabled him to undertake the distasteful task of ministering to such a patient. Theodore thanked him in a half-hearted sort of way, feeling that there was something not altogether grateful to himself in the spirit in which this offer was made. The doctor was far more cordial.

He told Bram he was doing a fine thing.

"But then," he added in his rough way, "fine things are what one expects of you, Mr. Elshaw."

And then he went out, leaving Theodore in much perplexity as to what the fellow could see in Elshaw to make such a fuss about.

Bram spent the night with him, doing his best to soothe and to comfort the unfortunate man, whose sufferings, both of mind and body, grew more acute as the hours wore on. His own worry about himself was the chief cause of this. Long before morning he had lost sight of the shame of his daughter's flight, and looked upon it solely as a wicked freak which had resulted in his own most cruel misfortune.

"Why, surely, man," broke out Bram at last, losing patience at his long tirades of woe and indignation, "it's better that you should be disfigured than her, at any rate."

"No, it isn't," retorted Theodore sharply. "Claire never cared half as much about her appearance as I did about mine. And, besides," he went on, with a sudden feeling that he had got hold of a strong argument, "if she had been disfigured, she would have had no temptation to do wrong!"

Bram jumped up, clenching his fist. He could bear no more. With a few jerked-out words to the effect that he would send Joan to get his breakfast, he rushed out of the house.

Poor Claire! Poor little Claire! Was this the creature she had wronged in going away? This shallow, selfish wretch who had turned her out, and who regretted the ministrations of her gentle hands far more than he did the shame her desperate act had drawn down upon her!

Bram went down to the works that morning a different man from what he had been the day before. He was waking from the dull lethargy of grief into which the first discovery of Claire's flight had thrown him. A smouldering anger against the Cornthwaites, father and son, was taking the place of sullen misery in his breast. He had gathered from Theodore that the elder Mr. Cornthwaite had taken his remonstrances not only coolly, but with something like relief, as if he felt glad of an excuse for getting rid of the relations whose vicinity had been a continual annoyance.

But Bram did not mean to be put off. Josiah, who had not been at the office at all on the previous day, should see him, and answer his questions. And Bram, maturing a grave resolution, strode down into the town with a steady look in his eyes.

Mr. Cornthwaite saw him as soon as he himself arrived, and, evidently with the intention of taking the bull by the horns, spoke to him at once.

"Ah, Elshaw, good-morning. Come in here a moment, please. I want to speak to you."

Bram followed in silence, and stood within the room with his back to the door, with a stern expression on his pale face.

Mr. Cornthwaite broached the unpleasant subject at once.

"Nice business this, eh? Nice thing Chris has done for himself now! Brought a hornet's nest about his ears and mine too! Old Hibbs and his wife have been down to my house blackguarding me; Minnie herself is fit for a lunatic asylum, and, to complete the business, the girl's rascally father has been to my house, trying to levy blackmail. But I've made up my mind to make short work of the thing! I start for London to-night; find out Master Chris (luckily he gave his address to no one but me, or he'd have had his wife's family about his ears already), and bring the young man back to his wife's feet—bring him by the scruff of the neck if necessary!"

"And—Claire—Miss Biron?" said Bram hoarsely.

"Oh, she must shift for herself. She knew what she was doing, running off with a married man. I've no pity for her; not the least. I wash my hands of the pair of them, father and daughter, now. He must just pack up his traps and be off after her. What becomes of her is his affair, not ours!"

"Mr. Christian can't get rid of the responsibility like that, sir," said Bram, with a note of sombre warning in his voice.

"I take upon myself the responsibility for him," retorted Mr. Cornthwaite coldly. "My son is dependent upon me, and he can do nothing without my approval. I am certainly going to give him no help towards the maintenance of a baggage like that. You know what my opinion of her always has been. Circumstances have confirmed it most amply. A young man is not much to blame if he gets caught, entangled, by a girl as artful and as designing as she is."

"I don't think you will find yourself and Mr. Christian in agreement upon that point, sir," said Bram steadily.

"Well, whether he agrees or not, he'll come back with me to-morrow," replied Mr. Cornthwaite hotly.

"Then, Mr. Cornthwaite, you'll please take my notice now, and I'll be out of this to-day. For," Bram went on, with a rising spot of deep color in his cheek, and a bright light in his eye, "I couldn't trust myself face to face with such a d—d scoundrel as Mr. Christian is if he leaves the girl he loves, the girl he's betrayed, and comes sneaking back at your heels like a cur, when he ought to stand up for the woman who loves him!"

"Upon my word, yours is very singular morality for a young man who goes in for such correctness of conduct as you do. Where does the wife come in, the poor, injured wife, in your new-fangled scheme of right and wrong? Is she to be left out in the cold altogether?"

"Where else can she be left, poor thing?" cried Bram with deep feeling. "Do you think if you brought Mr. Christian back 'by the scruff of the neck,' as you say, that you'd ever be able to patch matters up between 'em so as to make 'em live anything but a cat-and-dog's-life? No, Mr. Cornthwaite, you couldn't. The wife won't come to so much hurt; she wouldn't have come to none if you hadn't forced on this cursed marriage. Let her get free, and make him free; and let Mr. Christian put the wrong right as far as he can by marrying the girl he wants, the girl who knows how to make him happy!"

Mr. Cornthwaite's black eyes blazed. He hated even a semblance of contradiction; and Bram's determined and dogged attitude irritated him beyond measure. He rose from his arm-chair, and clasping his hands behind his back with a loud snap, he assumed towards the young man an air of bland contempt which he had never used to him before.

"Your notions are charming in the abstract, Elshaw. I have no doubt, too, that there are some sections of society where your ideas might be carried out without much harm to anybody. But not in that in which we move. If my son were to commit such an unheard-of folly as you suggest I would let him shift for himself for the rest of his days. And perhaps you know enough of Christian to tell whether he would find life with any young woman agreeable under those conditions."

Bram remained silent. There was a pause, rather a long one. Then Mr. Cornthwaite spoke again—

"Of course, you are sensible enough to understand that this is my business, and my son's; that it is a family matter, a difficulty in which I have to act for the best. And I hope," he went on in a different tone, "for your own sake, more than for mine, that you will not take any step so rash as leaving this office would be. Without notice, too!"

"As to that, sir, you had better let me go—and without notice," said Bram with a sullen note in his voice which made Mr. Cornthwaite look at him with some anxiety, "if it's true that you're going to make Mr. Christian leave Miss Claire in the lurch. For I tell you, sir," and again he looked up, with a steely flash in his gray eyes and a look of stubborn ferocity about his long upper lip and straight mouth, "if I was to come face to face wi' him after he'd done that thing I couldn't keep my fists off him; Ah couldn't, sir. That's what comes of my being born in a different section of society, sir, I suppose. And so, as Ah've loved Mr. Christian, and as Ah've had much to thank you and him for, sir, you'd best let me go back—to my own section of society, where a man has to stand by his own deeds, like a man!"

Mr. Cornthwaite's attitude, his tone, changed insensibly as he looked and listened to the man who told him his views so honestly, and stood by them so firmly. He saw that Bram was in earnest, and he began to walk up and down the room, thinking, planning, considering. He did not want to lose this clever young man; he could not afford to do so. Bram had something like a genius for the details of business, and was besides as honest as the day; not a too common combination.

The young man waited, but at last, as Mr. Cornthwaite made no sign of addressing him, he turned to touch the handle of the door. Then Mr. Cornthwaite suddenly stopped in his walk, and made a sign to him to stay.

"Well, Elshaw," said he in a more genial tone, "will you, if you must go, promise me one thing? Will you see Mr. Christian in my presence first, and hear what he has to say for himself?"

Bram hesitated.

"I don't want to hear anything," said he sullenly. "I'd rather go, sir."

"No doubt you would, but you wouldn't like to treat us in any way unfairly, would you, Bram? You acknowledge that we've not treated you badly, you know."

"Yes, sir."

"Well, then, you can hardly refuse to hear what the culprit has to say in his own defence. If, after hearing him, you are not satisfied, you can have the satisfaction of telling him what you think of him in good round terms before you go. Now, is that a bargain? You stay here until I come back from town—at least—with or without (for, of course, you may be right, and he may not come) my son?"

Bram hesitated; but he could not well refuse.

"All right, sir. I'll stay till you come back," he answered sullenly.

And, without another word or another look, he accepted his employer's satisfied motion of assent as a dismissal, and left the room.

CHAPTER XVIII
FACE TO FACE

Doggedly, sullenly, with a hard mouth and cold eyes, Bram went about his day's work in the office. His fellow-clerks knew that something of deep import had happened during that half-hour while he was shut up with Mr. Cornthwaite in the inner room; but so well did they know him by this time that no one made any attempt to learn from him what it was that had passed.

Quietly, unostentatiously, without any apparent effort, Bram had made himself a unique position, with his office companions as well as with his employers. Very taciturn, very stolid of manner, never giving an unasked opinion on any subject, he always seemed to be too much absorbed in the details of work to have time or inclination for the discussions, the idle chatter, with which the rest beguiled the monotonous hours on every opportunity.

But they had long since ceased to "chaff" him on his attitude, not through any distaste on his part for this form of attack, but as a natural result of the respect he inspired, and of the position he held with "the guv'nor" and his son. There was a feeling that he would be "boss" himself some day, and a consequent disposition to leave him alone.

But when the day's work was done, and Bram started on the walk back to Hessel, the look of dogged attention which his face had worn during office hours relaxed into one of keen anxiety. He had been able, by force of will, to thrust into the background of his mind the one subject which was all-important to him. Now that he was again, for fifteen hours, a free man, his thoughts fastened once more on Claire and on the question—Would Christian, obedient to his father and to self-interest, abandon her, or would he not?

Bram felt a dread of the answer. He would not allow to himself that he believed Christian capable of what he looked upon as an act of inconceivable baseness; but down at the bottom of his heart there was a dumb misgiving, an unacknowledged fear.

And Bram, his thoughts stretching out beyond the limits he imposed upon them, asked himself what he should do for the best for the poor child, if she were left stranded, as Mr. Cornthwaite made no secret of intending. He had unconsciously assumed to himself, now that the image of Claire had been deposed from the high pedestal of his ideal, the attitude of guardian to this most helpless of creatures, taking upon himself in advance the position which her father ought to have held.

If she were abandoned by her lover, it was he who would find her out, and care for her, and settle her in some place of safety. That she would never come back to the neighborhood of her own accord Bram felt sure.

When Bram got back to Hessel, he called at once at the farm, with a lingering hope that something might have been heard of Claire, that she might have sent some message, written some letter to her father or to Joan.

But she had not. He found Mr. Biron in the care of Joan, whose patience he tried severely by his fretfulness and irritability. The doctor had called again, and had expressed a growing fear of erysipelas, which had only increased the patient's ill-temper, without making him any more careful of himself. He was drinking whisky and water when Bram came in, and Joan reported that he had been doing so all day, and that there was no reasoning with him or stopping him, even by using the authority of the doctor.

Theodore was by this time in a maudlin and tearful condition, bewailing now the flight of his daughter, and now his own wounds, without ceasing.

Bram did what he could to cheer him, and to persuade him to a more reasonable course of conduct, but the effect was hardly more than momentary. And on the following day his condition had undoubtedly become worse. Bram, however, was obliged to leave him to go to the office, where the day passed without incident. Mr. Cornthwaite had gone up to town on the previous night, and had not returned. Bram began to hope that Christian had refused to come back.

Two more days passed, during which Mr. Biron's symptoms grew worse. The erysipelas had not only declared itself on the wounded part of the face, but was spreading rapidly. No attempt had been made to bring Meg Tyzack to book for the assault, in spite of Mr. Biron's frenzied adjurations. Bram could not bear to have the name of Claire dragged through the mire, as it must be if the jealous woman were brought into Court; and although Mr. Biron troubled himself less about this than he did about the revenge he wanted for his own injuries, Joan was so bluntly outspoken on the subject that even he had to give up the idea.

"You'd best tak' it quiet, sir," said the good woman coolly. "You see you couldn't coom into Coort wi' clean hands yourself, wi' the Joodge and everybody knowin' the life as Miss Claire led with you. Happen ye'd get told it served you roight!"

And Bram concurring, though less outspokenly, the indignant Theodore found himself obliged to wait for his revenge until he could see about it himself. This period promised to be a long time in coming, as the erysipelas continued to spread, and threatened to attack the membranes of the brain.

In the meantime, on the fourth day after the departure of Mr. Josiah Cornthwaite for London, Bram learned that father and son had returned home together.

Bram's heart sank. What of Claire? His mind was filled with anxious thoughts of her, as he awaited the expected summons to meet Christian face to face.

But the day passed, and the next. Neither father nor son appeared at the office at the works; and all that Bram could hear was that Mr. Christian was not very well. Bram looked upon this as a ruse, a trick. His sympathies were to be appealed to on behalf of the scoundrel of whose conduct he had spoken so openly.

Another day passed, and another. Still the work of the head of the firm was done by deputy; still the elder Mr. Cornthwaite remained at home, and his son, so Bram understood, with him.

So at last Bram, not to be put off any longer, wrote a short note to Mr. Cornthwaite, senior, reminding him of the latter's wish that he should see Christian before leaving the firm.

The answer to this note, which Bram posted to Holme Park on his way to the works, reached him by hand the same evening before he left the office. It contained only these words:—

> "Dear Elshaw,—You can come up and see my son at any time you like.—Yours faithfully,
>
> "Josiah Cornthwaite."

Bram started off to Holme Park at once, full of sullen anger against father and son. That this was the end he felt sure, the abrupt termination of a connection which had done so much for him, which had promised so much for his employers. Bram was not ungrateful. It was the feeling that this act had been committed by the man he loved and admired above all others, to whom he was indebted for his rise in life, which made the meeting so hard to him.

It was the knowledge that it was Christian, who had been so good to himself, who had ruined the life of the woman he loved, that made Bram shrink from this interview. He was torn, as he went, between memories of the pleasant walks he and Christian had had together, of the talks in which he had always opposed a rigorous and perhaps narrow code of morals to his companion's airy philosophy of selfishness, on the one hand; and thoughts of Claire, brave, friendless, little Claire, on the other. And the more he thought, the more he shrank from the meeting.

He knew by heart all Christian's irresponsible speeches about women and the impossibility of doing them any harm except by their express desire and invitation; knew that Christian always spoke of himself as a weak creature who yielded too readily to temptation, although he avoided it when he could. He knew every turn of the head, every trick of the voice, which could be so winning, so caressing, with which Christian would try to avert his wrath, as he had done many times before. He knew also that Christian had stronger weapons than these, in appeals to his affection, to the bond which Christian's own generosity and discernment had been the first to forge.

And knowing all this, Bram, determined to make one last appeal for justice and mercy for Claire, and if unsuccessful to pour out such fiery indignation as even Christian should quiver under, steeled himself and set his teeth, and strode up to the big house at dusk with an agitated heart.

In the gloom of the foggy night the lamp in the hall shone with a yellow light through the evergreens, and the whole place had a desolate look, which struck Bram as he went up. To his inquiry for Mr. Cornthwaite the servant who opened the door said, "Yes, sir," with an odd, half-alarmed look, and showed him into the study, where Mr. Cornthwaite sprang up from a chair at the sight of him.

"Ah, Elshaw," said he in a troubled voice, without holding out his hand, "you have come to see Christian. Well, you shall see him."

Without another word, without listening to Bram's renewed expostulations, he went out of the room, with a gesture of curt invitation to Bram to follow.

Up the stairs they went in silence. The fog seemed to have got into the house, to have shrouded every corner with gloom. On the first floor Mr. Cornthwaite opened a door, and beckoned Bram to come in. As the young man entered the room a shriek of wild laughter, in a voice which was like and yet unlike that of Chris, met his ears. A figure sprang up in a bed which was opposite the door, and a woman, in the dark gown and white cap and apron of a sick nurse, stood up beside the bed, trying to hold the sick man down. Bram stood petrified. There was the man of whom he was in search, unconscious of his presence, though he stared at him with bright eyes.

Christian was raving in the delirium of fever.

In a moment Bram experienced a revulsion of feeling so strong that he felt he could scarcely stand. Christian's follies, faults, vices, all were forgotten; there lay, dangerously ill, the lovable companion, the staunch friend. In that moment Bram, staring at the man he knew so well, who knew him not, felt that he would have laid down his own life to save that of Christian.

Suddenly he felt a hand laid gently on his arm. Mr. Cornthwaite, who had been watching him narrowly, saw the effect the sight had had upon the young man, and promptly drew him back, and shut the door behind them.

"Typhoid," said he, in answer to an imploring look from Bram. "He must have been sickening for it when he went away. I brought him back very ill, and the fever declared itself yesterday."

Bram did not ask anything for some minutes. He knew that Christian's life was in danger.

"His wife? She has forgiven him? She is with him?" asked Bram.

"Thank goodness no," replied Mr. Cornthwaite energetically. "I begin to hate the little canting fool. She offered to nurse him, I will say that; but we thought it better to refuse, and she was content."

"And—Claire?" said Bram.

Mr Cornthwaite grew impatient directly.

"I know nothing about her," said he coldly.

Bram straightened himself, as if at a challenge.

"You did not see her in London?" he asked.

"No."

"Nor trouble yourself about her?"

"No. And I sincerely hope, Elshaw, you are going to give up all thoughts of doing so either."

Bram smiled grimly.

"Not while I have a hand or a foot left, Mr. Cornthwaite."

"At any rate, you will not think of marrying her?"

There was a silence. Then Bram said, in a very low voice, very sadly—

"No."

He did not know whether he was not cruel, hard, in this decision. But he could not help himself. The feeling he had for Claire, for his first love, for his ideal, could never die; but it had changed sadly; greatly changed. It was love still, but with a difference.

Mr Cornthwaite, however, was scarcely satisfied.

"You will not think of leaving us, at least yet?" he said presently. Then, as he saw a look he did not like in Bram's face he hastened to add—"You are bound to wait until my son is better—or worse; until I am free to go to the office. I cannot be making changes now."

"Very well, Mr. Cornthwaite. But I must have a holiday, perhaps a two or three days' holiday, to start from to-morrow morning."

"All right. Good-night."

They were in the hall, and Bram, who had refused to re-enter the study, had his fingers upon the outer door.

"Good-night," said he.

And he went out. He was full of a new idea, which had suddenly struck him even while he was talking to Mr. Cornthwaite. He would not go to London; poor little Claire, abandoned by her lover, or rather by his father, would not have stayed there. It had flashed into his mind that there was one spot in the world to which she would direct her wandering steps if left all alone in the world. It was the little Yorkshire town of Chelmsley, where her mother lay buried.

On the following morning, therefore, Bram took train northwards, and, reaching before noon the pretty country town, went straight from the station to the big, square, open market-place, which, with the little irregular old-fashioned dwellings which surrounded it, might be called, not only the heart, but the whole of the town.

It was market-day, and at the primitive stalls which were ranged in neat rows, stood the farmers' wives and daughters before their tempting wares.

It was a cold but not unpleasant day, and the sight was a pretty one. But Bram had no eyes, no heart for any sight but one. He went to the principal inn, ordered some bread and cheese, and asked if there were any persons living in the town bearing the name of Cornthwaite; this he knew to have been the maiden name of Claire's mother.

The innkeeper knew of none. There had been a family of that name living at a big house outside the town; but that was years before.

Still Bram did not give up hope. It was something stronger than instinct which told him that to this, the spot where her mother's childhood had been passed, Claire would make her way. Disappointed in his inquiries, Bram set about what was almost a house-to-house search.

And towards the evening, when the lights began to appear in the houses, he was successful. He was searching the cottages on the outskirts of the town, and in one of them, crouching before the fire in a tiny room, where geraniums in pots formed a screen before the window, he saw Claire.

He stared at her for some seconds, until the tears welled up into his eyes.

Then he tapped at the window-pane, and she started up with a low cry.

CHAPTER XIX
SANCTUARY

With his heart in his mouth Bram waited. Would she come out to him? She stood up, with the firelight shining on her figure, but leaving her face in shadow, so that he could not tell what expression she wore.

He wondered whether she knew him. After waiting for a few moments he tapped again at the window, advancing his face as close as possible to the glass. Then, as she still did not move, he stepped back, and was going towards the door, when by a quick gesture she checked him, and seemed to intimate that he was to wait for her to come out to him.

At the same moment she left the room.

Bram waited.

When some minutes had passed, and still she did not come out, he began to feel alarmed, to wonder whether she had given him the slip. He walked round to the back, and saw that the cottage, which was one of a row of three, had a good garden behind it, and that there was a path which led from the garden across the fields.

Presently he went round to the front again, and knocked at the door. It was opened after the second knock, by a very respectable-looking old woman, with a kindly, pleasant face.

"Is Miss Biron staying here?" asked Bram, wondering whether Claire was using her own name or passing under another.

But the answer put to flight any doubts.

"Yes, sir," said the woman at once. "She is staying here, but she isn't in at present. She's just this minute gone out."

Bram felt his blood run cold. Claire was avoiding him then! The woman seemed to know of no reason for this sudden disappearance, and went on to ask—

"You are a friend of hers, sir?"

"Oh, yes, a very old friend of hers and her father's."

"And do you come from her father, sir?"

"Yes, I saw him this morning."

"Ah," cried she sharply. "And I hope he's ashamed of himself by this time for turning his daughter, his own daughter, out of his house!"

Bram said nothing. He did not know how much this woman knew, nor who she was, nor anything about her.

"I suppose he wants her back again?" she went on in the same tone.

"He does indeed. He's very ill. He has erysipelas all over his face and one of his hands, and is even in danger of his life. It has led to serious inflammation internally. He wants a great deal of care, such care as only his daughter can give him."

"Dear me! Dear me! Well, we must hope it'll soften his hard heart!" said the woman, coming out a step to listen. "He was always a light-minded, careless sort of a man. But I never thought he'd turn out so bad as he has done—never. He was a taking sort of a gentleman in the old days when he came courting Miss Clara, and married her and carried her off."

A light broke in upon Bram. This was some old servant of the family of Claire's mother, who had lived out her years of service, settled down, and "found religion" within sight of the old house, within the walls of which her girlhood had been passed. He had seen from the outside, as he looked in through the window at Claire, the framed texts of Scripture which hung on the walls, the harmonium in the corner, with a large hymn-book open upon it—the usual interior of the English self-respecting cottager.

"You lived in the family," said Bram, "did you not?"

"Why, yes, sir. I was under housemaid, and right through upper-housemaid to housekeeper with them in the old gentleman's and lady's time. Mr. Biron's told you about me, no doubt, sir," she added, with complacent belief that she was still fresh in that gentleman's mind. "And I don't suppose he had many a good word for me. I never did like the idea of his being half-French. I was always afraid it would turn out badly, always. I suppose he thought of me at once when he wanted his daughter back, sir?"

Bram thought this suggestion would do very well as an explanation of his own appearance at the cottage, so he did not contradict her. He asked if she knew where Claire had gone to.

"Well, no, sir, I don't. She ran upstairs, and put on her things all in a hurry, and went out at the back. I suppose she remembered something she'd forgotten this morning when she went out to do my little bit of marketing for me. And yet—no—she'd have gone out the front way for that." The old woman stared at the young man with wakening intelligence. She perceived some signs of agitation in him. "Maybe she saw you through the window, sir, and didn't want to speak to you," she suggested shrewdly.

Bram did not contradict her.

"Where does the path at the back lead to?" he asked, "I must see her. I think it's very likely, as you say, that she doesn't want to; but she would never forgive herself if her father were to die, would she?"

"Lord, no, sir. Well, she may have gone out that way and then turned to the left back into the town. Or she may—though I don't think it's likely—she may have gone on towards Little Scrutton. She's fond of a walk to the old abbey, that runs down to the left past Sir Joseph's plantation. But I should hardly think she'd go that far so late, and by herself too!"

"Thanks. Well, if she's gone that way I can catch her up, or meet her as she comes back," said Bram. "Thank you. Good-evening."

He hid as well as he could the anxiety which was in his heart, and set off, passing, by the woman's invitation, through the cottage kitchen, by the footpath across the fields.

He was half-mad with fear lest Claire, in an access of shame, should have fled from the shelter she had found under the good woman's roof, determined not to return to a hiding-place which had been discovered. It seemed clear to him that the old woman knew nothing but the fact that Theodore had sent his daughter away, and for one brief, splendid moment Bram asked himself whether that were indeed the whole truth, and the story of her flight with Christian an ugly nightmare, dishonoring only to the brains which had conceived it.

But then, like a black pall, there descended on his passionate hopes the remembrance of Claire's look when he last saw her at the farm; of the horror, the shame in her face; of her abrupt flight then; or her flight now. What other explanation could there be of all this? Was he not mad to entertain a hope in the face of overwhelming evidence?

But for all this he did hug to his heart a ray of comfort, of hope, as he reached the high-road, and quickly making up his mind to try the way into the country instead of that which led into the town started along between the bare hedges in the darkness with a quick step and an anxious heart.

The road was easy to follow, lying as it did, between hedges all the way. The plantation of which the old woman had spoken was some two miles out. Then Bram found a road dipping sharply down to the left, as she had said; and, after a few moments' hesitation, he turned into it. For some distance he went down the steep hill in the shadow of the fir trees of the plantation. At the bottom he came to a little group of scattered cottages, and following the now winding road he came suddenly upon a sight that made him pause.

The moon, clear, frosty, nearly at the full, shone down on a wide valley, shut in with gentle, well-wooded slopes, a very garden of peace and beauty.

Close under the nearest hill stood the ruined abbey, perhaps even more imposing in its majestic decay than it had been in the old days when a roof hid its lofty arches and tall clustered pillars from the gaze of the profane.

Coming upon it suddenly, Bram was struck by its massive beauty, its solitary grandeur. The walls, far out of the reach of the smoke of the town, were still of a glaring whiteness; the moon shone through the pointed clerestory windows, and cast long, black shadows upon the grass, and the broken white stones which lay strewn about within the walls. Here and there a mass of ivy, sturdy, thick, and bushy, broke the hard outline of tall white wall; or a clump of hawthorn, now bare, half-hid the small, round-headed tower windows of the transepts.

Bram went forward slowly, fascinated by the sight, and seized strongly by the conviction that little Claire would have found the stately old walls as magnetic in their attraction as he did. He came to the fence which surrounded the ruin, and climbed over it without troubling himself to look for a gate.

The ground was rough and uneven, encumbered with loose stones. He wandered about the transepts and the long choir, which were all that were left of the church itself, hunting in every corner and in the deep shadow of every bush. But he found no trace of Claire. Yet still he was haunted by the thought that it was here, within walls which had once been held holy, that the little fugitive would have taken shelter, would have hidden from him. So strongly did this idea possess him that he at last sat down on a stone in the ruined choir, determined to keep vigil there all night, and to make a further search when morning broke.

It was a cold night, and sleep in the circumstances was out of the question. He walked up and down and sat down to rest upon the flat stone alternately until dawn came. A long, weary night it was undoubtedly. Yet through it all he never lost for more than a few moments at a time the feeling that Claire was near at hand, that when daylight came he should find her.

The dwellers in the cottages outside the ruin were early astir, and one or two perceived Bram, and came up to the railings to look at him. But as none of them seemed to feel that his intrusion was any business of theirs he was left alone until the light was strong enough for him to renew his search. Then, not within the walls of the church itself, but in the refectory, which was choked up and encumbered with broken stones and rubbish which had made search difficult in the night, he found her.

There was a little stone gallery, with a broken stone staircase leading up to it, at one end of the refectory. And here crouched in a corner, fast asleep, with her head against the stone wall, was Claire. Her small face looked pinched and gray with the cold. He took off his overcoat and covered her with it very gently. But soft as his touch was she awoke, stared at him for a moment as if she scarcely knew him, and then sprang to her feet.

She was so stiff and cramped and chilled that she staggered. Bram caught her arm, but she wrenched herself away with a sound like a sob, and in her eyes there came a fear, a shame so deep, so terrible, that Bram looked away from her, unable to meet it with his own mournful eyes.

"Why did you run away from me?" asked he, so kindly, with such a brave affectation of rough cheerfulness that the tears came rushing into the girl's eyes. "You might have known I didn't want to do you any harm, mightn't you? I only wish I'd brought you some better news than I do."

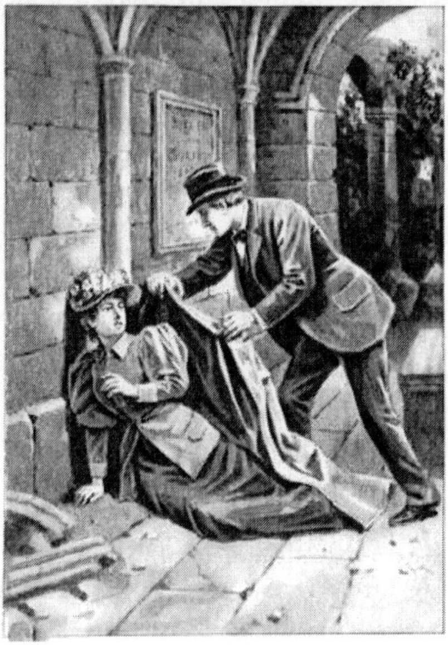

He took off his overcoat and covered her with it very gently.

He was looking away, through the tall, pointed arches, at the leafless trees beyond. He heard her draw a long breath. Then she asked, in a very low voice:—

"What news, then?"

"Your father wants you back. He's very ill—very ill. He's had an accident, and burnt his head and one of his hands badly. You've got to come back and nurse him; he doesn't mind what anybody says, and he does foolish and rash things that only you can save him from. You'll come back, won't you?"

There was a pause. Bram looked at her, and she bowed her head in silent assent. She would not meet his eyes; she hung her head, and he saw that she was crying.

"We'd better make haste and get back to Chelmsley," said he in a robust voice. "I forgot to look out a train; or rather I had hoped to have taken you back last night. But you gave me the slip; I can't think why. You've got nothing but a cold night and perhaps a bad cough by your freak."

Claire said nothing. She seemed to be petrified with shame, and scarcely to feel the cold without from the suffering within. It was pitiful to see her. Bram, long as he had thought over the poor child and her desolate situation, suffered new agonies on finding how deep her anguish was. A sense of unspeakable degradation seemed to possess her, to make every glance of her eyes furtive, every movement constrained.

"I will come," she said humbly, in a voice which was hoarse from exposure.

"Of course you will come," retorted Bram good-humoredly. "And put your best foot foremost too, for—"

She interrupted him hastily, coldly.

"But let me go alone, please. Thank you for coming; it was very good of you. But I want to go alone. And I want you not to come to see us at the farm. If you do—" Her voice grew stronger as Bram tried to protest, and suddenly she raised her head, and looked at him with a flash of excitement in her eyes. "If you do, I shall kill myself!"

"Very well," said Bram quietly. "Good-bye, then."

He jumped the stone steps, offering the assistance of his hand, which she declined. And he crossed the rough ground quickly, and went through the roofless church on his way back to Chelmsley.

Perhaps Claire's heart smote her for her ungraciousness. At any rate, when he glanced back, after climbing over the fence, he saw that she must have followed him very quickly, for she was only a few yards away. There was a look in her eyes, now that she was caught unawares, which was like a stab to his tender heart.

He stopped. She stopped also, and made a movement as if to turn back to run away. He checked her by an imploring gesture.

"You will come, really come; you've promised, haven't you?" said he.

She bowed her head. He dared not hazard another word. So, without so much as another glance from her, he went quickly up the hill on his return to Chelmsley.

What a meeting it had been, after so much anxious waiting! Nothing had been said that might not have been said any day by one casual acquaintance to another. And yet their hearts were nigh to bursting all the time.

Bram went straight to the station, hungry as he was. He thought Claire would tell the old woman a better story than he could make to account for her absence all night. And he thought that the sooner he was out of the place the sooner Claire would follow him back to Hessel. Within an hour and a half he was in the train, returning to Sheffield. He sent a message up to the farm on his arrival to prepare Theodore for his daughter's return, and then he set his mind to his office work for the remainder of the day.

When he returned to Hessel that evening he ventured to tap at the kitchen window of the farm. Joan came out to him. Yes, Miss Claire had come, the good woman said, wiping her eyes. And she hoped things might go right. But Meg Tyzack had been hanging about the place, and Joan was keeping all the doors locked.

"Ah'm in a terrible way abaht that woman," said Joan in a deep whisper. "Ah haven't towd her Miss Claire's coom back, and Ah hope nobody else will. For Ah don't think she's altogether in her roight moind, and Ah wouldn't have her in t' house again for summat!"

This was grave news. Bram, feeling that there was nothing he could do for the protection of the threatened household, stared out before him with trouble in his eyes.

"What did Mr. Biron say when he saw his daughter?" asked he.

Joan pursed up her lips.

"He didn't dare say mooch," said she, with a comprehensive nod. "He didn't even say how he'd coom by t' burns! It was me towd Miss Claire abaht Meg! And she heard me quite solemn, and didn't ask many questions. And when Ah towd her abaht Mr. Christian's having t' fever she joost shivered, and said naught."

Bram shivered too, and hurried away up the hill to his lodging.

CHAPTER XX
BY THE FURNACE FIRES

Then there began a strange time of dreary waiting for some crisis which Bram felt was approaching, although he could hardly foreshadow what the nature of it would be.

Things could not go on much longer at Duke's Farm in the way they had been doing for some time now. With nobody to look after him, the farm bailiff grew daily more neglectful of all business but his own. It went to Bram's heart to see ruin creeping gradually nearer, while he dared not put out a helping hand to arrest its approach. He did try. He wrote a note to Claire, studiously formal, saying that while her father's illness continued he should be glad to keep an eye on the management of the farm, as he had done some months ago. But the answer he got was a note still more formal than his own, in which Claire thanked him, but said she thought it better now that affairs had reached their present stage to let them go on as they were. After this to move a step in the direction of helping her would have been unwarrantable interference, which Bram would have undertaken once, when they were friends, but which he could not venture upon now.

Still he tried to perform the office of guardian angel, hampered as he was.

Joan, who was his good friend still, and who went daily to the farm to do the housework as usual, kept him fully acquainted with all that went on there. She told him that Mr. Biron, who was still suffering from erysipelas, which died away and broke out again, was growing more irritable every day, so that it was a marvel how his daughter could treat him with the patience and gentleness she showed. Claire herself, so Joan said, was altogether changed; and indeed Bram, when he caught a glimpse of her at the windows, could see the alteration for himself. She had grown quite white, and the set, hard expression her face wore made it weird and uncanny. All her youthful prettiness seemed to have disappeared; she never smiled, she hardly ever talked. No single word, so far as Joan knew, had passed between father and daughter on the subject of the latter's disappearance and return. Theodore was glad to get his patient nurse back; glad to have some one to bully, to grumble at, and that seemed to be all.

Claire never went out, and Joan never encouraged her to do so, for Meg Tyzack still hung about the place, Joan having encountered her early in the morning and late in the evening, on her way to and from the farm. Meg, so Joan said, would slink out of the way with a laugh or a jeering question about Claire or her father.

"Ah doan't believe," remarked Joan, when she had given Bram the account of one of these meetings, "as the lass is quite right. Yon young spark has a deal to answer for!"

The "young spark" in question, Christian Cornthwaite, was in the meantime doing something to expiate his misdeeds, for his illness was both dangerous and tedious. Day after day, week after week, there came the same bulletin to the many inquirers down at the works—"No change." Mr. Cornthwaite lost his grave, harassed look. He consulted Bram daily; took him, if possible, more into his confidence than before, over the details of the business; but he never talked about his son. He seemed, Bram thought, to have given up hope in a singularly complete manner; he spoke, he looked, as if Christian were already dead. In the circumstances, Bram found it impossible to bring before the anxious father the subject of Claire, and the distresses of the household at Duke's Farm.

Bram heard from Joan of the duns whose presence was now daily felt. Some of these he found out and settled with quietly himself; but he did not dare to pursue this course very far, lest Claire's feminine quickness should find him out.

The subject of ready money was a more delicate one still. Bram began by giving Joan small sums to supply the most pressing needs of the household at the farm, and for a little while she managed to evade Claire's curious questions, and even to pretend that it was she, Joan, who occasionally lent a few shillings for the daily purchase of necessary food.

But one evening, when Bram, as his custom was, waylaid her as she came from the farm, as soon as she was out of sight of the window, Joan looked at him with eyes full of alarm.

"Eh, but she's found me aht, Mr. Elshaw, an' she's led me a pretty dance for what you've done, Ah can tell ye."

"Why, what's that, Joan?"

"That there money! She guessed, bless ye! who 'twas as gave it to me. 'Joan,' says she, 'if ye take money from him again, if it's to keep us from starving, Ah'll go and throw mysen down t' pit shaft oop top o' t' hill!' And she means it, she do! Ah doan't like t' looks of her. What between her father and t'other one—" and Joan jerked her head in the direction of the works down in the town—"she's losing her wits too, Mr Elshaw, that's what she's doing!"

Bram was silent for some minutes.

"Well, it can't go on like this," said he at last. "The creditors will get too clamorous to be put off. If I could see Mr. Biron I should advise him to—"

But Joan cut him short with an emphatic gesture.

"Doan't you try it on, Mr. Elshaw!" cried she earnestly. "Doan't you try to get at Mr. Biron. That's joost what he wants, to get hold of you. Time after time he says to Miss Claire, 'If Ah could see young Elshaw,' says he, 'Ah could settle summat.' But she won't have it. It's t' one thing she won't let him have his way abaht. 'If he cooms in t' house,' says she, 'Ah'll go aht o' 't.' So now you know how she feels, Mr. Elshaw, and bless her poor little heart, Ah like her t' better for 't!"

Bram did not say what he felt about it. He listened to all she had to say, and then with a husky "Good-night, Joan," he left her and went home. He too liked the spirit Claire showed in avoiding him, in refusing help from the one friend whose hand was always held out to her. But, on the other hand, the impossibility of doing her any good, of even seeing her to exchange the warm handclasp of an old friend, gnawed at his heart, and made him sore and sick.

A dozen times he found himself starting for the farm with the intention of forcing himself upon her, of insisting on being seen by her, so that he might offer the help, the comfort, with which heart and hand were overflowing. But each time he remembered that, brave as he felt before seeing her, in her presence he would be constrained and helpless, easily repelled by the coldness which she knew how to assume, by the look of suffering, only too genuine, he could see in her drawn face.

And so the days grew into weeks, until one day, not long before Christmas, he was crossing from one room to another down at the works with a sheaf of letters in his hand, when he came face to face with Christian.

Bram stopped, almost fell back; but he did not utter a word.

Christian, who was looking pale and very delicate, held out his hand with a smile.

"Well, Bram, glad or sorry to see me back again?"

"Glad, very glad indeed, Mr. Christian," said Bram.

He wanted to speak rather coldly, but he could not. The sight of his friend, so lately recovered from a dangerous illness, and even now evidently suffering from its effects, was too much for him. Every word of that short speech seemed to bubble up from his heart. Christian, perhaps even more touched than he, and certainly, by reason of his recent illness, less able to conceal his feelings, broke into a sob.

"They told me—my father told me, you wouldn't be," said he, trying to laugh. "Said you came up to the house with the intention of punching my head, but that you relented, and consented to put off the gentle chastisement until I was on my feet again. Oh, Bram, Bram, for shame! When you knew I was always a *mauvais sujet* too, and never pretended to be anything else!"

"But, Mr. Christian," began Bram, who felt that he was choking, that the passions of love for Claire and loyalty to the friend to whom he owed his rise in life were tearing at his heartstrings, "when a woman—" Chris interrupted him, placing one rather tremulous hand lightly on his shoulder.

"My dear boy, d— the women! Oh, don't look shocked when I say d— the women, because I speak from conviction, and a man's convictions should be respected, especially when he speaks, as I do, from actual experience. I say d— the women; and, moreover, I say that until you can say d— the women too, you are incapable of any friendship that is worthy of the name. There! Now, go home, and ponder those words; for they are words of wisdom!"

And Chris, giving him a familiar, affectionate push towards the door of the room he had been about to enter, passed on.

The news of Christian's return to the office spread quickly, and was received with great personal satisfaction throughout the works, where the easy, pleasant manners of the "guv'nor's" son had made him a universal favorite. The tidings flew beyond the works, too, for Joan told Bram that Mr. Biron and his daughter had heard of Christian's return, and added that the mention of his name had been received by Claire in dead, blank silence.

"Poor lass! She looked that queer when she heard it," said Joan.

Bram, as usual, said nothing. The conflict between his feeling towards Claire and his feeling towards Christian grew hourly more acute.

"She wouldn't hear what Mr. Biron had to say," pursued Joan. "But she joost oop and went to her room, and Ah saw no more of her till Ah coom away. But she were that white! Ah wished she'd talk more, or else cry more; Ah doan't like them pains as you doan't hear nothing abaht. They gnaw, they do! It'd be better for her to go abaht calling folks names, like Meg!"

But this reference to Meg Tyzack in the same breath with Claire wounded Bram, who turned away quickly. Surely the life of patient self-sacrifice she was leading in constant attendance upon her selfish father was ample atonement for the error into which she had been driven.

It was a great shock to him when, on the afternoon of the following day, just before the clerks left the office, he heard a rumor that Miss Biron had come down to the works, and was asking to see Mr. Christian. Bram at first refused to believe the report. He went downstairs on purpose to find out the truth for himself, and saw in the yard, to his dismay, the figure of Claire in an angle of the wall. Well as he knew the little figure, he would not even then believe the evidence of his own eyes without further proof. He crossed the yard towards her. Claire ran out, passing close to him, so that he was able to look into her face. It was indeed she, but her face was so much changed, wore an expression so wild, so desperate, that Bram felt his heart stand still.

He called to her, but she only ran the faster. She disappeared into the building which contained the offices, and quickly as Bram followed he could not track her. When he reached the bottom of the staircase, he could neither see nor hear anything of her.

While he was wondering what would happen, whether she would present herself in the office of old Mr. Cornthwaite himself, and be treated by him with the brutal cynicism he always expressed while speaking of her, or whether she would find her way straight to Christian, he heard footsteps in the corridor above, and a moment later Chris himself, singing softly to himself, and swinging his umbrella as if he had not a care in the world, appeared at the top of the stair.

"Hallo, Bram!" cried he, catching sight of the young fellow, and laughing at him over the iron balustrade. "You look as solemn as a whole bench of judges. What's the matter?"

Bram hesitated. He did not know whether to tell Christian that Claire was about, or whether to hold his tongue. Doubt was cut short in a couple of seconds, however, when Christian reached the bottom of the staircase. For he came face to face with Claire, who had appeared as quickly and as silently as she had previously disappeared from one of the doors which opened on the ground floor.

Both stared at each other without a word for the space of half a minute. Both were pale as the dead; but while he shook from head to foot she was outwardly quite calm.

"I want—to speak to you," she said at last.

Her voice sounded hard, unlike her usual tones. There was something in them which sounded in Bram's ears like a menace.

Christian looked around, as if afraid of being seen.

"Not here," said he quickly. "In the works. I will go first."

He disappeared at once, and Claire followed him out through the door and across the first of the yards, where the work was slackening off, and where swarms of dusky, grimy figures, their eyes gleaming white in their smoke and dust-begrimed faces, were hustling each other in their eagerness to be out. Like a flash of lightning there passed through Bram's mind, brought there by the sudden contact with this black, toiling world from which Christian had rescued him, by the strong well-remembered smell of mingled sweat, coal-dust, and fustian, an overwhelming sense of love and gratitude for Chris, mingled with fear.

Yet what was he afraid of? What made him struggle through the crowd with a white face and laboring breath, in mad anxiety to keep close to the footsteps of the man and the woman? He could not tell. For surely he had no fear of poor, little, helpless Claire, however wild her look might be, however desperate the straits in which she found herself!

He had lost sight of both of them within a few steps of the office doors. They had been swallowed up in the stream of workmen who were pressing out as they went in.

Bram could only go at a venture in one direction through yards and past workshops, without much idea whether he was on the right track or not. He had a fancy that he might perhaps come up with them near the spot where he had first seen them together on that hot August afternoon eighteen months before, when Christian had picked him out for notice to his father, and so laid the foundation of his fortunes.

But when Bram got there, and stood where, rod in hand, he had stood that day, just outside one of the great rolling sheds, wiping the sweat from his forehead, he found the place deserted. The noise of the day had ceased; the steam hammers stood in their places like a row of closed jaws after an infernal meal. A huge iron plate, glowing red under its dusky gray surface in the darkness lay on the ground near Bram's feet—fiery relic of the labors of the day.

Bram passed on, peering into the sheds, where the machinery was still, and where the great leather bands hung resting on the grinding wheels. Past the huge presses he went, where the glowing plates of steel are curled into shape like wax under the slow descending, crushing weight of iron. Through the great room where the great armor-plates are shaved down, the steel shavings curling up like yards upon yards of silver ribbon under the slow, steady advance of the huge machine.

At last Bram fancied that he caught the sound of voices: the one shrill and vehement, the other deeper, lower, the voice of a man. He hurried on.

Through the heart of the works, which stretched for hundreds of acres on either side of it, ran the railway, at this point a wide network of lines, crossing and recrossing each other, carrying the goods traffic of the busy city. Bram came out upon it as he heard the voices, and looked anxiously, about him.

And at once he discerned, on the other side of the railway line, two figures engaged not merely in the wordy conflict which had already come to his ears, but in an actual physical struggle, the girl clinging, dragging; the man trying to push her off.

Bram's heart seemed to stand still. For, with a thrill of horror, he saw that a train had suddenly come out from under the bridge on his left, and was rapidly approaching the spot where the two struggling, swaying figures stood. He shouted, and dashed forward across the broad network of lines. Caution was always necessary when these were crossed, but he did not look either to the right or to the left; he could see only those struggling figures and the train bearing down upon them.

But his effort was made in vain. Before he could reach them the train had overtaken them, there was a wild, horrible shriek, and then a deep groan. Bram stood back shaking in every limb, until the train had passed by. Then, sick, blinded, he stared down at the line with a terrible sound in his ears.

On the ground before him lay a bleeding, mangled heap, writhing in agony, uttering the horrible groans and sobs of a man dying in fearful pain.

It was Christian Cornthwaite.

CHAPTER XXI
THE FIRE GOES OUT

A great sob burst from Bram's lips as he threw himself down beside Christian, whose moans were terrible to hear. He had been caught by the train, the wheels of the engine having passed over both his legs, crushing and mangling them in the most horrible manner. Bram saw at a glance that there was not the slightest hope of saving his friend's life, and that there was only the faintest chance of prolonging it for a little while.

Fortunately, help was at hand. A man, one of the hands employed at the works, ran out from the sheds which bordered the railway. He was in a panic of terror, and was at first almost incapable of listening to the directions Bram gave him.

Such first aid as it was possible to give Bram was already giving. But Christian himself shook his head feebly, and made a faint gesture to stop him.

"It's all of no use, Bram," said he, in a broken voice. "She's done for me; she's had her revenge now. You may just as well leave me alone, and then the next passing train will put me out of my pain. Oh, I would be thankful—thankful—"

Another moan broke from his lips, and his head, which was wet with great beads of agony, fell like lead in Bram's arms.

"Come, come, we can't leave you lying here," said Bram, in a deep, vibrating voice, as he hugged the dying head to his breast.

He had succeeded in getting the poor, wounded, mangled body from the line itself to the comparative safety of the space between that row of metals and the next. More than this he dared not attempt until further help came. He sent the workman to the office with directions that he should send in search of a surgeon the first person he met on the way. He was then to break the news, not to Mr. Cornthwaite himself, if he were still there, but to one of the managers or to one of the older clerks.

The man went away, and Christian, who had lain so still for some seconds that Bram feared he was past help already, opened his eyes.

"Hallo, Bram," said he, in a very weak, faint, and broken voice, but with something like his old cheerfulness of manner. "It's odd that I should peg out here, in the very thick of the smoke and the grime I've always hated so much, isn't it?"

Bram could not speak for a minute. When he did, it was in a ferocious growl.

"Don't talk of pegging out, Mr. Christian," said he. "You don't want to give in yet, eh?"

He spoke like this, not that he had the slightest hope left, but because he wished to keep in the flicker of life as long as he could, at least until the father could exchange one last hand-clasp with his dying son. And Bram judged that hope was the best stimulant he could administer. But Chris only smiled ever so faintly.

"Oh, Bram, you don't really think it would be worth while to rig me up with a pair of wooden legs, do you? I shouldn't be much like myself, should I? And the guv'nor wouldn't have to complain of my running after the girls any more, would he?"

Bram shivered. These light words had a terrible import now, and they sent his thoughts back from the sufferer to the author of the outrage. He glanced round instinctively, and an involuntary sound escaped his lips as he saw, standing on the edge of the network of lines, only a few feet from himself and Chris, the figure of Claire.

With head bent and hands clasped, she stood, neither moving nor uttering a sound, but watching the two men with wild eyes, and with a look of unspeakable, stony, horror on her gray white face.

Chris looked up, caught sight of her, and uttered a cry.

"Claire! Claire!" he called, in a voice hoarse and unlike his own.

She did not move, did not seem to hear him.

Then Bram called to her.

"Come. He wants you to come."

At the sound of Bram's voice she looked up suddenly, shivered, and came slowly nearer.

"Look out! Take care! Come here between the lines!" said Bram.

She obeyed his directions mechanically, stumbling as she came. When she found herself beside the two men, she fell to trembling violently, but without shedding a single tear.

Chris tried to raise himself, and Bram lifted him up so that he could meet her eyes.

"Claire!" said the dying man in a whisper, "come here. Don't look down. Look at my face—my face."

But her eyes had seen enough of the nature of the injuries he had received to render her for a few moments absolutely powerless to move. She seemed not even to hear his voice, but stood beside him without uttering a sound, possessed by a horror unspeakable, indescribable. Christian tried to speak in a louder voice to distract her attention from his injuries, to draw it upon himself.

"Claire," said he, "remember I haven't much time. Stoop down, kneel down; listen to what I have to say."

There was a short silence. At last her eyes moved; she drew a long breath. She looked at his face, and the tears began to stream down her cheeks.

"Oh, Chris, Chris!" she sobbed out in a voice almost inaudible. "It is too awful, too horrible! Oh, won't you, can't you—get well?"

"No, no," said he impatiently. "Surely you can't wish it! I want to speak to you, Claire; you can't prevent my saying what I like now, can you?"

She only answered by a sob, as she sank down on her knees beside him. Bram, in an agony of uneasiness—for the space between the lines where they all three were was a narrow one, and another train might pass at any minute, and shake the little life there was remaining in Christian out of his maimed body—kept watch a few feet away. He was afraid of some rash movement on the part of the miserable, grief-stricken girl, whom he believed to be suffering such agonies of remorse as to be incapable of controlling herself if an emergency should arise. He could hear the voice of Christian as he whispered into Claire's ear; he even caught the sense of what he said, with a terrible sense of gnawing sorrow for the wasted life that was ebbing so fast away.

"I've been a fool, Claire, the biggest fool in the world," said Christian, still in the old easy tones, though his voice was no longer that which had raised the spirits of his friends by the very sound of it. "If I hadn't been a fool, I should have taken Bram's advice and married you. I know you didn't want me; I believe you liked old Bram better; but that wouldn't have mattered. You'd have had to marry me if I'd made up my mind you should."

"Oh, Chris, don't tell me. It's too horrible!"

"No, it isn't horrible to talk about it, to me, at least. And you have to let a fellow be selfish when he's only got a few minutes to live. If I'd married you, I should have been happy, even if you hadn't been. You're the only girl I ever really cared about. Claire—yes, you can't stop me, and it's no use talking about my wife, because the only consolation I have in this business is the knowledge that I can't ever see her again! I loathe her! I know I ought to have found it out sooner, but I've been punished for that mistake with the rest."

He stopped, his voice having gradually grown weaker and weaker. Bram turned quickly, and came down to him. But the moment Claire put her hand under his head he raised it again, and a faint tinge of color came into his cheeks.

"Kiss me, Claire," said he.

For a moment, to the surprise and indignation of Bram, she seemed to hesitate. Then she obeyed, putting her lips to Christian's forehead, after a vain attempt to check her tears. Then there was a silence. They heard the voices of Mr. Cornthwaite and another man asking—"Where? Where is he?" And Christian opened his eyes.

"Bram," said he, in a voice which betrayed agitation, "take her away. Don't let my father see her. Take her away. Never mind leaving me. Quick."

But there was no time. Mr. Cornthwaite was already close to the group. He touched Claire, and shrank back with an exclamation of horror and disgust. Bram seized her arm, and almost lifted her from the spot where she stood, dazed and incapable of movement. She, however, was evidently unconscious both of Mr. Cornthwaite's touch and of his utterance. She was like a bewildered child in Bram's hands, and she allowed him to lead her across the lines, obeying his smallest injunction with perfect, unresisting docility.

When he had brought her to a place of safety within the works, he turned to her.

"I want to go back to him," he said. "It will only be for a moment, I'm afraid. Then I'll come back and take you home. Will you wait for me?"

"Yes," she answered in the same obedient manner, as if his wish were a command.

He looked searchingly into her face. In mercy, it seemed to Bram, a cloud had settled on her mind; the terrible events of the past half-hour had become a blank to her. The little creature, who had been a passionate fury such a short time ago, had changed into the most helpless, the most docile, of living things. Did she understand what it was that she had done? Did she realize that it was her own act which had killed her cousin? Bram could not believe it. He gave one more look into her white face, hardly daring to tell himself what the outcome of this terrible scene would be for her, and then he left her, and went back across the rails to the spot where he had quitted his friend.

They had raised him from the ground in spite of his protests, and were bearing him by his father's orders into the shelter of the works. When they stopped, and laid him down on a couch which had been hastily made with coats and sacks, he was so much exhausted that it was not until they had forced a few drops of brandy down his throat that he was able to speak again. Then he only uttered one word—

"Bram!"

"Elshaw, he wants you!" cried Mr. Cornthwaite, who was leaning over his son, with haggard eyes.

Bram came forward. Christian put out his right hand very feebly, let it rest for a moment in Bram's, which he faintly tried to press, and looked into his face with glazing eyes. Bram, holding the hand firmly in a warm, strong grip, knew when the life went out of it. Even before the hand fell back, and the eyes closed, he knew that the fingers he held were those of a dead man.

CHAPTER XXII
CLAIRE'S CONFESSION

Bram held the hand of his dead friend for some minutes, not daring to tell the father that all was over. But Mr. Cornthwaite suddenly became aware of the truth. He started to his feet with a cry, beckoning to the doctor, who had stepped back a few paces, knowing that he could do nothing more.

"He has fainted again!" cried Mr. Cornthwaite. But Bram knew that the unhappy man was only trying to deceive himself. The doctor's look, as he knelt down once more by the body of Christian, made Mr. Cornthwaite turn abruptly away. Bram, who had stepped back in his turn, carried that scene in his eyes for weeks afterwards—the shed where they all stood, the silent machinery making odd shapes in the background. The dead body of Christian on the ground, with his face upturned, the crowd of figures around, all very still, very silent, the only two whose movements broke up the picture being Mr. Cornthwaite and the doctor. A flaring gas jet above their heads showed up the white face of the dead man, the grave and anxious countenances of the rest.

Quite suddenly there appeared in the group another figure—that of Claire. They all stared at her in silence. She seemed, Bram thought, to be absolutely unconscious of what had happened until she caught sight of the body of her cousin. Then, with a low cry, like a long sob, she put her hands to her face, covering her eyes, turned quickly, and ran away.

Mr. Cornthwaite, however, had seen her, and, his face darkening with terrible anger, he followed her rapidly with an oath. Anxious and alarmed, Bram followed in his turn. The girl had not much of a start, and although she was fleet of foot, Mr. Cornthwaite, with his superior knowledge of the works, gained upon her rapidly, and would have seized her roughly by the arm if Bram had not interposed his own person between them, giving the girl an opportunity of escape, of which she availed herself with great adroitness.

"Elshaw!" cried Mr. Cornthwaite in astonishment. A moment later he went on in a transport of anger—"How dare you stop me? You have let her get away, you have helped her, the vile wretch who has killed my son! But don't think that she shall escape punishment. You can't save her; nobody shall. She has murdered my son, and—"

"Not murdered, sir," cried Bram quickly. "It was an accident—a ghastly accident. The girl is dazed with what has happened. She hardly knows herself. Pray, don't speak to her now. It is inhuman—inhuman. She is suffering more than even you can do. Give her a chance to recover herself before you speak to her."

Mr. Cornthwaite freed himself with a jerk from Bram's restraining hand. But Claire had disappeared.

"Well, she's got away this time, but your interference won't save her much longer. My son—to be killed—by a jade like that! My God! My God!"

He had broken down quite suddenly, overcome by an overwhelming sense of his loss. Although he had never been a very tender or a very indulgent father, he had loved his son more than he himself knew. He recognized, now that Christian lay dead, what hopes, what ambitions had been bound up in him. Even the works, the true darling of his heart, seemed suddenly to become a mere worthless toy when he realized that with himself would die the interest of his family in the enterprise he had founded. He had imagined that he should see his descendants sitting in his own place in the office, carrying on the work he had begun. Now, in one short hour, his hopes and dreams were demolished. Nothing was left to him but revenge upon the woman who had taken the color out of his life by killing his son.

Bram was awed by the depth of his so suddenly manifested despair. He felt with a most true instinct that there were no words in the human tongue which could do any good to the miserable man. He could only stand by, in solemn silence, while Mr. Cornthwaite put his head down between his hands, drawing long sobbing breaths of grief and despair.

But presently the doctor, who was an old friend of Mr. Cornthwaite's, came in search of him, and put his hand through his arm. Then Bram stole quietly away, and went in search of poor Claire.

He had not to go far. He had not, indeed, walked twenty paces, when, turning a corner among the innumerable buildings which formed the great works, he came upon her, standing, like a lost child, with her arms down at her sides, and her head bent a little downwards. As soon as he appeared she turned to accompany him without a word, much as a dog does that has been waiting for its master.

This change in the spirited girl to such a helpless, docile creature, frightened Bram even more than it touched him. He felt that some great, some awful change, must have taken place in the girl who was too proud to allow him to enter her father's house. Was it the feeling of the awful thing she had done, of the vengeance she had drawn down upon herself which had brought about the change?

He could not see her face. She walked beside him in silence till they came to the gate of the works, and there she stopped for a moment to look through the door by which Christian had come out with her an hour before. And then in the gaslight Bram saw her face at last, read the very thoughts which were passing in her mind—remembrance, remorse—the horror of it all. But she uttered no word, no cry. With a shudder she passed out, putting her hands up to her eyes as if to shut out the terrible pictures her brain conjured up.

Bram followed her, at first without speaking. She did not seem to know that he was beside her; at least she never looked at him, never spoke to him. He, on his side, while longing to say some kindly word, was afraid of waking her old pride, of being told to go about his business, if he broke the spell of silence which hung over them both.

So, as silent as the dead, they walked on side by side through the crowded streets, with the groups of rough factory hands, of grinders, of lassies with shawls round their heads, extending far over the road. A drizzling rain had begun to fall, and the stones of the streets were slimy, slippery and black. Claire went straight on through the crowds, threading her way deftly enough, but mechanically, and without turning her head. Bram following always. A vivid remembrance flashed into his mind of the previous occasion on which he had followed her, when Mr. Cornthwaite had told him to see her home from Holme Park, and she had dashed out of the house like an arrow to escape the infliction. Unconscious of his proximity she had been then; unconscious she seemed to be now.

When she reached the hill near the summit of which the farmhouse stood, however, her strength seemed suddenly to desert her; the slight, over-taxed frame became momentarily unequal to its task, and she staggered against the stone wall which fenced the field she had to pass through. Then Bram came up, and, after standing beside her a few moments without speaking, and without eliciting a word from her, he drew her hand through his arm, and led her onwards up the hill.

It was now dark, with the pitchy blackness of a wet, moonless night. The ground was slippery with rain, and the ascent would have been toilsome in the extreme to the girl's weary little body but for Bram's timely help. So tired was she that before they reached the farmhouse gates Bram put his arm round her waist, and more than half-carried her without a word of protest.

There was no light in the front of the farmhouse; but when they got to the gate of the farmyard, through which it was Claire's custom to enter, they saw a light in the kitchen window; and when they opened the door Joan jumped up from a seat near the big deal table.

"Eh, Miss Claire, but Ah thowt ye was lost!" cried she. Then at once realizing that something untoward had happened, she glanced at Bram, who shook his head to intimate that she had better ask no questions.

"Where's my father?" asked Claire at once, drawing her arm away from that of Bram, and stopping short in the middle of the floor at the same time.

"He's gone oop to t' Park," said Joan, with a look at Bram as much as to say there was no help for it, and the truth must come out.

Claire, sinking on the nearest chair, uttered a short, hollow laugh.

Joan, who had been waiting with her bonnet on for Claire's return, hardly knew what to do. She saw that the young girl was ill and desperately tired, and, on the other hand, she was anxious to get back to her own goodman and to her little ones. In her perplexity she looked at Bram, the faithful friend, whom she was heartily glad to see admitted again.

"Ah doan't suppose Mr. Biron'll be long coming back," she said. "If Ah was to make ye both a coop o' tea, Mr. Elshaw, and then run back to my home for an hour, would you stay here till Ah coom back? Ah'd give a look in to see all was reght. She doan't look as if she ought to spend t' neght by herself."

This was said in a low voice to Bram, whom she had beckoned to the door of the back kitchen, while Claire remained in the same attitude of deep depression at the table.

"No," said he at once. "She mustn't be left alone to-night. I'll stay till you come back, whether her father comes back before then or not. She's had a great shock—an awful shock. But," and he glanced back at the motionless girl, "I won't tell you about it now. And you can go now. You needn't trouble about the tea; I'll make it."

Joan looked at him, and then at Claire with round, apprehensive eyes.

"Will she let ye stay?" she asked, in a dubious whisper.

"Poor child, yes. She's almost forgotten who I am."

But Claire had lifted up her head, and was rising to come towards them. Bram dismissed Joan by a look, and she slipped out by the back way, and left the two together.

Claire followed Joan with dull eyes as the good woman, with a series of affectionate little smiles and nods, went out, shutting the door behind her. Then she remained staring at the closed door, while Bram, without taking any notice of her, went quietly across to the cupboard where the tea was kept, took out the tea-caddy, and put the kettle on the fire to boil. She did not interrupt him, and when he glanced at her again he saw that she had sunk down again in her chair, and had dropped her head heavily upon her hands, leaning on the table drowsily.

Presently she made a little moaning noise, and began to move her head restlessly from side to side. Bram put a cup of tea down in front of her, and said gently—

"Got a headache, Miss Claire?"

She raised her head as if it was a weight too heavy for her to lift without difficulty.

"Oh, Bram, it's so bad, worse than I've ever had before," said she plaintively.

In her eyes there was no longer any grief; only a dull sense of great physical pain. She seemed to have forgotten everything but that burning, leaden weight at her own temples.

"Will you drink this, and then lie down for a little while?" asked he.

With the same absolute docility that she had shown to him all the evening, she took the cup from his hands, and tried to drink. But she seemed unable to swallow, and in a few moments he had to take it from her, lest her trembling hands should let it drop on the floor.

"Now, you had better lie down," said he. "Come into the drawing-room; there's a fire there. I saw it flickering as we came along. If you lie down on the sofa till Joan comes back, she'll take you upstairs and put you to bed."

He saw that she had no strength left to do anything for herself. She got up as obediently as ever; but when she reached the door a fit of shivering seized her. She staggered, fell back, and whispered as Bram caught her—

"No. Don't make me go in there. Let me stay here."

There was an old broken-down horsehair covered sofa against the wall in the big kitchen, and Bram hastened to make it as comfortable as he could by bringing the cushions from the drawing-room. Before he had finished his preparations she complained of feeling giddy; and no longer doubting that she was on the verge of being seriously ill, Bram led her to the sofa, and going quickly to the outer door looked out in hope of finding some one whom he could send for the doctor. He was unsuccessful, however; the rain was coming down more heavily than ever, and there was not a living creature in sight. The farm hands lived in the cottages at the top of the hill, and Bram did not dare to leave Claire by herself now that the torpor in which she had come home was beginning to give place to a feverish restlessness. So he shut the door, and seeing that Claire's eyes were closed, he began to hope that she had fallen asleep, and crossed the floor with very soft steps to his old place by the fire.

A strange vigil this! By the side of the woman who had been so much to him, who, even now that she had lost the lofty place she had once held in his imagination, seemed to have crept in so doing even closer into his heart. So, at least, the chivalrous man felt now that, by an act of mad, inconceivable folly and rashness, Claire had endangered her own liberty, and perhaps even her life. For that Mr. Cornthwaite would press his conviction that the act was murder Bram could not doubt. Hating the very sound of the girl's name as he had long done, believing that Christian's attachment for her had been the cause of his estrangement from his wife, of his entire ruin, it was not likely that he, a hard man naturally, would flinch in his pursuit of the woman to whom he imputed so much evil.

And Bram hardly blamed him for it. He would not have had him feel the loss of his son one whit less than he did; he knew what pangs those must be which pierced the heart of the bereaved father. Bram himself felt for both of them; for Mr. Cornthwaite and for Claire. Her he excused in the full belief that her sufferings had brought on an attack of frenzy in which she was wholly unaccountable for her actions. How else was it possible to explain the bewildered horror of her look and attitude when called to Christian's side by the dying man himself? And had not Chris, in his words, in his manner to her, absolved her from all blame? Not one word of reproach had he uttered, even while he lay dying a fearful death as the result of her frenzied attack! Surely there was exoneration of her in this fact? Bram felt that this was the point he must press upon the aggrieved father.

As this thought passed through his mind, and instantly became a resolve, Bram raised his head quickly, and was struck with something like horror to find that Claire was sitting up, resting her whole body on her arms, and staring at him with glittering eyes.

As these met his own astonished look, she smiled at him with a strange sweetness which made him suddenly want to spring up and take her in his arms. Instead of that, he rose slowly, and advancing towards the sofa with a hesitating, creeping step, asked gently if she wanted anything.

She shook her head, smiling still; and then she put out one hand to him. He took it; the skin was hot and dry. Her lips, he now perceived, looked dry and parched.

"Bram," she said in her old voice, bright and soft and clear, "I forget. What day is it we are to be married?"

Bram stood beside her, holding her hand, such a terrible rush of mingled feelings thronging, surging into his heart that he was as incapable of speech as if he had been a dumb man. She looked at him with the same gentle smile, inquiringly. Presently, as he still kept silence, she said—

"It seems a strange thing to have forgotten. But was it Tuesday?"

Bram nodded slowly, as if the head he bent had been weighted with lead. Then she drew her hand out of his with a contented sigh, and fell back on the couch. Again she closed her eyes, and again Bram, who was in a tumult of feelings he could not have described, of which the dominant was pain, cruel, inextinguishable pain, hoped that she was asleep. He sat down on a chair near her, and watched her face. It was perfectly calm, peaceful, and sweet for some minutes. Then a slight look of trouble came over it, and she opened her eyes again.

"Bram," she called out in a voice of alarm. Then perceiving him close to her, she drew a breath of relief, and stretched out her hand to him. "It's so strange," she went on, with glittering eyes. "Whenever I shut my eyes I have horrible dreams of papa, always papa! Where is he? Is he here? Is he safe?"

Bram patted her hot, twitching hand reassuringly.

"He is quite safe, I've no doubt," he said. "He's gone out, and he hasn't come back yet."

Claire stared at him inquiringly, and frowned as if in perplexity.

"But what has happened?" she asked. "Why does everything seem so strange? Your voice, and the ticking of the clock, and my own voice too—they sound quite different! And my head—oh, it aches so! Have I been ill? Where's Joan?"

She wandered on thus so quickly from one subject to another that Bram was saved the trouble of finding answers to any of her questions except the last.

"Joan will be back in a little while," said he. "She's gone home to see to her children. But she won't be long."

"Is she coming back to-night? Why is she coming back to-night?"

"Well, to look after you."

"Then I have been ill?"

"You're not very well now," said Bram gently.

"Why not? Something has happened? Won't you tell me what it is?"

There was a pause. Then she gave his hand an affectionate, clinging pressure.

"Never mind, Bram. You needn't tell me unless you like. I don't mind anything when you're here. You won't go away, will you?"

The loving tone, the caressing manner, stirred his heart to the depths. Surely this tender trust was her own real feeling for him, suddenly revealed, free from all restraints of prudence, of necessary coldness. What did it mean? Was this the woman who had ruined her life for another man, this girl who looked at him with innocent eyes full of love, who seemed to be thrilled with pleasure at the touch of his fingers? Was this the woman who had struggled with Christian in the shadow of the great works two hours before, whose mad passion of hate and revenge had given her fragile limbs power to fling him down on the railway line? Bram sat in a state of wild revolt from the terrible ideas, which had, indeed, till that moment seemed real, inevitable enough. What was the miracle that had happened? What was the explanation of it all? While he still asked himself those questions, with his head on fire, his heart nigh to bursting, the soft, girlish voice spoke again.

"Bram, what was the difficulty? There was a difficulty, wasn't there? Only I can't remember what it was. Why was it that you stayed away? That you didn't come here as you used to? You don't know what a long time it seemed, and how I used to long for you to come back again! Why, I used to watch for you when I knew it was time for you to go past, and I used to kiss my hand to you behind the curtains, so that you couldn't see me! But why—why didn't I want you to see me, Bram? I can't remember."

"Oh, my darling!" burst from Bram's lips in spite of himself.

That one word was answer enough for her. She smiled happily up into his face, and closed her eyes, as if it hurt her to keep them open, the lids falling heavily. Bram wished—he almost prayed—that they could both die that moment; that neither might ever have to live through the terrible time which was in store for them. The delirium which had so mercifully descended upon her overwrought mind had shut out the horrible secrets of the past from Claire.

As Bram sat, as still as a statue lest he should disturb her by a movement, he heard the sound of footsteps outside, and a moment later the door was burst open, and Mr. Biron, pale, haggard, dripping with rain, begrimed with mud, a horrible spectacle of fear and terror, stole into the room, and shutting the door, bolted it, and then sank in a heap on the floor, with his eyes turned in a ghastly panic of alarm towards the window.

CHAPTER XXIII
FATHER AND DAUGHTER

Bram was struck by the entire change which had taken place in Theodore Biron, a change which had, indeed, been creeping over him ever since Meg's attack, and his consequent disfigurement, but which seemed to have culminated to-night in what was almost a transformation.

As he crouched on the floor, and looked anxiously up at the window, there was no trace in the cowering, shrivelled figure, in the scarred, inflamed face, out of which the bloodshot eyes peered in terror, of the gay, easy-mannered country gentleman *en amateur*, who had impressed Bram so strongly with his airy lightness of heart only sixteen months before.

"Lock the door, Bram," said he, presently, in a hoarse voice when he suddenly became conscious of the young man's presence. "Lock the door!"

Bram hastened to do so. He wanted to open it first to look out and see who it was that had inspired Mr. Biron with so much alarm. But Theodore restrained him by a violent gesture.

"Lock it, lock it!" repeated he, as, evidently relieved to find a man in the house, he got up from the floor, and went with shivering limbs and chattering teeth towards the fire. "And now bolt the shutters—quick—and then on the other side!"

He indicated with a nod the front of the house, but when Bram walked towards the door he shuffled after him, as if afraid of being left alone. Bram turned to cast a glance at the sofa and its occupant before leaving the room. Theodore, in a state of nervous alarm which made him watch every look, glanced back also. On seeing his daughter lying back with closed eyes on the cushions, he uttered a cry.

"Claire, oh, oh, what will become of her? What will become of me?"

And, utterly broken down, he covered his face with his shivering hands, and sobbed loudly.

Bram wondered if he had heard all.

"Come, come, be a man, Mr. Biron," said he. "What is it you're afraid of?"

"That sh—she—devil who—who half-blinded me, who threw that stuff over me!" sobbed Theodore. "She's followed me—from Holme Park—I managed to dodge her among the trees of the park; but she knows where I live. She'll come here, I know she will." Suddenly he drew himself up, in another spasm of fear. "See that the door is locked in the front, and the windows—see to them!" cried he, with a burst of energy.

"All right," said Bram. "I'll see to that. You stay here with her," and he indicated Claire with a movement of the head.

But Mr. Biron shrank into himself, and tried to follow Bram out.

"I'm afraid of her! She's gone mad; I know she has," whispered he. "Haven't you heard what she did to-night—down at the works?"

And Theodore, whose face had in a moment gone ashy white, all but the inflamed patch on the left side, which had become a livid blue, crept closer still to Bram. But the young man's face as he again looked towards the unconscious girl wore nothing but infinite pity, infinite tenderness.

"You're right, Mr. Biron. The poor child is mad, I believe," he said gravely. "And, thank God, she hasn't come to herself yet. One could almost wish," he added, more to himself than to his companion, "that she never may."

Mr. Biron shuddered.

"Do you mean that she is ill?" he asked querulously.

"Yes, she's very ill—delirious."

Mr. Biron shot right out of the room into the hall with all his old agility. He was evidently as much afraid of his unhappy daughter as he was of Meg herself.

"Oh, these women, these women! They never can keep their heads!" moaned he. "And just when I'm as ill as I can be myself! I've been shivering all the way home, I have, indeed, Elshaw."

Bram, who had left the door of the kitchen open so that he might be within hearing of a possible call or cry from Claire, was locking the front door and barring the shutters of the windows in deference to Mr. Biron's wish.

He was too much used to Theodore's utter selfishness to feel more than a momentary pang of disgust at this most recent manifestation of it. He was sorry for the poor wretch, whose prospects were certainly now as gloomy as he deserved. He recommended him to go upstairs and change his wet things, promising to come up and see him as soon as Joan arrived. And Mr. Biron, though at first exceedingly reluctant to move a step by himself, ended by preferring this alternative to returning to the room where his unconscious daughter lay.

He detained Bram for a few moments, however, to tell him of his adventures at Holme Park.

"When I got there, Bram, I was told that my brother-in-law was out. But as I had very particular business with him, I said I would wait. Well, you may hardly believe it, but they didn't want even to let me do that. But I insisted; a desperate man will do much, and I made such a noise that Hester came out, and told the wretched creature who was refusing me admittance that I was to be let in. Well, I was wet through then, and they left me in a room with hardly any fire. And, would you believe it, the wretched man had the impudence to lock up my brother-in-law's desk before my eyes! It was an intentional insult, Elshaw, inflicted upon me just because I am not able to keep up a big establishment of useless, insolent creatures like himself! But these people never will understand that there is anything in the world to be respected except money! And, after all, can one blame them when their masters and mistresses are no better? It's all money, money, with Josiah Cornthwaite!"

Bram, who was anxious to get back to the kitchen that he might keep watch over Claire, cut him short.

"Well, and Mr. Cornthwaite? He arrived at last?"

Theodore's face fell at the remembrance.

"Ye-es, and I shall never forget what he did, what he said. He came into the room with glaring eyes—'pon my soul, I thought he had been bitten by a mad dog, Elshaw! He flew at me, showing his teeth. He shook me till my teeth chattered; he called me all the names he could think of that had anything brutal and opprobrious in the sound. He told me my daughter had killed his son, murdered him; and he said that he would get her penal servitude if they didn't bring it in what it was—murder! What do you think of that? What do you think of that? And I, in my weak state, to hear it! I give you my word, Elshaw, I never thought I should get home alive!"

There was a pause. Mr. Biron wiped his face. His hands were shaking; his voice was tremulous and hoarse. He looked as pitiful a wretch as it was possible to imagine.

"Did he tell you—how it happened?" asked Bram in a low voice.

He was hoping, always hoping against hope, that some new fact would come to light which would shift the blame of the awful catastrophe from Claire's poor little shoulders. But Mr. Biron had no comfort for him.

"Yes," sobbed he. "He told me she had gone down to the works to see her cousin—"

"Ah, if she had only not done that! Not been forced to do that," broke from Bram's lips.

Theodore grew suddenly quiet, and stared at him apprehensively.

"How was she forced to do it?" he asked querulously.

But Bram did not answer.

"Well, yes. What else did Mr. Cornthwaite say?" asked he.

"And that they quarrelled close to the railway line. And that she—she—'pon my soul, I can't see how it's possible—a little bit of a girl like that! He says she dragged Christian down, and flung him in front of a train that was coming along! Of course, we know that woman is an incomprehensible creature; but how one of only five feet high could throw down a young man of stoutish build like Christian is more than even I, with all my experience of the sex, can understand!"

Bram was frowning, deep in thought. Again he did not make any answer.

"That's all I heard. Have you learnt any more particulars yourself, Elshaw?"

"I was there," replied Bram simply.

This gave Mr. Biron a great shock. He began to shiver again, and subsided from the buoyant manner he had begun to assume into the terror-stricken attitude of a few minutes before. He turned to clutch the banisters to help him upstairs.

"Well," said he in a complaining voice, as he began to drag himself up, "if she did it, that's no reason why everybody should be down upon me! Meg Tyzack, too! A fury like that! What right has she to follow me, to persecute me?"

"The poor creature's had her brain turned, I think, by—by the treatment she's received," said Bram.

"But I had no hand in the treatment! She has no right to visit Christian's follies and vices upon me! *Me!* And yet, when I came out of the house at Holme Park, and I came upon her on her way up to it, she turned out of her way to go shrieking after me! There's no reason in such behavior, even if she is off her head!"

"Well, there's just this, Mr. Biron, that she knows you used to encourage Christian to come to your house, and to urge Claire to go and meet him," said Bram sturdily, disgusted with the airs of martyrdom which the worst of fathers was assuming. "And there's enough of a thread of reason in that, especially for one whose mind is not at its best."

To Bram's great surprise, these words had such an effect upon Theodore that he said nothing in reply, but with an unintelligible murmur shuffled upstairs at once.

Bram felt rather remorseful when he saw how the little man took his words to heart, and wondered whether he was less easy in his mind than he affected to be. He returned to the kitchen, where Claire was sitting up on the sofa listening intently.

"Who's that?" she said in a husky voice of alarm.

Bram, who had heard nothing, listened too. And then he found that her ears were keener than his own, for in another moment there came Joan's heavy rap-tap-tap on the door.

He let her in, and saw at once that she had heard something of the occurrences of the evening. Her good-natured face was pale and alarmed; she looked at Claire with eloquent eyes.

"Oh, sir, do you think it's true?" she asked in an agitated whisper. "That she did it, that our poor, little Miss Claire killed him, killed Mr. Chris?"

"Don't let us think about it," said he quickly. "It was nothing but a shocking accident, if she did; of that you may be sure."

"But will they be able to prove that?" asked the good woman anxiously.

"We'll hope they may," said he gravely. "In the meantime she's so ill that she can tell us nothing; she's forgotten all about it. You must get her upstairs."

Joan set about this task with only the delay caused by the necessity of lighting a fire in the invalid's bedroom. Claire meanwhile remained silent, keeping her eyes fixed upon Bram with an intent gaze which touched him by its pathetic lack of meaning.

Not until Joan came back and put strong arms round the little creature to carry her upstairs did some ray of intelligence flash out from the black eyes.

"No, don't take me away," she said. "I want to stay here to talk to Bram."

And she stretched out feebly over Joan's shoulder two little hands towards him.

He took them in his, and pressed upon each of them a long, passionate kiss.

"No, dear. It will be better for you," he said simply.

And then, with a sudden return to the extreme docility she had shown to him all the evening, she smiled, and let her hands and her head fall as Joan started with her burden on the way upstairs.

CHAPTER XXIV
MR. BIRON'S REPENTANCE

Then Bram went upstairs also, and knocked at Mr. Biron's door.

"I'm going for the doctor now, Mr. Biron," he called out without entering. "I've come up to ask if there's anything I can get for you before I go."

"Come in, Elshaw, come in!" cried Theodore, in a voice full of tremulous eagerness. "I want to speak to you."

Bram obeyed the summons, and found himself for the first time in Mr. Biron's bedroom, which was the most luxurious room in the house. A bright fire burned in the grate, this being a luxury Theodore always indulged in during the winter; the bed and the windows were hung with handsome tapestry, and there were book-shelves, tables, arm-chairs, everything that a profound study of the art of making oneself comfortable could suggest to the fastidious Theodore.

He himself was sitting, wrapped in a cozy dressing-gown, with his feet on a hassock by the fire. But he looked even more wretched than he had done in his drenched clothes downstairs. There was an unhealthy flush in his face, a feverish glitter in his eyes.

Bram saw something in his face which he had never seen there before, something which suggested that the man had discovered a conscience, and that it was giving him uneasiness.

"Sit down," said he, pointing to a seat on the other side of the fireplace. Bram wanted to go for the doctor, but the little man was so peremptory that he thought it best to obey. "Elshaw, I think I'm going to die."

He uttered the words, as was natural in such a man, as if the whole world must be struck into awe by the news. Bram inclined his head in respectful attention, clasping his hands and looking at the fire. He could not make light of this presentiment, which, indeed, he saw reason to think was a well-founded one. Mr. Biron's never robust frame had been shaken sorely by his own excesses in the first place, by erysipelas and consequent complications, and it was evident that the experiences of this night had tried him very severely. He was still shivering in a sort of ague: his eyes were glassy, his skin was dry. He stood as much in need of a doctor's aid as did his daughter.

But still Bram waited, struck by the man's manner, and feeling that at such a moment there was something portentous in his wish to speak. Mr. Biron had something on his mind, on his conscience, of which he wanted to unburden himself.

"Elshaw," he went on after a long pause, "I've been to blame over this—this matter of Claire and—and her cousin Chris." He stared into Bram's face as if the young man had been his confessor, and rubbed his little white hands quickly the one over the other while he spoke. "I did it for the best, as I'm sure you will believe; I thought he was an honorable man, who would marry her and make her happy. You believe that, don't you?"

Up to this moment Bram had believed this of Theodore; now for the first time it flashed through his mind that it was not true. However, he made a vague motion of the head which Theodore took for assent, and the latter went on. He seemed to have become suddenly possessed by a spirit of self-abasement, to feel the need of opening his heart.

"There was no harm in my sending her to meet him—until—last night," pursued the conscience-stricken man. "I know I did wrong in letting her go then!"

Bram sat up in his chair with horror in his eyes.

"You sent her? Begging, of course, as usual?"

The words were harsh enough, brutal, perhaps, in the circumstances. But Bram's feeling was too strong for him to be able to choose the expression of it. That this father, knowing what he did know, suspecting what he did suspect, should have sent his daughter to ask Christian for money was so shocking to his feelings that he was perforce frank to the utmost.

"What could I do? How could I help it? One has got to live, Claire as well as I!" muttered Theodore, avoiding Bram's eyes, and looking at the fire. "Besides, we don't know anything. We may be doing her wrong in suspecting—what—what we did suspect," said he earnestly, persuasively. "She never told me that she went away with him, never! I believe it's a libel to say she did, the mere malicious invention of evilly-disposed persons to harm my child."

Bram was silent. These words chimed in so well with the hopes he would fain have cherished that, even from the lips of Mr. Biron, they pleased him in spite of his own judgment. Encouraged by the attitude which he was acute enough to perceive in his companion, Theodore went on—

"No, you may blame me as much as you like. You have more to blame me for than you know. I'm going to tell you all about it—yes, all about it." And he began to play nervously with his handkerchief, and to dart at Bram a succession of quick, restless glances. "But I will hear nothing against my child. It's not her fault that she's the daughter of her father, is it? But she's not a chip of the old block, as you know, Elshaw."

Bram, who was getting anxious about leaving Claire so long without medical attention, got up from his chair. He did not feel inclined to encourage the evident desire of Mr. Biron for the luxury of confession, of self-abasement. Like most vain persons, Theodore was almost as willing to excite attention by the record of his misdeeds as by any other way. And in the same way, when he felt inclined to write himself down a sinner, nothing would content him but to be the greatest sinner of them all. So he put up an imploring hand to detain Bram.

"Wait," he said petulantly. "Didn't I say I had something to tell you? It's something that concerns Claire, too."

At the mention of this name Bram, who had moved towards the door, stopped, although he was inclined to think that all this was a mere excuse on the part of Theodore to detain him, and put off the moment when he should be left by himself.

"You remember that a box was sent to you—a chest, by the man at East Grindley who left you his money?"

Bram nodded. His attention was altogether arrested now. Even before Mr. Biron uttered his next words it was clear that he had a real confession to make this time, that he was not merely filling up the time with idle self-accusations.

"I went to your lodging the day it came, just to see that it was safe. Your landlady had sent to ask me if I could take care of it for you, as it was something of value. But I preferred to leave the responsibility with her. In—in fact, Claire thought it best too."

Bram read between the lines here, knowing what strong reasons poor Claire would have for taking this view. Mr. Biron went on—

"There was a key sent with it."

Bram looked up. He had found no key, and had been obliged to force the padlock.

"The key was in a piece of paper. I found it on the mantelpiece. I—I—well, of course, I had no right to do it; but I thought it would be better for me to look over the contents of the chest to make sure they were not tampered with in your absence."

Bram was attentive enough now.

"So I unlocked the box, and I just glanced through the things it contained. You know what I found; with the exception of this, that there was some loose cash—"

Bram's face grew red with sudden perception. But he made no remark.

"I forget exactly what it was, something between two and three hundred pounds. Now, I know that in strict propriety," went on Mr. Biron, in whom the instinct of confession became suddenly tempered with a desire to prove himself to have acted well in the matter, "I ought to have left the money alone. But it was strongly borne in upon me at the moment that my dear daughter was worried because of unpaid bills; and—and that, in short, it would be just what you would wish me to do if you had been here, for me to borrow the loose sovereigns, and apply them to our pressing necessities. I argued with myself that you would even prefer, in your delicacy, that I should not have to ask for them. And—in short, I may have been wrong, but I—borrowed them."

A strange light had broken on Bram's face.

"Did Miss Claire know?" he asked suddenly in a ringing voice.

"Well—er—yes, in point of fact she did. She came to look for me, and she, well, she saw me take them. She—in fact—wished me to put them back; and I could not convince her that I was doing what you would have wished."

Bram's brain was bursting. His heart was beating fast. He came quickly towards Mr. Biron, and seized him by the wrist. There was no anger in his eyes, nothing but a fierce, hungry hope. For he could not despise Theodore more than he had done before, while the fact of Claire's shame on meeting himself might now bear a less awful significance then it had seemed to do.

"She knew you had taken it? And you forced her to say nothing?" cried he in passionate eagerness.

Mr. Biron was disconcerted.

"Well, er—I thought that—that perhaps, until I could see my way to paying it back, it would be better—"

But Bram did not wait for more explanations. Indeed, he needed no more. He saw in a flash what the shame was which he had seen in Claire's eyes when she met him after his return. It was the knowledge that her father was a thief, that he had robbed Bram himself, and that she could neither make restitution nor confession for him.

And with this knowledge there flashed upon him the question—Was this the only shame she had to conceal? He was ready, passionately anxious, to believe that it was.

Mr. Biron was quick to take advantage of this disposition in Bram. His mood of self-abasement seemed to have passed away as rapidly as it had come. Not attempting to draw his hand away from Bram's grasp, he said buoyantly—

"But I could not let the matter rest. I felt that you might suspect her, my child, of what her father, from mistaken motives perhaps, had done—"

Bram cut him short.

"Oh, no, I shouldn't have done that, Mr. Biron," he said rather dryly. "But you were very welcome to the money. And I am glad to think you enjoyed yourself while it lasted."

This thrust, caused by a sudden remembrance of the hunter and the new clothes in which Theodore had been so smart at his expense, was all the vengeance Bram took. He tore himself away as speedily as possible, and ran off for the doctor with a lighter heart than he had borne for many a day. Might not miracles happen? Might they not? Bram asked himself something like this as he ran through the rain over the sodden ground.

When he returned to the farmhouse with the doctor, Bram received a great shock. For, on entering the kitchen, he found Mr. Cornthwaite himself pacing up and down the room, while Joan watched him with anxious eyes from the scullery doorway.

Josiah stopped short in his walk when the two men entered. He nodded to Bram, and wished the doctor good-evening as the latter passed through, and went upstairs, followed by Joan.

"Will you come through, sir?" said Bram. "There's a fire in the drawing-room."

Mr. Cornthwaite, over whom there had passed some great change, followed him with only a curt assent. Bram supposed that even he had been touched to learn that the woman of whom he had come in search was so ill as to be past understanding that her persecution had already begun. He stood in front of the fire, with his hat in one hand and his umbrella in the other, with his back to Bram, in dead silence for some minutes.

Then he turned abruptly, and asked in a stern, cold voice, without looking up from the floor, on which he was following the pattern of the carpet with the point of his umbrella—

"Did that scoundrel Biron get back home all right?"

"He's got home, sir, but he's very ill. He's caught cold, I think."

"He was not molested, attacked again, by the woman, the woman Tyzack, who threw the vitriol over him before?"

"No, sir. She followed him, but he lost sight of her before he got here."

Mr. Cornthwaite nodded, and was again silent for some time. Bram was much puzzled. Instead of the fierce resentment, the savage anger which had possessed the bereaved father immediately after the loss of his son there now hung over him a gloomy sadness tempered by an uneasiness and irresolution, which were new attributes in the business-like, strong-natured man.

The silence had lasted some minutes again, when he spoke as sharply as before.

"I came to see the daughter, Claire Biron. But I'm told—the woman tells me—that she is ill, and can't see any one. Is that true?"

"Yes, sir. She is delirious."

Mr. Cornthwaite turned away impatiently, and again there was a pause. At last he said in the same sharp tone—

"You brought her back home, I suppose?"

"Yes. At least I followed her, and when she grew too tired to walk alone I caught her up, and helped her along."

Mr. Cornthwaite looked at him curiously. The little room was ill-lighted, by two candles only and the red glow of the fire. He could see Bram's face pretty well, but the young man could not see his.

"Still infatuated, I see?" said Josiah in a hard, ironical voice.

Bram made no answer.

"You intend to marry her, I suppose?" went on Mr. Cornthwaite in a harder tone than ever.

Bram stared. But he could see nothing of Mr. Cornthwaite's features, only the black outline of his figure against the dim candle-light.

"No, sir," said he steadily. "I only hope to be able to save her life."

"And how do you propose to do that?"

"Sir, you know best."

His voice shook, and he stopped. There was silence between them till they heard the footsteps of the doctor and Joan coming down the stairs. Mr. Cornthwaite opened the door.

"Well, Doctor," said he, "what of the patients?"

There was more impatience than solicitude in his tone.

"They're both very ill," answered the doctor. "They ought each to have a nurse, really."

"Very well. Can you engage them, Doctor? I'll undertake to pay all the expenses of their illness."

The doctor was impressed by this generosity; so was Bram, but in a different way. What was the reason of this sudden consideration, this unexpected liberality to the poor relations whom he detested, and to whom he imputed the death of his son?

"What's the matter with them?" went on Mr. Cornthwaite in the same hard, perfunctory, if not slightly suspicious tone.

"Pneumonia in Mr. Biron's case, brought on by exposure to wet and cold, no doubt. He has just had a severe shivering fit, and his pulse is up to a hundred and four. We must do the best we can, but he's a bad subject for pneumonia, very."

"And the daughter?"

"Acute congestion of the brain. She's delirious."

"Ah!"

Mr. Cornthwaite seemed satisfied now that he had the doctor's assurance that the illness was genuine. He made no more inquiries, but he followed the medical man into the hall and to the front door. The doctor perceived that it was locked and bolted at the top and bottom.

"All right," said he, "I'll go through the other way."

And he made his way to the kitchen, followed by Mr. Cornthwaite and Bram.

As he opened the door which led into the kitchen, the wind blew strongly in his face from the outer door, which was wide open. The rain was sweeping in, and the tablecloth was blown off into his face as he entered. At the same moment Joan, who had gone into the back kitchen to prepare something the doctor had ordered, made her appearance at the door between the two rooms.

"I shouldn't leave this door open," said the doctor as he crossed the room to shut it. "The wind blows through the whole house."

Joan stared.

"Ah didn't leave it open, sir," said she. "Ah've only just coom through here, and it were shut then. Some one's been and opened it."

Bram gave a glance round the room, and then opened the door through which he and the others had just come to examine the hall.

"What's the matter?" asked Mr. Cornthwaite sharply. He had bidden the doctor a hasty good-bye, afraid of the condolences which he saw were on the tip of his tongue.

Bram, with a candle in his hand, was peering into the dark corners.

"I was just thinking, sir, that perhaps Meg Tyzack had got in while we were talking in the drawing-room," said he. "Mr. Biron made me bolt the doors to keep her from getting in. He seemed to be afraid she would follow him into the house."

The words were hardly uttered, when from the floor above there came a piercing scream, a woman's scream.

"Claire!" shouted Bram, springing on the stairs.

But before he could mount half a dozen steps a wild figure came out of Claire's room, and rushed to the head of the staircase in answer to his call. But it was not Claire. It was, as Bram had feared, Meg Tyzack, recognizable only by her deep voice, by her loud, hoarse laugh, for the figure itself looked scarcely human.

Standing at the top of the stairs, with her arms outstretched as if to prevent any one's passing her on the way up, the gaunt creature seemed to be of gigantic height, and looked, with her loose, disordered hair and the rags which hung down from her arms instead of sleeves, like a witch in the throes of prophecy.

"Stand back! Stand back! Leave her alone!" she cried furiously, as Bram rushed up the stairs, and struggled to get past her. She flung her arms round him, laughing discordantly, and clinging so tightly that without hurting her he would have found it impossible to disengage himself.

"What has she done? What has she done?" asked Mr. Cornthwaite in a loud, hard, angry voice as he came to Bram's assistance.

At the first sound of Mr. Cornthwaite's voice, Meg's rage seemed suddenly to disappear, to give place to a fit of strange gloom, quite as wild, and still more terrible to see. Releasing Bram, who ran past her, she leaned over the banisters, and looked straight into Mr. Cornthwaite's haggard face.

"What has she done? What have I done?" said she in a horrible whisper. "Why, I've done the best night's work that's ever been done on this earth, that's what I've done. I've sent the man and the woman I hated both to—. Ha! ha! ha!"

With a shrieking laugh she leapt past him to the bottom of the stairs.

CHAPTER XXV
MEG

Bram Elshaw heard Meg's wild words as he rushed along the corridor towards the room out of which she had just come—Claire's room, as he guessed, with a sob of terror rising in his throat.

The door was open. On the floor, just inside, lay what Bram at first thought to be Claire's lifeless body. Meg had dragged her off the bed, and flung her down in an ecstasy of mad rage.

But even as he raised her in his arms, before the frightened Joan had run up to his aid, Bram was reassured. The girl was unconscious, but she was still breathing. Joan wanted to send him away.

"Leave her to me, sir, leave her to me. You can goa and fetch t' doctor back," cried she, as she tried jealously to take Claire out of his arms.

But Bram did not seem to hear her. He was staring into the unconscious face as if this was his last look on earth. He hung over her with all the agony of his long, faithful, unhappy love softening his own rugged face, and shining in his gray eyes.

"Oh, Claire, Claire, my little Claire, my darling, are you going away? Are you going to die?"

The words broke from his lips, hoarse, low, forced up from his heart. He did not know that he had uttered them; did not know that he was not alone with the sick girl. Joan, whose tears were running down her own face, suddenly broke into a loud sob, and shook him roughly by the shoulder.

"Put her down; do ee put her down," she said peremptorily. "Do ye go for to think as your calling to her will do her any good? Goa ee for t' doctor. And God forgive me for speaking harsh to ye, sir."

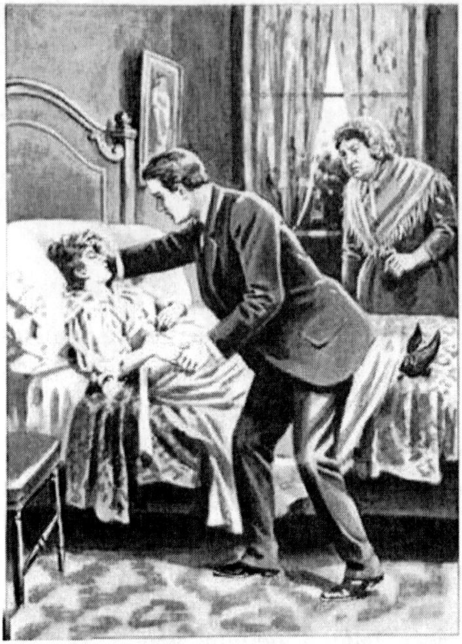

"Oh Claire, Claire, my little Claire, are you going to die?"

And the good woman, seeing the strange alteration which came over Bram's face as he raised his eyes from the girl's face to hers as if he had come back from another world, changed her rough touch to a gentle pat of his shoulder, and turned away sobbing.

Bram lifted Claire from the floor with the easy strength of which his spare, lean frame gave no promise, and placed her tenderly on the bed. Then he held one of her hands for a moment, leaned over her, and kissed her forehead with the lingering but calm tenderness of a mother to her babe.

"A' reght," muttered he to Joan, falling once more into the broad Yorkshire he had dropped for so long, "Ah'm going."

At the foot of the stairs he was brought suddenly to full remembrance of the hard, matter-of-fact world of every day. Mr. Cornthwaite was standing, cold and grave, buttoning up his coat, ready to go.

"Where are you going?" asked he shortly.

"For the doctor again, sir. Meg has nearly done for her, for Miss Claire."

Mr. Cornthwaite uttered a short exclamation, which might have been meant to express compassion, but which was more like indifference, or even satisfaction. So Bram felt, in a sudden transport of anger.

"And the old man—Mr. Biron, what did she do to him?"

Bram was silent. He remembered Meg's ferocious words, her triumphant cry that she had killed both the woman and the man she hated; and as the remembrance came back he turned quickly, and went in the direction of Theodore's room. But Mr. Biron was lying quietly in bed, apparently unaware that anything extraordinary had happened. For when he saw Bram he only asked if he were going to stay with him. Bram excused himself, and left the room.

"Mr. Biron's all right, sir," he said to Mr. Cornthwaite, who had by this time reached the door, impatient to get away.

The only answer he got was a nod as Mr. Cornthwaite went out of the house.

Bram had not to go far before he found some one to run his errand for him, so that he was able to return to the house. His mind was full of a strange new thought, one so startling that it took time to assimilate it. He sat for a long time by the kitchen fire, turning the idea over in his mind, until the doctor returned, and went away again, after reporting that Claire was not so much injured by the woman's violence as might have been feared.

It was very late when a nurse, the only one to be got on the spur of the moment, arrived at the farmhouse. Bram was still sitting by the kitchen fire. When she had been installed upstairs Joan came down for a little while.

"What, you here still, Mr. Elshaw?" cried she.

"Well, you might have known I should be," he answered with a faint smile. "I'm here till I'm turned out, day and night now!"

"Why, sir, ye'd best goa whoam," said Joan kindly. "Ye can do no good, and Ah won't leave her, ye may be sure. Ah've sent word whoam as they mun do wi'out me till t' mornin'."

"Ah, but I've something to say to you, Joan. Look here; doesn't it seem very strange that Mr. Cornthwaite when he is half-mad with grief at his son's death, should come all the way out here to see his niece? And that he should say nothing more about—about the death of his son? And that he should give orders for a nurse to come, and undertake to pay all the expenses of her illness? Doesn't it look as if—"

Joan interrupted him with a profound nod.

"Lawk-a-murcy, ay, sir. Ah've thowt o' that too," said she in an eager whisper. "And don't ye think, sir, as it's a deal more likely that that poor, wild body Meg killed Master Christian wi' her strong arms and her mad freaks than that our poor little lass oop yonder did it?"

Bram sprang up.

"Joan, that's what I've been thinking myself ever since the woman rushed out from here. She said she'd sent to h— the woman and the man she hated, didn't she? Well, if Claire was the woman, surely Mr. Christian must have been the man!"

They stared each into the face of the other, full of strong excitement, each deriving fresh hope from the hope each saw in the wide eyes of the other. At last Joan seized his hand, and wrung it in her own strong fingers with a pressure which brought the water to his eyes.

"You've got it, Mr. Bram, you've got it, Ah believe!" cried she in a tumult of feeling. "Oh, for sure that's reght; and our poor little lass is as innocent of it as t' new-born babe!"

Full of this idea, Bram conceived the thought of making inquiries at Meg's own home, and he started at once with this object.

It was now very late, past eleven o'clock; but his uneasiness was too great to allow him to leave the matter till the morning. So, at the risk of reaching the farmhouse, where Meg's parents lived, when everybody was in bed, he took a short cut across the wet, muddy fields, and arrived at his destination within an hour.

The rain had ceased by this time, and the moon peeped out from time to time, and from behind a mass of straggling clouds. The little farm lay in a nook between two hills, and as Bram drew near he saw that a light was still burning within. In getting over a gate he made a little noise, and the next moment he saw a woman's figure come quickly out of the farmhouse.

"Meg, is that you, Meg?" asked a woman's voice anxiously.

"No," said Bram, "it isn't Meg, ma'am. It's me, from Hessel, come to ask if she'd got safe home."

She came nearer, and peered into his face.

"And who be you?"

"My name's Bram Elshaw. I'm a friend of the Birons at Duke's Farm."

"Ah!"

There was a world of sorrow, of significance, in the exclamation. After a pause, she said, not angrily, but despondently—

"Then maybe you know all about it? Maybe you can tell me more than I know myself? Have you seen anything of Meg—she's my daughter—this evening?"

Bram hesitated. The woman went on—

"Oh, don't be afraid to speak out, sir, if it's bad news. We've been used to that of late; ever since our girl took up with t' gentleman that has treated her so bad. It's no use for to try to hide it; t' poor lass herself has spread t' news about. She's gone right out of her mind, I do believe, sir. She wanders about, so I often have to sit up half t' night for her, and she never gives me a hand now with t' farm work. And as neat a hand in t' dairy as she used to be! Well, sir, what is it? Has she made away with herself?"

"She came to Duke's Farm to-night, and attacked Miss Biron," said Bram.

"Well, she was jealous," said Meg's mother, who seemed to be less afflicted with sentiment concerning her daughter than with vexation at the loss of her services. "The lass found it hard she should lose her character, and then t' young gentleman care more for his cousin all t' time. Not but what Meg was to blame. She used to meet him when she knew he was going to Duke's Farm, up in t' ruined cottages on top of t' hill at Hessel. So I've learnt since. Folks tell you these things when it's too late to stop them!"

Bram remembered the night on which he had heard the voices in the dismantled cottages, and he remembered also with shame that he had conceived the idea that Christian's companion might be his cousin.

"Did she tell you where she was going when she went out to-night?" asked Bram.

"She hasn't been home since this afternoon," replied Meg's mother. "She went out before tea, muttering in her usual way threats against him and her,—always him and her. She never says any different. I've got used to her ravings; I don't think she'd do any real harm unless to herself, poor lass!"

"I'm afraid she has this time," said Bram gravely. "I don't know anything more than I've told you; but I'm afraid you must be prepared for worse news in the morning."

Startled, the woman pressed for an explanation. Bram, having really nothing but suspicion to go upon, could tell her nothing definite. But his suspicion was so strong that he felt no diffidence about preparing Meg's mother for a dreadful shock. On the other hand, he was able to assure her that, whatever she might have done, her manifestly disordered state of mind would be considered in the view taken of her actions.

Then he returned to Hessel, tried the door of Duke's Farm, and found it locked for the night. He went round to the front, looked up at the dim light burning in Claire's room with a fervent prayer on his lips, and then climbed the hill to his own lodging.

On inquiry at the farm next morning on his way to his work Bram learnt from the nurse, who was the only person he could see, that while Mr. Biron had had a very bad night, Claire was as well as could be expected. No decided improvement could be reported as yet, nor could it indeed be expected. But she was quieter, and her temperature had gone down, temporarily at least.

He went on his way feeling a little more hopeful, after impressing upon the nurse to keep the doors locked for fear of any further incursions from poor, crazy Meg Tyzack.

On arriving at the works, he saw, as was to be expected after the tragedy of the preceding evening, an unusual stir among the workmen, who were standing about the entrance, talking in eager and excited tones. One of the workmen saluted Bram, and asked him if he had "heard t' fresh news."

"What's that?" asked Bram.

"Coom this weay, sir; Ah'll show ye."

Bram, with a sick terror at his heart, asking himself what new horror he should be called upon to witness, followed the man through the works. The rain had come on again, a drizzling, light rain, which was already turning the morning's dust into a thick, black paste. They passed across the yards and through the sheds, until again they reached the spot where the railway divided the works into two parts.

An exclamation broke from Bram's lips.

"Not another—accident—here?"

For there was quite a large throng of workmen scattered over the lines on the opposite side, and culminating in one dense group not far from the spot where he had found Christian on the previous night.

"Ay, sir, it's a woman this time." And his voice suddenly fell to a hoarse whisper. "T' woman as killed Mr. Christian! T' poor creature was crazed, for sure! She got in here, nobody knows how, this morning; an' she must ha' throwed herself down on t' line pretty nigh t' place where she throwed him down last neght. She must ha' waited for t' mornin' oop train. Anyway, we fahnd her lyin' there this mornin', poor lass!"

Bram had reached the group. He forced his way through, and looked down at the burden the men were carrying towards the very shed under the roof of which Chris had died.

The mutilated body, which had been decapitated by the heavy wheels of the train, was only recognizable by the torn and stained clothing as that of Meg Tyzack.

Bram staggered away, with his hand over his eyes.

CHAPTER XXVI
THE GOAL REACHED

No sooner had Bram recovered himself, and gone to the office without another question to any one, avoiding the group and the sickening sight they surrounded, than he found one of the servants from Holme Park with a letter from Mr. Cornthwaite, asking him to come up to the house at once.

He found his employer sitting in the study alone, in the very seat, the very attitude, he had seen him in so often. While outside the house looked mournful in the extreme with its drawn blinds; while the servants moved about with silent step and scared faces, the master sat, apparently as unchanged as a rock after a storm.

It was not until a change of position on the part of Mr. Cornthwaite suddenly revealed to Bram the fact that the lines in his face had deepened, the white patches in his hair grown wider, that the young man recognized that the tragedy had left its outward mark on him also. He had summoned Bram to talk about business. And this he did with as clear a head, as deep an apparent interest as ever. Even the necessary reference to his lost son he made with scarcely a break in his voice.

"I shall only have the works shut on one day, the day of the funeral, Elshaw," said he. "But in the meantime I shan't be down there myself. I—I—" At last his voice faltered. "I should like to be at work again myself—to give me something to think about, instead of thinking always on the same unhappy subject. But I couldn't go down there so soon after—after what I saw there."

Bram could not answer. The remembrance was too fresh in his own mind.

"So I want you to take my place as far as you can. You can telephone through to me if you want to know anything. You have to fill your own place now, you know Elshaw, and—another's."

Bram bowed his head, deeply touched.

"Now you can go. If you want to see—him, one of the servants will take you up. And the ladies, poor things, are sure to be about. They bear up beautifully, beautifully. His wife bears up a little too well for my taste. But—perhaps—we must forgive her!"

He shook Bram by the hand, and the young man went out.

In the death-chamber upstairs he found Mrs. Christian, dry-eyed, on her knees beside the bed. She sprang up on Bram's entrance, and remained beside him, without speaking a word, while he looked long and earnestly at the placid face, looking handsomer in death than it had ever looked in life, the waxen mask, refined and delicate beyond expression, the long golden moustache, the fair hair, silkier, smoother than Bram had ever seen them.

And presently a mist came before his eyes, and he went hastily out.

He found Mrs. Christian still beside him. She was very pale, but quite calm.

"I am glad you are come. You were poor Christian's great friend, were you not?" said she.

"Yes, madam," said Bram rather stiffly.

Her little chirping voice irritated him. Although he understood that the neglected, unloved wife could not be expected to feel Christian's death as those did who had loved and been loved by him, he wished she would not bear up quite so well, just as Mr. Cornthwaite had done.

But she insisted on following him downstairs, and then she opened the door of the morning-room, and asked him to come in. She would take no excuses; she would not keep him a moment.

"I wish to ask you about Miss Biron," said she, to Bram's great surprise, when she had shut the door of the room, and found herself alone with him. "Oh, yes," she went on with a little nod, as she noticed his astonished look, "I bear her no malice because my husband loved her better than he did me. I only wish he had married her! I do sincerely hope and pray that I nourish no unchristian feelings against anybody, even the poor, mad girl who killed him, and who has since made away with herself in such a dreadful manner!"

She had heard of it already then! Bram was appalled by the manner in which she dismissed such an awful occurrence in a few rapid words.

"And, of course," she went on, "I cannot feel that I have any right to blame Miss Biron, since we know that she did not run away with Christian, as we had supposed."

Bram was overwhelmed with relief unspeakable. This was the first time he had heard anything more than doubt expressed as to Claire's guilt in this matter. He had, indeed, entertained hopes, especially since last night, that Claire had been wrongfully accused. But what was the strongest hope compared with this authoritative confirmation of it? He was shrewd enough, strongly moved though he was, to control the emotion he felt, and to put this question—

"Did Mr. Cornthwaite—did his father—did Mr. Cornthwaite know that he had done his son and Miss Biron—an injustice, thinking what he did?"

"Why, of course he knew," replied Mrs. Christian promptly. "When he found Christian in London he accused him at once, and, of course, Christian told him—indeed, he could see for himself—he was wrong. Christian knew no more where his cousin had gone to than anybody else did."

Bram was silent. He resented Mr. Cornthwaite's behavior in leaving him in ignorance of such a fact. But his resentment was swallowed up in ineffable joy.

"What I wanted to learn was whether Miss Biron has all the nursing she wants," chirped in little Mrs. Christian, "because I should be quite glad to do anything I could for her out of Christian charity. I have done a good deal of sick nursing, and I like it," pursued the poor, little woman. "And I should be really glad of something to occupy my thoughts now in this dreadful time. I have been living with my parents, you know, since this misunderstanding first came about. His father brought Christian here, and when he got well he showed no wish to come back. But when I heard late last night of what had happened, of course I came here at once. And you will ask Miss Biron if she will have me, won't you? I would nurse her well. And, indeed, they are not very kind to me here."

Over the round, pale, freckled face there passed a quiver of feeling which awoke Bram's sympathy at last. The unattractive little woman had been rather cruelly treated from first to last in this affair of Christian's marriage. The Cornthwaites, one and all, had thought much of him and little of her from the beginning to the end of the matter. And the offer to tend the girl Christian had loved so much better than herself had in it something touching, even noble, in Bram's eyes.

He stammered out that he would ask; that she was very good; that he thanked her heartily. Then, exchanging with her a hand-pressure which was warm on both sides, he left her, and went out of the gloomy house.

Of course, Joan would not hear of accepting the kindly-offered services of poor Mrs. Christian. But when she heard of the welcome information which Bram had obtained from her she went half-mad with a delight which found expression in clumsy leaps and twirls and hand-clappings, and even tears.

"And so it's all reght, all reght, as we might ha' knowed from t' first. Oh, we ought to die o' shame to think as we ever thowt anything different! Oh, sir, an' now ye can marry her reght off, an' we can all be happy as long as we live! Oh, sir, this is a happy day!"

Bram tried to silence her, tried at least to check this confident expression of her hopes for the future. Not that his own heart did not beat high: if she was happy in this newly-acquired knowledge, he was happier still. The idol was restored to its pedestal. It was he now, and not she, who had a shameful secret—the secret of his past doubts of her.

Bram could not forgive himself for these, could not now conceive that they had been natural, justifiable. He had doubted her, the purest of creatures, as she was the noblest, the sweetest. He felt almost that he had sinned beyond forgiveness, that he should never dare to meet her frank eyes again.

In the meantime, as day after day passed slowly by, the news he got of her grew better, while that he received of her father grew worse.

At last, two days after the funeral of Christian, he learnt, when he made his usual morning inquiry at the farm on his way down to the works, that Mr. Biron had passed away quietly during the night.

His last words, uttered at half-past two in the morning, had been a characteristic request that somebody would go up immediately to Holme Park with a note to Mr. Cornthwaite.

Bram heard from Joan that they tried to keep the intelligence of her father's death from Claire, who was now much better, but who was still by the doctor's orders kept very quiet. But she guessed something from the looks and sounds she heard, and before the day was over she had learnt the fact they tried to conceal; and then she spent the rest of the day in tears.

Mrs. Cornthwaite and Hester visited her on the following day, and begged her to come back with them. But Claire refused very courteously, but without being quite able to hide her feeling that their offers of kindness and of sympathy came too late.

As, however, the farm and everything Mr. Biron had left were to be sold, it was necessary that she should go somewhere. So, on the day after the funeral, Claire returned to the cottage of the old housekeeper at Chelmsley, who had written inviting her most warmly to return.

Bram, who had not dared to ask to see her, feeling more diffidence in approaching her than he had ever done before, felt a pang whenever he passed the desolate farmhouse on his way to and from his work. All the news he got of Claire was through Joan, who received from the grateful and affectionate girl letters which she could not answer without great difficulty and many appeals to her children, who had had the advantage of the School Board.

Joan gradually became sceptical as the time went on as to the fulfilment of her old wish that Bram should marry Claire. Winter melted into spring, and yet he made no effort to see her; he sent her no messages, and she, on her side, said very little about him in her letters. Indeed, as the leaves began to peep out on the trees, there cropped up occasional references in those same letters of hers to the kindness of a curate, who was teaching her to sketch, and encouraging her to take such simple pleasures as came in her way.

Joan spelt out one of the letters which referred to these occupations to Bram on the next occasion of their meeting. Then she looked up with a broad smile, and gave him a huge nod.

"Ye'll get left in the lurch, Mr. Elshaw, that'll be t' end of it!" she said, with great emphasis.

"Well," said Bram with apparent composure, "if she takes him, it will be because she likes him. And if she likes him, why shouldn't she have him?"

But he was ill-pleased for all that. The vague hopes he had long ago cherished had become stronger, more definite of late; he had forced himself to be patient, to wait, telling himself that it would be indelicate to intrude upon the grief, the horror of the awful shock from which she must still be suffering.

He had long since heard all the particulars of the terrible death of Chris, and of the manner in which the mistake between Meg and Claire had come to be made. A workman had seen Christian and Claire in earnest conversation not far from the railway line; had seen her give him the note from her father which had brought her down. Christian had spoken kindly to her, had bent over her as if with the intention of kissing her, when suddenly the stalwart figure of Meg, who had followed them from some corner where she had concealed herself in the works, rushed between them, threatening them both with wild words. Claire had crept away in alarm, and Meg had gradually dragged Chris, talking, volubly gesticulating all the time, out upon the railway lines. She must have calculated to a nicety the hour at which the next train might be expected, so the general opinion afterwards ran. At any rate, it was she who was with Christian when the train came by; and as every one believed, as, in fact, poor Chris himself had said, she had flung him of malice prepense down on the line just as the train came up to them.

The workingman who gave Bram most of these details was the person who disabused Mr. Cornthwaite of his idea that the murderess was Claire. He had given his information at the very time that Bram was on his way to Hessel in the company of poor little Claire.

Although Claire herself had not witnessed the catastrophe, she had had the awful shock of coming suddenly, a few minutes later, upon the mangled body of her dying cousin. And Bram felt that he could not in decency approach her with his own hopes on his lips until she had in some measure recovered, not only from that shock, but from her father's death, and the loss of her beloved home.

The farm now looked dreary in the extreme. April came, and it was still unlet. The grass in the garden had grown high, the crocuses were over, and there was no one to tie up their long, thin, straggling leaves. The tulips were drooping their petals, and the hyacinths were dying. There was nobody now to sow the seeds for the summer.

Bram was on his way back home early one Saturday afternoon, when the sun was shining brightly, showing up the shabby condition of the house and grounds, the absence of paint on doors and shutters, the weeds which were shooting up in the midst of the rubbish with which the farmyard was blocked up.

As he leaned over the garden gate and looked ruefully in, with painful thoughts about the little girl who was forgetting him in the society of the curate, he fancied he heard a slight noise coming from the house itself.

He listened, he looked. Then he started erect. He grew red; his heart began to beat at express speed.

There was some one in the house, stealing from room to room, not making much noise. And from the glimpse he caught of a disappearing figure in its flight from one room to another Bram knew that the intruder was Claire.

He stole round to the back of the house with his heart on fire.

The door was locked; she had not got in that way. Bram had never given up the workman's habit of carrying a few handy tools in a huge knife in his pocket, and in a few seconds he had taken one of the outside kitchen shutters off its hinges, and shot back the window-catch.

The next moment he was in the room.

But what a different room! The deal table where he had so often done odd jobs of carpentering for Claire; the old sofa on which she had lain on the night of Christian's death while she uttered those precious words of love for himself, which he had treasured in his heart all through the dark winter; the three-legged stool on which she used to sit by the fire; the square, high one he used to occupy on the other side—all these things were gone, and there was nothing in the bare and dirty apartment but some odds and ends of sacking and a broken packing case.

Suddenly Bram conceived an idea. He dragged the packing case over the floor, taking care not to make much noise, put it in the place of his old stool, and sat down on it, bending over the dusty ashes which had been left in the fireplace just as he used to do over the fire on a cold evening.

And presently the door opened softly, and Claire came in.

He did not look round. He was satisfied to know that she was there, there, almost within reach of his arm. And still he bent over the ashes.

A slight sob at last made him look up.

Oh, what a sight for him! The little girl, looking smaller than ever in her black frock and bonnet, was standing in the full sunlight, smiling through her tears; smiling with such unspeakable peace and happiness in her eyes, such a glint of joy illuminating her whole face, that as he got up he staggered back, and cried—

"Eh, Miss Claire, you're more like a sunbeam than ever!"

She did not answer at first. She only clasped her small hands and stared at him, with her lips parted, and the tears springing to her eyes. But then she saw something in his face which brought the blood to hers; and she turned quickly away, and pretended to find a difficulty in making her way through the rubbish on the floor.

"Miss Claire!" said he. "Oh, Miss Claire!"

That was the sum and substance of the eloquence he had been teaching himself; of the elaborate and carefully-chosen words which he had so often prepared to meet her with, words which should be respectful and yet affectionate, sufficiently distant, yet not too cold. It had all resolved itself into this hapless, helpless exclamation—

"Miss Claire! Oh, Miss Claire!"

"I'm not surprised to find you here, Bram," said she with a little touch of growing reserve. "When I heard a noise in here I knew I should find you—just the same."

There was a very short pause. Then Bram said breathlessly—

"Yes, Miss Claire, you'll always find me just the same."

The words, the tone, summed up all the kindness he had ever shown her; all the patient tenderness, the unspeakable, modest goodness she knew so well. Claire's face quivered all over. Then she burst into a torrent of tears. Bram watched her for a minute in dead silence. Then, not daring so much as to come a step nearer, he whispered hoarsely—

"May I comfort you, Miss Claire, may I dare?"

"Oh, Bram—dear Bram—if you don't—I shall die!"

Which, when you come to think of it, was a very pretty invitation.

And Bram accepted it.

And they were married, and they *were* happy ever afterwards, though, in these despondent days, it hardly does to say so.